Lost Without a Trace is Patricia's fourth published book and tells a harrowing story of loss and separation.

The story is set in England, where Patricia grew up and developed a love of literature, sport and art. Her passions are gardening and fishing and being with her close family.

Although Patricia now calls Australia her home, her roots are firmly entrenched in England, where she returns for holidays as often as she can.

Patricia attended university in Australia as a mature student and obtained her Bach. App. Sc. in Recreation.

I would like to dedicate this book to my four grandchildren, Olivia, David, Jessica and Regan.

Patricia Ilich

Lost Without a Trace

Austin Macauley Publishers™
London • Cambridge • New York • Sharjah

A CIP catalogue record for this title is available from the British Library.

ISBN 9781035857975 (Paperback)
ISBN 9781035857982 (ePub e-book)

www.austinmacauley.com

First Published 2024
Austin Macauley Publishers Ltd®
1 Canada Square
Canary Wharf
London
E14 5AA

Many thanks to Barry Sharp for his invaluable help with my many computer problems.

Prologue

Jack knew he had a duty to return to war-torn England but, as Ida had pointed out, he was better off staying where he was. He had been badly hurt with severe lacerations, broken ribs and a broken and dislocated arm. The main problem was Jack couldn't speak a word of German and it was the middle of winter, freezing cold. The German army was looking for him and escape back to England seemed impossible. As he was not in uniform, if he was caught he knew he would be shot as a spy.

He was safe with Ida for the time being, providing he didn't speak to anyone. When he finally decided the time was right to leave, as duty dictated, she blackmailed him into staying with the threat of turning him in to the German authorities. Jack could have killed her; she was the enemy, but he was no murderer and she had, after all, saved his life.

In her efforts to keep Jack working on the farm, Ida fed him lies about the progress of the war. She exaggerated and reported false claims of the domination of the German forces and the capitulation of the British Government. The repercussions of this deception were to last for many years, affecting the reuniting of Jack with his child and mother.

The work on the farm was not difficult and as he laboured in the paddocks, he had time to consider his options. Time to remember the child he had left behind, his mother and his life in England. He went back in his mind, remembering a happier time; a time of optimism and excitement, when he was on the cusp of adulthood, when all the world and its opportunities were open to him. War was then, nowhere on his personal horizon.

The result of the years of lies and deceit meant Jack was dislocated from his little family, his mother and young son.

Chapter 1
Jack Singleton

Jack remembered kissing his tearful mother goodbye at home. She had clung to him, going over and over all the promises she wanted him to make. With his eyes rolling heavenwards he wearily answered, as he had been doing all the past week, "Yes Mum, I'll be careful. Yes Mum, I'll be very, very careful. Yes Mum, I'll write every week. Yes Mum, I'll not talk to strangers. Yes Mum, I'll always take a clean hanky with me. Yes Mum, I'll not go out alone at night. Yes Mum, I'll always wear clean underwear."

"For goodness' sake, Lizzie, give it a break. Leave the boy alone," admonished Jack's father. "He's all grown up now and he's a sensible boy. He'll be just fine."

Jack and his father had taken the train down to the docks at Southampton, where the two shook hands manly. Unexpectedly, his normally reserved father suddenly embraced Jack and, overcome with embarrassment, then stood back and shook hands once again. Jack climbed the steep gangplank with backward glances, still able to see his father. He boarded the ship and waved his father goodbye, with a little sadness at the parting but with no regrets whatsoever. Jack Singleton was setting sail from Southampton on the M.V. Olympic, bound for New York.

It was the 8 May 1934 and the jubilant, skinny 18-year-old Jack was fairly jumping out of his skin. He was, at this moment, completely free; the world was his oyster, his future was open to anything he wanted it to be.

Jack was tall for his age with a shock of unfashionable bright red curls which bounced every time he turned his head. His expressive blue eyes seemingly joined forces with his oscillating eyebrows. So many people commented on how this unusual attribution gave his face a fast changing animation and expression. One moment he could look sad and depressed, the next he would light up with quixotic joyousness.

Like his face, his mood could change, one moment contemplative and introspective and the next frivolous, happy and excited. His conversation could change too from expectant questioning accompanied by furrowed brows, doubting and disagreeing or sometimes with one eyebrow raised and a quizzical look on his young face. Either way, his poor parents had a hard time keeping up with him and his youthful disposition and exuberance.

Jack loved his father dearly but had been away from home for many years; a boarder at one of England's finest educational institutions, Monmouth Public School. Monmouth School was on the south-eastern edge of Wales and lay where the two rivers, the Monnow and the Wye, met.

Jack had been a county and school representative at rowing and thoroughly enjoyed the sporting side of school life, but not the bullying, strict traditional life of a border, subservient to the prefects and stick wielding masters. He'd had his fair share of caning as a junior boy and resolved never to cane or in any way bully a junior boy when he himself was a senior and he never did. He was more than glad to put school life behind him and join the workforce at the same bank as his father, Martins Bank.

However, banking was not Jack's choice; banking was always something his father wanted for him and, being a good son, Jack acquiesced and fell into the expected role of junior banker for the most tedious and seemingly endless year of his young life. Jack had "itchy feet" and longed to get out into the real world and spread his young wings.

After much complaining, Jack's father offered to write to his brother, who was also a banker and lived in New York, asking him to take his nephew into his care for guidance and further education. Letters of credit and introduction were sent to America and it was agreed that Jack would live with his uncle and aunt for a year to broaden his education and to give him an insight into the realm of international banking.

When Jack first told his parents that he wanted to go travelling, his mother implored him not to be so foolish. "You're too young to be out there on your own. You don't know anything about the real world." All to no avail, Jack wouldn't listen to his mother's entreaties, all fell on Jack's deaf ears. His mother appealed to his father, "For goodness' sake, George, talk some sense into the boy."

"Well, to be honest, Lizzie, I think it would do Jack the world of good. He's been cloistered in the school all his life and even when he's been home on holidays, he's not had to face up to any of life's real challenges. No, I think it will do him a world of good, make him grow up a bit, give him a sense of independence, stand on his own two feet for a change. He's had a sheltered childhood and maybe it's time he saw the real world. If we send him off to Alan and Amy in New York, he'll still be watched over and taken care of but he'll have much more independence. No, Lizzie, I think it will be good for the boy and at least he's not going off into the wilds of Australia."

Since Jack was about eleven years old, he'd had an obsession with Australia. Geography at school had never appealed to him until his class started learning about Australia. For some reason that country captured his imagination. At the end of that term, when he was home on holiday and, as usual, being questioned by his parents about what sort of things he was doing at school, he enthusiastically related to them all that he was learning about Australia.

"Did you know, dad, that Australia was discovered less than two hundred years ago and it was an Englishman, Captain Cook, who found it?"

"Well, actually, son, I think it was a Dutch navigator who spotted it first."

"No, dad, it was Captain Cook and he set sail from Whitby on his ship called The Endeavour. They didn't have engines, only sails. It must have taken them months, years maybe."

"That's interesting, dear," commented his mother, trying to sound interested.

"Yes and guess what they found when they got there? Gold! Tons and tons of it, just lying around."

"I don't think that's quite right, son," intercepted his father. "I think they found the gold a lot later and I'm pretty sure it wasn't just lying around."

"Honest, dad, it was. We're learning all about it. And guess what else, they have kangaroos, they're funny animals that don't walk, they only jump. And guess what else, they have sticks that if you throw them away, they come back to you."

"Yes, dear," sighed his mother, "dinner's ready, go wash your hands and then come to the table."

Once at the table, Jack started in again on the subject of Australia. "I think, dad, when I grow up I want to go and live in Australia and go to find a lot of gold. I'll make us all rich and we can have a car for you and a diamond necklace for mum and, well, everything."

The subject of Jack living in Australia came up time and time again over the years. Jack's parents thought he would eventually get over his obsession with it but it was never far from Jack's young mind. They had no idea why Australia appealed to him so much. It just did.

Jack's whole life seemed to him to have been one of subservience to authority, to the discouragement of any free will. Once he had left school life, as the son of a banker, it was not much different, really. It was all fairly strict and quite constrained and Jack expected life would be the same with his uncle, but that was in the future. For now, he was alone and free.

He had ample funds and not a worry in the world. No one to tell him to go to bed or get up at a certain time. No one to remind him to clean his teeth or wear warm underwear, no one to reprimand him for putting his elbows on the table or talking too much at dinner. No one to tell him to "straighten your tie," or "clean your shoes. Don't forget to say your prayers, eat your greens!" Freedom at long last. The ocean in front of him seemed to speak on the wind off the waves, "Come on, come on, the world is waiting for you, all life's wonders are in front of you."

Chapter 2
The Crossing

Although the weather was chilly, the wind was kind for the crossing, nevertheless many people were seasick, but not Jack. He loved the bracing wind on his face and spent hours just gazing at the ocean in front of the boat and the rolling of the enormous bow wave as the ship rent the ocean asunder as it tore its way through the water. He loved the squealing of the seagulls that followed the boat and the taste of the salt spray that kept getting blown back into his face. The smell of the ocean and the keen biting wind that turned his pink face a red rosy hue all contributed to his elation and excitement. The late evening sun turned the clouds to orange and the ocean to gold.

Jack spread his young arms and shouted in the wind, "Is this all for me, god? Are you putting on a display just for me? Are you trying to tell me something?"

He wasn't in the least bit religious, but like most people in times of great stress or times of great happiness, he looked to god either for help and assistance or to give special thanks.

He had been to the library back home in London and read as much as he could about America and New York in particular. He was desperate to see the Statue of Liberty and his father had given him a box camera as a parting gift and he couldn't wait to use it. An elderly American couple noticed that Jack was alone and tried to befriend him but he sensed their good intentions and didn't want anyone wrapping him in cotton wool, he didn't want any surrogate parents smothering and suffocating him, he'd had enough of authority and well-meaning adults so he avoided them when he could.

At the evening meal, he was questioned by two elderly spinster ladies about his life in London and about his aspirations once he got to New York. He wasn't exactly rude to them but he just didn't want to talk about his hopes and plans, simply because he didn't have any plans. He knew he would have to stay with his aunt and uncle but he really thought that there was more to life than living within the constraints of relatives who would watch over him. He didn't want to be "watched over" he wanted freedom, to do what he wanted, to be what he wanted, even though he didn't know what he wanted to be or what he wanted to do.

There were only one or two young girls on the boat and Jack chatted amiably enough to them. In actual fact he had absolutely no experience with girls. His had been a boys only school and girls were as foreign to him as Bulgarians or Russians or even aliens from the moon. But they were girls and as such now were of great interest to him. After a while, he realised that they were just ordinary girls, ordinary people really and although he found he could talk to them quite easily, he wasn't excited by them at all.

However, there was one girl who was different. She was an Indian and wore a sari and this girl was closely chaperoned by her parents, but he did get to speak to her on quite a few occasions. They exchanged stories of their lives and he was fascinated by her tales of a girl's boarding school in England which were so different to his experiences attending a boy's boarding school.

There was no corporal punishment at her school and junior girls were never made to be servants for the senior girls. The teachers were in charge of the girls, not the prefects. Sports were different, of course, but the girl did tell him about the rowing club she had joined, very much against her parent's wishes and how much she had enjoyed rowing. They apparently didn't want their daughter to play any kind of sport, neither netball nor hockey. They just wanted her to grow up to be a lady.

The girl told him all about her holidays in Bombay and the house they had on the coast with twenty servants. He was impressed with the girl and her way of life. That was what he was craving, something different, something out of the ordinary. He just wanted to break free from his oppressive, narrow world and experience other worlds, other people, other cultures. His life, he thought, of his own making, was just beginning.

The elderly couple did eventually corner him one afternoon and were able to answer his questions about the Statue of Liberty. They told him how she guards the entrance to New York Harbour on Liberty Island. She was a gift from France, they told him, to commemorate the signing of the Declaration of Independence and has been a symbol of democracy and hope since 1886. Jack couldn't wait to see the 305 feet tall statue, the Empire State Building and all the skyscrapers.

As they neared the end of their journey, Jack was keen to see the New York skyline and to record his first sights on his camera, however, that was not to be as a mist descended and obscured the view. The approach to New York was marked by a lightship: the mist became a heavy fog and the Olympic was sailing very close, homing in on the radio beacon of Nantucket Lightship.

Jack was leaning over the guardrail and was shocked to see, appearing out of the gloom, another, much smaller vessel. He screamed into the fog, but no one took any notice of him as the larger boat, the one Jack was on, sliced through the smaller vessel which broke apart and immediately sank. Men were in the water; shouting; screaming; it was a nightmare as the Olympic tried to stop.

It all happened so quickly. The ship's crew members were shouting orders at each other and running around trying to get organised. It was panic and chaos. Jack watched helplessly, not knowing what to do, watching the drama unfold. He was sort of frozen to the spot, with his hand over his mouth, watching, not able to do anything, not wanting to get in the way, overcome by feelings of desperate helplessness.

The Olympic crew, after much shouting and screaming at each other, lowered the lifeboats and managed to rescue seven men. They were hauled out of the water, some unconscious, some shouting for help. The water turned red with blood and some of the men were quite possibly dead, but some, while obviously seriously hurt, were very much alive. Jack was young and had never witnessed anything horrific in his life, he was traumatised and ran to his cabin in tears and confusion. He wanted to feel like a man, but at that moment he wanted his mother; he was a little boy again.

Chapter 3
New York

Jack was met at the vast International Terminal by his aunt and uncle. He really didn't need any introduction, his uncle Alan was almost identical to his father, though they were not twins. His aunt Amy crushed him to her ample bosom and he was hustled through Customs and Immigration before he could catch his breath. The ride out to their apartment was hair-raising for Jack.

To start with, everyone drove on the wrong side of the road, taxis honked their horns with infuriating regularity and all cars were being driven at breakneck speed. The smell of the city was different from anything he had known before. No unpleasant smells, just very different. They seemed to be driving through vast canyons; the buildings were so tall and the road just seemed like a narrow valley snaking its way through the mountainous skyscrapers.

There was steam rising from gutters and grey pigeons everywhere. Heady smells drifted into the car from the street sellers cooking something, he didn't know what and spicy aromas that make Jack's mouth water. He would have loved to stop the car and buy whatever it was that was being sold, but he was polite and said nothing that could be taken as an insult.

Two miles further on, the spicy aromas changed to sickly perfumed air and, even further on, changed again to a cloying, overpowering smell of decaying garbage. He resolved, however, that once settled, he would explore the city and experience everything that was different from what he had left at home.

His aunt and uncle had American accents, although Jack knew that they were both English by birth. Alan was a staid, laconic, conservative pot-bellied bank manager, exactly like George, his younger brother. They were both prematurely balding and could have been book ends they looked so much alike. Aunt Amy had the same temperament and disposition of her husband. They had grown together and almost merged into one being, except, of course, for their looks.

She had a soft feminine face with a small pointed chin but her staid, conservative manner, however, was a mirror image of her husband. They were a natural pair and complemented each other. They pointed out landmarks on the journey and kept up a barrage of questions about George and Elizabeth, Jack's parents. They asked no questions about the two ships colliding and Jack assumed that the news hadn't hit the headlines of the papers yet. He didn't offer any information on the tragedy and he wasn't asked for any. He decided to keep it to himself; he didn't want to talk about it; he didn't want to even think about it.

The next few days flew by in a flurry of sightseeing and acclimatisation, getting used to the different money, the traffic, the food, the people. All too soon, it came time to accompany uncle Alan to the office and to commence duties as a junior bank clerk. Jack came down from cloud seven with a wallop.

This was the real world, the world his father knew well, the world of commerce, banking, boredom, monotony. Jack didn't want any part of it, but he had no choice. It was the only work he could do and the recession in America had only been a short while back, so he was grateful for the employment, no matter what. His aunt and uncle were very good to him; he had his own room and freedom to come and go in the evenings, as he wished.

He made friends with another young clerk in the office who told him of a youth club that had a team of basketball players and who were looking for more players, especially those who were quite tall. Jack took after his father and was 6ft 3inches in his stocking feet.

Jack's only sporting prowess was as a rower, he had never played basketball and didn't even know the rules, but he agreed to meet his friend there the next evening and promised to have a look at it. Once the coach saw Jack, he approached him and asked if he would like a game. Jack readily accepted the invitation but once he started playing wished he had never agreed.

He was pushed and pummelled, ridiculed and rejected. It was embarrassing; he didn't know the first thing about basketball. The coach apologised and appointed a junior coach to take Jack to one side and teach him the rudiments of the game. It was not as easy as it looked. He was taught to bounce the ball with great regularity and much monotony, in front of his legs, around his legs, through his legs. To throw it into the hoop, to weave and dodge from side to side, to avoid losing the ball to an opponent.

Jack was not one to give up easily and so went to the club three times a week, just to practise on his own. After two months, the coach, who had been watching him, invited him to join a group in a game. This time Jack could hold his own and, being quite tall, was able to give a good account of himself. He was no champion, but he wasn't an embarrassment either, he even managed to put the ball into the hoop three times.

Jack was eventually put into a "C" grade team as a substitute. He was tickled pink and determined to move up the ranks until he would be accepted as a "B" or even an "A" grade player.

At this time all the basketball teams were either black or white, that is Negro or Caucasian. There were very few competitions where the two groups would meet and compete but at the end of the Jack's first year in America, he was asked to join his team to play a match against an all-black team. The competition was fierce but the "Glory men," Jack's team, won with five points in hand.

After the game, there were to be drinks and a buffet dinner. The two teams mingled, somewhat stiffly and it was there that Jack noticed the most beautiful negress he had ever seen, actually one of the very few negresses he had actually ever seen, beautiful or not. She took his breath away, he actually stopped breathing as his body froze for just a moment.

She was tall, as tall as Jack himself. Slender with a delicate neck covered in colourful beads. Her name was Harriet and her brother had been playing in the game. She congratulated Jack on his team's win and they chatted about the game in general.

He was fascinated by her height, her exotic looks, her openness, her views on the game and on life in general. She in turn was amazed at his wonderful English accent, his fiery red hair, his freckles and his good humour, but mostly she was amazed at how he was willing to talk openly to her, most of the boys and men she met wouldn't talk to a black girl at all and if they did, it was very much frowned upon by both sides, black and white.

Harriet was a stenographer with a Civil Rights Legal Team and worked downtown New York, just a short ride from the bank where Jack was working. Although they both realised that their families would absolutely disapprove of their meeting, nevertheless they agreed to have lunch in a small café, halfway between their two offices. Whether it was the danger of "forbidden fruit" or the excitement of flouting of authority, Jack didn't care, he was very much attracted to Harriet.

She was like nothing he had ever known or experienced and that thrilled him. They saw each other quite often after that first meeting. In fact, they had begun to have quite strong, if inadvisable, feelings for one another.

He had the good sense not to flaunt his friendship around. It wasn't exactly a secret, he just didn't want his aunt and uncle to disapprove of anything he did and he didn't want anyone at the office knowing who he was seeing either, he also didn't want any reports going back to England to his parents telling them that he was seeing a coloured girl, he didn't think that would go down too well at all. Not that his parents were particularly colour prejudiced as far as he knew, but it was just not the thing in England.

As the two grew closer and closer, they discussed every manner of topic and Jack was interested in everything Harriet told him, especially about the struggles of black people in America. It all seemed so unfair to him; he who had never known inequality, segregation or cultural differences. He had been brought up in a world where everyone was accepted for what he was.

There were social differences in England but Jack was mostly unaware of other people's lives and other social classes, apart from his own. He had been a cloistered, protected childhood and he was appalled to think that people were discriminated against, just because of the colour of their skin.

Harriet explained to Jack that although she came from a very humble home and quite poor family her elder brother was doing well in the plumbing trade and had wanted to have Harriet educated to enable her to go out in to the world with her head held high and have every chance that life might present to her, not only in the world of coloured people but on an equal footing within the white community too. He had paid for her to learn shorthand and typing and she had been lucky enough to obtain a good job in New York, well away from her home and background.

Harriet told him all about her hero, Charles Houston, her boss at the National Association for the Advancement of Coloured People (NAACP). She related stories to him about the work she did, typing documents for several very important civil rights cases that went before the United States Supreme Court about how her boss had played a major role in nearly every civil rights case for the last five years.

Towards the end of 1935, Jack asked his uncle if it would be alright if he could help him to find a suitable small apartment as he would like to be independent. Aunt Amy was a trifle upset and felt that this request was a direct reflection of her failure to make Jack feel at home. He was quick to reassure her that she had been the perfect "adopted" mother but he was growing up and needed a place of his own. Uncle Alan understood perfectly and agreed to help his nephew find a place. He thought there might be a girl involved but was wise enough not to enquire.

In the back office of the bank was a small noticeboard for any of the staff to use to advertise goods for sale, notices of social outings and sometimes advertising of apartments for rent. It was one of these notices that drew the attention of uncle Alan, who was quick to get details and take Jack out to see the property.

They both agreed that while it was quite small, it would be affordable and close enough to the city to enable Jack to commute quite easily. The apartment had just one room, which served as a lounge and kitchen, a separate bathroom and a tiny, but adequate bedroom.

In England, it would have been described as a bedsitter or simply a bedsit. There were three flights of stairs, but Jack was young and healthy and stairs were no problem to him at all. The stairwell and entrance were grubby and smelt of boiled cabbage mixed with garlic but once inside the apartment it was clean and airy. The sparse furniture, especially the mattress, looked new and the bedroom looked out over the river and park. It was just what Jack wanted. Jack never did take Harriet to see his aunt and uncle, his instincts told him that they wouldn't approve and there was no need upsetting them. Such were the circumstances in America at that time.

Chapter 4
Married Life

Jack was now nineteen and his thoughts about Harriet were not as pure as he knew they should be. His imagination ran wild and he wanted more than just a goodnight kiss from her when he took her home each evening.

His first fumbling under her blouse were met with a sharp reprimand, "What are you doing? Get off!"

"Ohhhh, Harriet, I, I, I, just let me touch you a little bit."

"Jack Singleton, behave yourself." His embarrassment was acute and he turned without a word and left for home. His discomfort was as physical as mental.

He pondered on his feelings all the way home and thoughts of Harriet took up his working hours, his leisure hours and his sleeping time over the next few days. He decided he had to do something, his feelings for Harriet were taking over his life, his physical needs were becoming more and more urgent.

Jack had not yet taken Harriet to see his apartment, his tiny flat, but decided he would invite her home at the weekend and cook a meal for her and then, well, who knows what might happen. She agreed to meet him as usual after work and he shyly asked if she would come to his apartment for a meal on the Saturday night.

Harriet was no fool and knew what was in the back or even in the front of Jack's mind. She had been brought up to be a good girl and had never let a boy touch her inappropriately, but she was nineteen too and her feelings for Jack were as profound as his feelings for her. She wanted to see his little apartment and she smiled to herself when she thought that he probably had a motive other than giving her an evening meal.

Harriet's sex education was sparse, to say the least. Certainly no information came from her parents or her school. She knew the rudiments of sex, basically what went where, but as for details, she was totally ignorant. She knew how babies were conceived and had been warned by the girls in school, "Don't sit on a toilet seat that a boy had sat on. That's one way of getting pregnant. Don't let a boy put his tongue in your mouth, that's another way."

The white boys always told the coloured girls, "Black girls can't get pregnant if they have sex with a white boy."

Harriet instinctively knew this was all nonsense but had no close girlfriends who had actually experienced sex and so had no second hand true knowledge of the situation either. Harriet also knew that there was no way she could ask her mother such questions. Harriet's mother would have given the poor girl a severe lecture on morality based on her southern state's Christian beliefs and the lecture would in all probability be accompanied by a sharp slap or worse.

Harriet was too embarrassed to ask anyone and so resorted to the only source of information that she felt she could trust. She went to the library to see if she could find a book that would explain things, but even when she found one, she was too embarrassed to sit and read it or even take it home.

Jack was no better educated. His sex education came mostly from secretive whisperings in the school dormitory. One boy had managed to secrete a "men's only" magazine into the school and this magazine was passed from boy to boy in the dormitory and discussed in whispered awe. The pictures of women in the magazine bore absolutely no resemblance to any woman he had ever seen. He just couldn't imagine his mother without her clothes on and he was absolutely sure that she would look nothing like the women in the magazine.

Sex education was never a part of the public school curriculum and Jack's parents never gave any thought to his needs for such information. Jack, like Harriet, knew where babies came from, how they were conceived, what went where, but nothing further. Jack tried to imagine his parents doing what he knew they must have done, at least once, to conceive him, but it was just impossible. His imagination just didn't stretch to such wild thoughts. He had no knowledge of the female reproductive system or anything about a female's monthly cycle.

Ignorance was not bliss, he knew that he knew nothing, but he desperately wanted to know everything. His body had an urgency and he knew he had to do something about that and something had to be done as soon as possible.

Jack's tiny apartment sported a two ringed gas cook top and never having had to cook for himself before coming to America, Jack was no cordon bleu chef. Since moving into the apartment, he had existed mainly on take-away meals, sandwiches, cereal and fruit, but on this night, this special occasion, he had wracked his brains to come up with a meal fit for an evening to remember.

Some of his take-away meals came from the tiny Italian restaurant that was situated on the ground floor of the apartment block. Jack had made friends with Nino, the owner and asked for his advice. Nino was sympathetic to Jack's needs and offered to prepare a take-away meal for Jack, but the young Romeo was determined to cook the meal himself. Nino gave Jack plenty of advice and they both eventually agreed upon a simple two course dinner with a nice (if somewhat cheap) bottle of Italian Chianti.

Jack opened a tin of soup as a starter and then, following Nino's advice, prepared a chicken and mushroom risotto that he was able to cook in the one single frying pan that the kitchen boasted. Jack's education had been sufficient to let him know that a bottle of wine would relax both of them and maybe, well maybe, who knows, his luck might be in.

He had gone over in his mind, time and time again, not only the simple meal and its preparation but also his moves to try and coax Harriet into letting him explore her body, just maybe, to ease, not tease his mind.

Harriet sensed what the evening was really all about and was nervous with a sort of tingling anticipation, but was not half as nervous as Jack himself. He had bought a small tablecloth and laid the table with a tiny bunch of flowers in the middle. His plates and glasses didn't match but hoped she wouldn't notice these small defects.

As soon as she arrived, he kissed her gently and without speaking, took her warm coat and hung it in the closet. Gingerly, he opened the bottle of wine and, taking care not to spill any due to his trembling hands, poured them both a glassful. A second kiss was inevitable and as the bed was so close, he manoeuvred Harriet towards it. She let herself be lowered to the bed and as Jack's hands reached under her blouse, he realised he needed to get rid of the encumbrance of her brassiere, but she was on her back and he couldn't reach to undo the thing.

Frustration mixed with over eager anticipation, along with the sure knowledge that Harriet wasn't resisting him, caused Jack to have the most terrifying and embarrassing moment of his young life. His young, healthy body exploded in an unwanted shaming premature ejaculation, along with a strangled cry and some rude blaspheming that shocked both of them.

He was still fully dressed and Harriet wasn't exactly sure what had just happened, only that Jack was apologising over and over as he retreated into his bathroom. He came out from a lukewarm shower with a towel draped around him, grabbed a clean outfit and retreated back into the bathroom.

Harriet turned the gas rings off, dinner could wait. More or less realising what had happened, decided to take matters into her own hands. She slipped out of all her clothes and climbed into bed. When Jack emerged from the bathroom fully dressed, he was shocked and amazed to find Harriet in his bed with the sheets pulled up to her neck as she patted the space next to her, indicating her need for him to join her. He didn't need a second invitation. His clean clothes came off and landed on the floor where they stayed all night waiting for the morning clean -up. Breakfast consisted of warmed up soup and reheated risotto.

Where formal sex education was lacking, human needs and nature were not.

Harriet had a furious argument with her brothers, who shared an apartment with her, but, nevertheless, moved in with Jack the very next day. She had never told her family that Jack was Caucasian and they assumed that she was in a relationship with one of her own kind.

Jack and Harriet had everything they needed in life, a comfortable, if somewhat small apartment, good jobs and no financial worries. They had their health and each other, life was sweet. Jack had been promoted to the "B" team at basketball and Harriet would have liked to be able to go along to all his games to cheer him on, but there was so much colour prejudice and outward hostilities towards coloureds that they both agreed it was better that they keep a low profile and not make an outward show of their relationship.

For these two young people, their love flowed unobstructed by their different cultures and background. They had no need for other people's approval, they were content to bask in each other's love and admiration. Together they formed a cocoon of love, so encompassing, so all engrossing that they both felt completely safe, absolutely free from outside influences. Once home of an evening, they closed the door to their apartment and left the world outside, they were complete in their love had for each other.

For two and a half years, the two lived a quiet life with Jack visiting his aunt and uncle each Sunday for lunch. He felt really guilty for not telling them about Harriet but argued that if he told them he had a partner that they would want to meet her and if they met her that they would disapprove, as everyone they knew would disapprove also; not just the white community, but the black community too.

Harriet came from a large family and she knew her parents, two brothers and three sisters would never approve of her inter-colour relationship with Jack. "No," she reasoned, she wouldn't exactly tell lies about her private life, if questioned, but on the other hand she wouldn't volunteer information about her relationship with Jack either. However, in the March 1938 Harriet's doctor confirmed what she had suspected for a few weeks, that she was pregnant and the baby was due for the end of November.

She told Jack on the Saturday morning, after she had thrown up in the bathroom. He took her out to lunch to celebrate, but Harriet hardly ate a thing and after taking her home, he went shopping on his own. That evening he made Harriet put her feet up while he cooked dinner. They celebrated their news with a bottle of wine and after the dishes had been done, he asked Harriet to go for a walk with him.

It was a beautiful night and as they strolled through the local park Jack took a furtive look around them to see that no one else was near and then he dropped to one knee and in a very shaky voice declared, "Harriet Watkins, I love you, will you do me the greatest honour by becoming my wife?"

Harriet took a step backwards and looked him up and down and then slowly replied, "Jack, you don't have to do this, you don't know what you're asking, it's not that easy in this country."

"Yes it is, I made enquiries and it's quite legal here," he informed her.

"No," she explained, "I didn't mean that exactly, I mean people aren't going to accept us as a married couple, I know it's actually legal here, although it's not legal in most other states, but I mean you can never present me in any company as your wife, you will be ostracised from all society."

Jack stood up quickly and almost shouted, "To hell with society. I don't want to marry them, I want to marry you. I want us to have this baby and be an ordinary family, I want to be a father and you my baby's mother."

Harriet had tears in her eyes as she held on to him and said, "Alright, Jack Singleton, I'll marry you if that's what you want, but we will never be ordinary, that's just not possible."

Jack slipped a small diamond ring on her finger and they strolled home, arm in arm, as happy as any young couple could be.

The paperwork and notices were not too difficult and one month later, Jack and Harriet married at City Hall with no friends or relatives in attendance. The necessary witnesses had to be called in from the offices at the back of the hall and it was all over in a matter of ten minutes. They had made an appointment with a local photographer for some photographs to be taken and while they were still in their wedding outfits, the newlyweds dined in style to celebrate.

Harriet wore a simple white organza summer dress and carried a small bouquet of white rosebuds. Jack was feeling so guilty for not telling his aunt and uncle or even his family back home, but they both agreed that it was the best policy.

The two lovers settled down to married life and patiently waited for their bundle of joy to be born. Harriet learnt how to knit and made many little "things" for their expected infant. Jack bought a cot and a small stroller. It was going to be a tight fit getting everything into the small apartment but they reasoned that the baby wouldn't need "running around" space for two or three years.

Jack took a daily newspaper and was becoming increasingly worried about the situation in Europe, it looked like England might be drawn into a European war and he was afraid for his parents who still lived in London.

Harriet knew how worried he was and one day she read out to him an article about the British Prime Minister, Neville Chamberlain, who had just returned from Germany, landing at Heston Aerodrome on 30 September 1938. The report quoted Chamberlain as saying:

"The settlement of the Czechoslovakian problem, which has now been achieved is, in my view only the prelude to a larger settlement in which all Europe may find peace. This morning I had another talk with the German Chancellor, Herr Hitler and here is the paper which bears his name upon it as well as mine. Some of you, perhaps, have already heard what it contains but I would just like to read it to you. We regard the agreement signed last night and the Anglo-German Naval Agreement as symbolic of the desire of our two peoples never to go to war with one another again."

The report went on to state that later that day Chamberlain stood outside 10 Downing Street, the official home of the Prime Minister and again read from the document and concluded:

"My good friends, for the second time in our history, a British Prime Minister has returned from Germany bringing peace with honour. I believe it is peace for our time. We thank you from the bottom of our hearts. Go home and get a nice, quiet sleep."

Jack didn't get a "nice quiet sleep" he was worried and was starting to feel that he needed to go home, to take care of his parents, to bring his child up in a free society where there wouldn't be so much prejudice. He was feeling also that if there was to be a war, he had a duty to his country to help where he could. He wouldn't want people thinking that he had deliberately stayed abroad and neglected his patriotic duty.

He discussed the issue with Harriet and told her that he thought it was time that he informed his parents of his marriage and of the impending arrival of their grandchild.

He also thought it would be best if the baby was born in England and therefore would have British nationality.

Harriet had always wanted to see England and so not only readily agreed, but was thrilled at the prospect of going to Europe.

Jack wrote to his surprised parents telling them all his latest news and they replied how delighted they were firstly to hear that he was married, secondly that a child was on the way and thirdly that Jack was returning home. He didn't tell them that Harriet was coloured and, of course, they didn't ask. Jack did, however, tell his aunt and uncle at the weekend that he was married and they were surprised and somewhat shocked that he hadn't told them sooner.

Again, though, he didn't take Harriet to meet them and he didn't tell them she was coloured. They did ask when were they going to meet this mysterious wife and Jack fobbed them off with the excuse that she had to return to her own family to inform them of their plans and to say her goodbyes.

Jack had booked them on a transatlantic crossing for the following month, in October. It was a busy time organising a passport for Harriet, giving notice to leave the apartment and notice to leave their respective workplaces, but they were excited at the prospect of leaving America and starting a new life in England.

Jack had booked them to return on the M.V. Georgic, which was a Cunard White Star Line ship. When Harriet saw the ship tied up alongside the New York Harbour wall, she gasped. It was so beautiful and large with one fat funnel, already smoking. The deck was some 700 feet long and the inside, luxury, like she had never seen before. Their cabin was tiny but had its own bathroom, everything was wonderful.

The baby was due in six weeks' time but Harriet was so tall and slim and wore her clothes so well that it was difficult to see her "baby bulge" unless you were specifically looking for it.

Most of the passengers were fellow Brits trying to get home before war was declared and then it would be impossible. The crossing was fairly rough being in October and Harriet started to get seasick after the first few hours. There was a doctor on board who gave her some tablets and admonished her for travelling so late in her pregnancy.

"You're a very foolish young woman travelling in your condition. Honestly, if you had told the shipping line that you were so far gone, I doubt very much if they would have granted you a passage to travel. As it is, you appear to be quite healthy apart from the seasickness and I see no reason why there should be a problem."

Jack had his meals in the dining room and ordered her a simple tray be brought to their cabin as Harriet felt she just couldn't face a full meal. "What a pity," he told her, "as the food's just fabulous."

For the whole week of the journey, Harriet hardly ate a thing, she could only sip water and stayed in bed every day. The end of the voyage couldn't come quick enough for the two. Jack was beside himself with worry and just wanted to get Harriet onto dry land and get her to eat something. He would spend most of his time in their cabin reading to her and trying to reassure her that all would be well. He occasionally walked around the deck for fresh air and exercise but the salt spray and breaking waves no longer excited him. His spirits were low and he felt the weight of responsibility for his wife and their unborn child.

By the time the ship docked at Southampton, there was a gale blowing and the rain was pelting down. All the passengers had to disembark using the gangway, which was open to the elements, but once inside the terminal, it was warm and sheltered from the wind.

Unfortunately, the gangway was at an angle sloping down to the terminal and so the rain was collecting at the bottom and puddling annoyingly. Passengers were taking a large step across the puddle and some tried to jump over it so as not to get their feet wet. Harriet was weak, but felt able to walk from their cabin and was eager to disembark as quickly as possible. Jack was struggling with their two suitcases and didn't notice Harriet take a long stride across the puddle.

Unfortunately, the wooden floorboards were sodden and had become quite slippery. Her feet slipped from under her and down she went in a contorted, soggy heap. She screamed at the pain that shot through her stomach as she twisted to try and save herself.

Jack appealed to the other passengers to help him and together with two officials from the Customs and Immigration, they managed to get Harriet to a bench and laid her down. An ambulance was called for and they rushed her to the local hospital.

It was a night long vigil and Jack was beside himself with worry. The nurses kept coming to him with updates on her progress but it was a difficult time. Harriet had gone into labour prematurely and was threatening to lose the baby. Apparently she had haemorrhaged very badly and the doctors were having a difficult time stabilising her.

Eventually, the chief surgeon came to see Jack and took him into a side room to tell him the awful news that Harriet had not survived the trauma, her body was too dehydrated from being seasick and as she was painfully thin normally and had very narrow hips. Well, everything had conspired against her and unfortunately her body just couldn't take it.

However, Jack now had a beautiful, but very tiny baby boy and that should be his consolation. The baby was healthy enough but would have to stay in hospital, in the Intensive Care Unit for at least three days.

Chapter 5
Back Home in England

George and Elizabeth Singleton were thrilled to hear that their only son was returning home and were shocked, but thrilled to hear that he was not coming alone. In fact, he had married and was bringing his wife with him; also that a baby was due in a few weeks' time. It was all so very exciting. Elizabeth was miffed with Jack for not telling them before that he was dating a girl and had even married her, but she loved her son and forgave him. She did tell George, though, that she fully intended to box Jack's ears for not telling them sooner.

George laughed at her and shook his head knowingly, "I don't think so Lizzie, I've never known you punish that child for anything. You've always been too soft with him."

"Oh, George Singleton and I suppose you're going to tell me you are the disciplinarian in the family. When did you ever raise your hand to the child?" They both laughed and enjoyed the excitement of looking forward to the return of their son and meeting his bride.

They knew Jack was due home in the next few days but he hadn't told them which boat he was taking or the exact time of his expected arrival and so they couldn't go down to Southampton to meet the boat and just had to be content with waiting to greet the pair at home.

That night, Elizabeth noticed George was taking a couple of pills before getting into bed. George was normally quite averse to taking any medicine or pills and she questioned him worriedly, "What's wrong? What are you taking and why?"

"Oh, it's nothing. I just feel a little queasy, it's probably just the excitement of seeing Jack again." Elizabeth put her hand on George's forehead and declared, "My god, George, you're all cold and clammy and you're actually sweating. What's wrong?"

"Nothing I tell you, just give me a few minutes. I'll be fine."

With that, George put his hand out to steady himself and then just collapsed into a heap by the side of the bed. Elizabeth knew in her heart that this was serious. George was never ill, he never complained about anything, even when he had a cold or a cough, he always declared himself, "Just fine."

Elizabeth tried to make George more comfortable but he was too heavy for her to lift him into a more comfortable position and he kept drifting in and out of consciousness. She knew she had to get help and immediately went to the phone and dialled 999. The ambulance came within a few minutes and took George, with Elizabeth, in tow to the large local hospital.

The doctors did all sorts of tests on George and had wires and tubes coming in and out of his body. It was all very serious and Elizabeth was terrified for her husband. While doctors and nurses scurried around him, Elizabeth just sat quietly holding his hand, watching her husband's laboured breathing. The senior doctor eventually took Elizabeth to one side and told her that George had suffered a severe stroke and may not actually survive and even if he did, he would be paralysed down one side of his body.

With tears flowing freely, Elizabeth returned to her husband's side to hold his hand and do her best to coax him back into life for her. Eventually all the hospital staff, save for one nurse, left the pair alone and after a while, George opened his eyes and saw the grief on Elizabeth's face. He was able with his one good hand to rest it on top of hers and with tears in his eyes which were overflowing down his now slightly misshapen face, he tried with some trouble to coax his tongue to behave and allow him to speak. His words were slurred but Elizabeth was able to make out what he was trying to say.

Painfully, George dragged his words through careful thoughts. Elizabeth stiffened at the tortured sound of her husband's voice. Her eyes, like his, were filled with emotional tears of love and devotion as she lay her head next to his face and whispered, "Don't try and talk, my love, just rest and you'll be just fine."

"No," he slowly and carefully formed the words, "I'm not fine. I know this is the end."

"No, George, don't say that."

"I'm sorry, Lizzie, but I think it's my time. I don't think I'll last the night. I've always believed in god and I do believe that I'll go to a good place where I will wait for you to come to me."

"No, George, please don't say that. You're going to be fine."

"Please tell Jack I'm sorry. I really wanted to see him and his new wife." As Elizabeth sat upright and took her handkerchief to her free flowing tears, she watched as her husband raised his good hand and cupped her wet face and tried to stroke his wife's hair. She took hold of his hand and kissed his palm. Their love was pure and both felt a desolation at the thought of eternal separation. Elizabeth reached across her husband and laid her head gently on his chest, listening to the faint beat of his heart. George stroked her back and ran his fingers through her hair, trying to remember the first time he touched his wife, more than twenty-five years earlier.

"You have always had my heart, Lizzie. I never loved anyone but you. Be happy for the memories we share, I'll take those memories with me and when it's your turn, I'll be close by, waiting for you."

The tears were flowing fast and Elizabeth wanted to say so much but was choked with her emotions. She knew she was losing her soulmate, her strength, her ally, her best friend.

Elizabeth couldn't bear to leave his feeble embrace and remained with her head on his chest, even as the nurses came in and out of the room to check his progress. It was sometime in the night that Elizabeth realised George was no longer breathing and his heart was no longer feebly beating. She didn't call the nurses, she just lay still, clinging to the final moments of contact. Her misery hung heavy in the air as she accepted what she knew had happened. She had no more tears to cry. The nursing staff left her alone and allowed those last few hours to pass privately, quietly, without intrusion.

Jack had told his parents that he was coming home but hadn't told them which ship, so he hadn't expected them to be at the dock waiting for him. On reflection, he was so glad that he had done it this way, it meant that he was able to make arrangements for Harriet's funeral and write to her parents, all without encumbrances and without other people weeping all over him. He did, of course, write to his own parents informing them of the tragedy and that he would be coming home in three days with his baby, but no mother.

He had taken a room in a small hotel in Southampton and two days later, he got a telegram from his mother, first of all sympathising with him for his terrible loss and secondly, sadly telling him that his father had recently suffered a major stroke and unfortunately had not been able to recover.

Jack didn't think he could take any more bad news, he was just glad that he was alone and in a private place so that he could mourn the loss of the two people who meant so much to him. Unmanly though it was, he cried himself to sleep every night for those three days. He had no idea how he was going to cope with a baby on his own and how he was going to take care of his mother. Jack was only twenty-two, he was only a young man, but at that time he felt old, really old, overnight he aged and was never to regain his youthful joie de vivre.

The hospital gave Jack a bag with basic essentials for the baby; some clothes, nappies, bottles and milk formula. He bought a small foldaway stroller and took delivery of his tiny baby. He had been interviewed in the hospital by the office staff and had registered the baby as Harry, in memory of Harriet.

He left the small hotel and took the train up to London. Fortunately, the baby slept all the way and was no trouble at all. At the station, he took a taxi to his parent's house and was greeted with hugs and kisses from his mother. There were tears flowing, both tears of joy at seeing each other, mingled with tears of sorrow at the loss of George and the loss of Harriet. The baby was in the stroller, wrapped in a mountain of baby blankets and once in the house, Elizabeth couldn't wait to have a look at her only grandchild.

When Jack took the baby from the stroller, Elizabeth took a step backwards with her hand over her mouth: she gasped, "Oh, my god, he's black!"

"No mum, he's not black, he's Harry and he's a half-caste and, therefore, deep coffee coloured."

The baby was indeed a dark coffee colour, more of a dark chocolate colour, really. He was a brown skinny little thing with enormous eyes and the makings of a little patch of bright red curly hair. Elizabeth didn't take the baby from Jack, she just sat down and put her hands over her face saying over and over, "Oh, how could you Jack, how could you? Oh, what would your father have said? Oh, Jack, how could you?"

"Mum, this is my baby. I loved Harriet, she was an educated good woman and I loved her. Please try to understand, I haven't committed any crime, I have a beautiful half-caste baby and I love him and I hope you can love him too. If you can't, I shall just have to go somewhere and bring him up on my own, but I really had hoped you would be able to love him and help me bring him up; please?"

Turning her head from side to side, Elizabeth just kept repeating, "Oh, Jack, how could you, how could you?"

At that, the baby started crying and Jack asked if there was any milk in the house as he needed to make up a bottle. He also needed to change the baby's nappy and get settled into his old room, unless his mother just didn't want him there. Elizabeth pulled herself together and told Jack to take the baby and his suitcases up to his room and she would organise a bottle for the child.

Once the baby had been changed and fed, he settled down to sleep, Jack was then able to sit and talk over the situation with his mother. Elizabeth told Jack that George hadn't yet been buried, she wanted Jack to be home as she didn't feel she could make those arrangements herself, it was all just too much for her, too upsetting.

She agreed to help Jack with the baby but with grave reservations, much tut tutting and shaking of her head. Jack agreed to go over to the local funeral parlour to organise the funeral. He asked Elizabeth would it be alright if she stayed home and watched over the baby while he was gone. She agreed and Jack left for the undertakers almost immediately.

When Jack got to the undertakers, he asked the receptionist, an overweight middle-aged woman whose uniform barely stretched across her huge bosom, for the paperwork and forms which needed to be completed. She fumbled through some files, took a sip from her cup of tea and then was able to tell Jack that his father was still in the morgue at the hospital and would need official authority before he could be transported to the funeral parlour; also when his father's body had been moved to the parlour, then Jack would need to formally identify his father.

Jack had been through the same procedure only days before and didn't think he could bear going through all the trauma of a funeral again. Jack took a taxi to the hospital and was nauseated by the overpowering smell of disinfectant. Documents needed to be signed and certain formalities completed, but eventually Jack managed to organise for his father's body to be transported to the undertakers.

First, though, he had to formally identify his father's body. He was taken down to a subterranean part of the hospital where it was cold, terribly cold. A hospital orderly took Jack into a large room which had metal drawers built into the side of the walls. He checked his filing system and after much fumbling proceeded to open one of the drawers. Jack hardly recognised the man he knew as his father, he was almost a complete stranger, he was thinner, much thinner than Jack remembered and there were deep furrows in his face. His eyes were sunk into his head, closed and unseeing.

The hospital orderly departed the room and left Jack alone with his father's body. Jack put his trembling hand to his father's face and recoiled with shock at the incredibly cold, hard feel of the old man's skin. He was not a religious person but managed to mumble a few words in prayer and bent over and kissed his father goodbye.

Before departing, Jack asked to see the senior doctor who had attended his father. The doctor was sympathetic to Jack's loss and explained how George Singleton had suffered a second massive stroke and had just passed in his sleep. He assured Jack that his father had not suffered, he had never been in pain and it was all for the best. He explained that even if Jack's father had regained consciousness, he would not have retained all his faculties; so in the end this was all for the best.

A nurse took Jack into an anteroom where there were some formalities and then he was allowed to go home to his mother and baby. He should have gone straight home but instead he went walking through the local park and sat on a bench and just gave way to his emotions. He thought his heart would break, how can anyone suffer two losses in such a short space of time. He was devastated and sat on that park bench for the best part of two hours. It seemed every nerve and sinew in his body refused to work, he was numb.

Eventually, he had to face his mother and when he did, he had no need for words. They embraced and then Elizabeth went to her room, to grieve in private; to mourn the loss of the only man she had ever really, truly loved and Jack retired to his room to mourn for his wife, for the only romantic love he had ever known.

Chapter 6
Back to Work

George Singleton had been a good provider for his wife and son. He had risen to the post of General Manager at the city branch of the Bank. He was well respected and there was a good turnout at the funeral, friends and work colleagues all paid their respects and spoke well of George.

Jack had managed to get a babysitter for the few hours that the funeral took but hurried back to the house as soon as it was decent to leave the mourners. Before he left, one of the directors of the bank took him to one side and asked him what his plans were, now that he was back in England. Jack told him that he hadn't given it any thought as life had taken an unexpected turn and he didn't know what he was going to do. The director was very sympathetic to Jack's loss and offered him a job, as a fully-fledged clerk in the Foreign Affairs Department, based on Jack's experience in America.

Jack was so grateful that he shook the man's hand vigorously, thanking him for his kind consideration. It was agreed that Jack would commence work on the following Monday. Sad though Elizabeth was, she was elated to hear that Jack would be working at the bank. George had left her reasonably well provided for, but Jack would need employment and this was a godsend. It was work he was well qualified to do and she hoped he would settle down and forge a career for himself.

Elizabeth had never followed a career or taken any form of employment. George was old-fashioned like that, he had always felt it was his duty as "man of the house" to provide for his family and never expected Elizabeth to take up paid work of any kind.

However, she explained to Jack that she would have to let the gardener and the housekeeper go; with just savings and George's pension to live on, she could no longer afford the luxury of home help. Jack, of course, readily volunteered to keep the garden looking good and told his mother he would help out with the work around the house, well, as much as he could, anyway.

Elizabeth really didn't want to spend the rest of her life looking after a baby, a child, but realised there was nothing else they could do. Jack needed help and she needed something or someone now to fill her life. With George gone, her life would be empty, have no purpose.

So they agreed that Jack would go to work at the bank and that Elizabeth would look after the baby. She had got over the shock of seeing a dark-skinned half-caste Harry and couldn't help warming to the tiny bundle who was so helpless and such a good baby.

However, she knew that tongues would wag and she didn't want friends or neighbours to criticise her son and his choice of bride and so just separated herself from the people she used to meet and socialise with.

They all assumed that she was grieving and no one bothered her. She never went back to the bridge club or to the golf club but kept herself to herself. She cooked and cleaned and cared for the baby; life was full and there was no time to feel sorry for herself, no time really to mourn for George, she had to get on with life, to care for this helpless infant who needed her. She realised being "needed" is probably one of the best feelings in the world and got on with the job, with as little complaining as she could manage.

Jack worked at the bank and his boss was impressed with Jack's knowledge of international banking. As far as Jack was concerned, the work was not difficult, just tedious and boring, he couldn't see himself remaining in banking for the rest of his life. He needed more stimulation, more challenge but for the time being, it was a solid job and brought in good money and he was just grateful to be employed.

Jack would bring home a newspaper each day and mother and son would discuss the daily news as well as catch up on the day's events. Elizabeth was a caring grandmother and Harry was thriving. He was too young to know, but Father Christmas came that December and left him a stocking full of goodies, clothes, toys and baby furniture. There were homemade coloured paper chain streamers across the living room and Jack brought a large Christmas tree, which he could barely fit through the front door.

They both laughed at the stupidity of it but enjoyed decorating the tree with all manner of decorations, most left over from previous years, but many that Jack made from coloured paper and he also hung in the tree silver paper covered chocolates. Elizabeth cooked a large chicken for Christmas dinner and made an amazing plum pudding with brandy sauce.

Mother and son got on really well and enjoyed the festive season: Harry was too young to know what was going on but gurgled happily in his crib. So long as he was fed and changed, he was the perfect baby. Elizabeth loved him and loved looking after him, but just couldn't get over the hurdle of him being coloured, it rankled her and she knew she just had to accept it and get over it, but it always bothered her whenever she looked at him.

Chapter 7
Preparations for War

Shortly after Christmas, Jack brought a copy of *Time* magazine home and both he and Elizabeth were shocked to see that Adolf Hitler had been voted Man of the Year.

"How could Time magazine honour that madman?" Elizabeth asked. "Everyone knows that Germany has occupied Czechoslovakia and it looks like they mean to do the same to Poland. Hitler is just a thug, a bully and a dictator, I just can't understand how the German people can't see him for what he is."

Jack just shrugged his shoulders and said, "There's going to be a war and we'll be in the thick of it, just you wait and see."

They discussed the conference that had been held in Germany back in September when four of the world's leading statesmen had met to supposedly redraw the map of Europe. Neville Chamberlain had attended along with Edouard Daladier of France, Benito Mussolini and Adolf Hitler. Elizabeth agreed that Chamberlain's "Peace with Honour" promise had actually achieved nothing.

Jack was quite angry at the thought that Britain should try and appease the dictators, whom he thought only wanted abject surrender from Britain and the rest of Europe. He told Elizabeth that if war was declared he wanted to volunteer and do his bit to fight off any invasion of England, the thought of surrender was abhorrent and he for one would never submit to German rule.

Elizabeth took from her apron pocket a letter that she had received that morning from Uri Zwick. Jack vaguely remembered a friend of his father's; a Max Zwick, a German who had been involved with George's bank. "Yes," said Elizabeth, "that's the one, well the son Uri has written me a letter and it's all quite upsetting and I don't think there's anything we can do, but I'll read it out to you."

Dear George and Elizabeth,

I hope this letter finds you both fit and well. I don't know if you will get this letter actually as getting a letter out of Germany is very difficult but I have friends who are helping me. I just wanted you (and maybe others in Britain) to know what we are going through here.

The other day, three SS men entered our jewellery store and demanded the keys from my father. They started looting the shop and when my father refused to give them the keys and tried to stop them from taking the stock, they beat him with clubs and knocked all his teeth out. We were both arrested and detained in the 9th District with about a thousand other Jews.

At about 3 o'clock in the morning, they released all those under 18 and allowed us to go home. Outside, there was a mob waiting to beat us all and we had to run for our lives. I got home severely bruised and battered and found the shop completely demolished. All the windows had been broken and the stock had been looted. There is nothing we can do and my father has been taken away with the other adults.

I don't know what will happen, I think the world has gone mad. If it was a foreign army doing this to us, I could sort of understand it, but it's our own people, Germans, persecuting us, just for being Jewish; whatever did my father do to deserve this, I don't know. I have heard that they are rounding up all the Jewish people and putting them into a separate area, but that's only a rumour. They know who we are, what religion we are and where we live. They got all that information from the census that was done a few years ago.

My father says now, that we, the Jewish people, were stupid to answer all their questions, especially the question about religion, but it's too late now, they have all the information they need. I don't know if you will get this letter; I have to trust my friend, but if I get a chance, I will write again.

Best wishes

Uri Zwick

As she read the letter, Elizabeth's voice cracked and tears were running down her cheeks. Jack got up from his chair at the table and put his arms around his mother to comfort her. They both clung to each other and mourned for the world gone crazy, for their lost loved ones and for the terrible future that they felt the world was coming into.

Jack settled down at the bank and got on well with everyone and worked hard. Everyone at the bank was worried about the possibility of war and it was always the topic of conversation at lunch times. There were those who believed Chamberlain's "Peace in our time" speech and those who said Germans couldn't and shouldn't be trusted; that Germany wanted to take over the world. It caused many a heated argument between staff and the papers were scoured each day for fresh news.

Elizabeth was worried too, she could remember the first world war and the difficulties that Londoners went through. She was determined that if there was to be a war, then she would plan for their survival, their food and things that the baby would need. If the war was going to last a few months or even a few years, the baby would be growing and would need clothes and toys and furniture; fit for a toddler or even a two, three or four-year-old.

The house was a good size, having four bedrooms and a large back garden. She walked out to the garden and had a good look at it. "Well," she said to herself, "we really don't need all those flowers, you can't eat flowers and those shrubs too, they'll all have to go. I'm going to clear everything and put in vegetables and fruit and even, maybe a chicken coop; nothing wrong with fresh eggs for a growing child."

She talked over the project with Jack and they agreed that at the weekend they would set to, to pull out everything in the back garden and replant with things they could eat. Jack was no carpenter but had seen chicken coops before and offered to do his best to make one for Elizabeth.

That weekend and each weekend for many months, Jack and Elizabeth worked to transform the back garden. It was hard, backbreaking work but they had a purpose and were keen to see their project come to fruition. Elizabeth was forty-eight but after so much gardening felt about ninety-two. They laughed as they worked and the baby grew as he watched from his pram.

The chicken coop was erected with many pieces of salvaged timber; it looked a bit rickety but it was the best that Jack could do, he was no woodworker. There were two nesting boxes next to two perches and a sloping gangplank with ridges on it for the chickens to waddle up. Elizabeth was delighted with it and left Jack with the baby one day as she went to the market to order three bales of straw, one bag of sawdust to be delivered and four chickens.

The straw and sawdust came first and Jack distributed it all in the nesting boxes and on the ground inside and around the coop. He had put posts up and erected wire netting. At the back of the chicken run he showed Elizabeth how she could open the nesting boxes and take any eggs out, without actually going into the chicken run, but there was a door to the run and she could get into the run to give the chickens food and water.

When the chickens were delivered, they immediately started digging into the straw and looked very happy. Elizabeth had bought in a huge amount of corn and pellets and couldn't wait for the chickens to do their bit and start producing eggs. There was one brown chicken, one black and two white. With not much originality, she gave them all names, Brownie, Blackie, Whitey One and Whitey Two. She couldn't distinguish between Whitey One and Whitey Two, but it really didn't matter. They were all going to give her eggs and so she determined she would love them all.

The next weekend, Elizabeth went to the market again and discussed her vegetable and fruit needs with the gardening section manager. The manager's name was Albert Robertson and he advised her what vegetables would grow in the London area, what fruit might be possible, what fertiliser and manures she would need. It was all quite bewildering to her but he sold her a good book, which explained just about everything in detail. Elizabeth took his advice and ordered all the things he recommended, including a nice big new wheelbarrow as her old one had worn through and developed a hole in the bottom.

Once Jack and his mother had stripped the garden completely of all its flowers and shrubs, it looked quite bare and pathetic, however Jack set to with the spade and turned over all the earth. The manures and fertilisers were delivered and again Jack turned over the earth, incorporating all the manure and fertiliser.

As recommended by Albert, they left the garden alone for a month and allowed it all to settle, then the good part of gardening could commence. Elizabeth went back to the market to ask Albert for more advice about setting out the garden. He was very interested in her project and offered to go around to the house and have a look at the garden before giving any further advice: he needed to see the shadows, how the house was aligned, where the winds would come from and what fences were already there.

Albert was fifty-two, a widower and walked with a heavy limp. He was what some people would call swarthy, being of Italian descent, not very tall and quite stocky, but he had black sparkly eyes and quite liked the look of Elizabeth. She had noticed his eyes and liked the look of him too, but was still in mourning for George so put all thought of romance behind her. However, she was glad of Albert's interest in her garden and welcomed the visit and listened attentively to his advice as to the layout of the garden.

Albert was acutely aware of the necessity of planting fruit trees so that they faced south, collecting as much sun as they could. Some vegetables he told her needed more sun than others and she should not plant exotic fruit and vegetables, as they would only disappoint her when they wouldn't flourish.

Albert recommended she plant some seedlings and some packet seeds, along with six fruit trees. She had bought two apple trees, two pear trees and two plum trees and together they planted them against the back fence to take advantage of the summer sun. He told her not to expect any fruit for at least three years, but it was exciting for Elizabeth to think of growing her own fruit, a thing she had never done before.

Albert helped Elizabeth divide the garden into sections and advised her which vegetables would be best in each section. The sections were divided by pathways that would enable her to tend the beds without trampling all over the plants. Jack was happy to assist with the paving of the pathways and between the three of them, the garden was laid out and had a professional look about it.

Elizabeth was very grateful for all Albert's help and cooked him a meal of gigantic proportions before he had to head off back home. He promised he would look in on her in a month's time and see how it was all getting on.

Chapter 8
Joining Up

Every day, Jack and his mother would discuss the daily news about the impending war. Jack was adamant that he wanted to volunteer even though his mother pleaded with him to consider Harry and tried to talk him out of the idea of telling him that he now had responsibilities and couldn't just run off to join the army.

Jack was still a young man and discussed endlessly with his mother the notion that he had to "do his bit" if England was threatened.

On 1 September 1939, it was reported that German troops had swarmed across the Polish border and unleashed what was called a Blitzkrieg, the first the world had ever seen. Apparently, Hitler had been planning his attack since March, ever since the German troops had occupied Czechoslovakia. German warships and U-boats attacked Polish naval forces in the Baltic Sea. Hitler apparently was claiming that the invasion was a defensive action, but no one was fooled and Britain knew that was rubbish.

The Poles had readied their defences, but they based their defensive strategy on the experiences of the first world war.

Jack's mother was of the opinion that the Polish cavalry troops would defend their country, as they were considered to be the best horsemen in the world. Jack laughed at his mother's naivety and told her, "Honestly mum you're living in the dark ages, the Poles probably are the best horsemen in the world, I'm not disputing that, but horses can't put up any defence against tanks."

Jack's mother retorted, "They'll repel any attack the Germans can make, mark my words, you'll see."

Jack just rolled his eyes and shook his head, "You don't understand mum, modern warfare just isn't like that anymore."

Britain and France had sworn to defend Poland and the two countries sent ultimatums to Hitler, demanding his withdrawal from Poland. There was no response to this demand and on 3 September Chamberlain announced on the British radio that a state of war now existed between Britain and Germany. World War II began with this broadcast.

It was announced on the radio that the king would shortly be broadcasting a message. Jack and his mother sat in awed silence, listening to King George address the nation. It was a scratchy reception on their little brown Bakelite kitchen radio and the speech was delivered slowly and deliberately. It started by the king addressing everyone as if he were speaking to them personally. He explained how, for the second time in the lives of most people, Britain was now at war.

The king pulled no punches and declared that if Britain and her allies did not prevail then the peoples of the world, under a German rule, would be kept in bondage and fear and all hopes of a settled peace and security of justice and liberty among nations would be ended.

The king ended his speech by calling on god to "bless and keep us all".

Jack sat quietly reflecting on all that had been said while his mother sobbed gently, rocking herself backwards and forwards; eventually she did the English thing and made them both a strong cup of tea.

Over the next few days, Jack read aloud to his mother that the German troops were advancing steadily on Poland and the Soviet forces were also marching into Poland from the east. Warsaw surrendered on 27 September and by 6 October Poland ceased to exist as a country.

Outside the bank where Jack worked was a large colourful poster showing a young airline pilot dressed in all his flying kits climbing into his airplane. He was waving cheerfully and the writing on the poster read: "Coming?—then hurry!"

It went on in smaller print eventually to explain "air crews wanted NOW for the RAAF." This poster was advertising for the Australian Air Force. Jack was attracted to the poster and the notion of joining the Air Force, but the thought of joining the Australian Air Force was even more appealing. The young pilot in the picture looked so happy and confident.

Jack decided he would try and find out more about joining the Royal Air Force or the Australian Air Force; the very thought of learning to fly just gave him such a thrill and he thought if he could join the Australians, well that would just be the icing on the cake, Australia had always appealed to his need for adventure, something different, something exotic even.

Chapter 9
Royal Air Force Training

Jack discussed his desire to volunteer with his mother. He told her how he would just love to learn to fly, especially if he could be part of an Australian force, even if he wasn't Australian. Maybe they would ship him off to Australia for training, it was something he would just love to do. Elizabeth was beside herself with anger and frustration at him.

She told him over and over, "You have a child, you have a responsibility, you have me, a widow woman, you can't just run off when you feel like it. We need you here, Harry and I need you. I'm sure you won't be called up as you are a supporting father and son. You can't do this to us. You just can't. And if you really must, then at least be with your own people, not foreigners, like the Australians."

"Oh, mum, Australians aren't really foreigners, they're the same as us, white and basically, mostly British born anyway."

"No matter, son, if you really must join up then have the good sense to be with your own kind, English, British, I'm serious, I don't want you mixing with a load of colonials. I've heard those Australians are a wild bunch and what's more, they're all descendants from convicts who were deported there a hundred years ago."

"Oh, mum, you're priceless!" laughed Jack.

"Well, I'll reconsider the Australian thing, but sorry, mum, it's my duty to join up and I intend to do it. What if I don't go to war and the Germans win, how will I ever be able to hold my head up in any sort of company? I need to do my bit, I can't leave it to all the other chaps. Harry is your grandson, you love him, I can see that. I'm sure you will look after him, care for him and bring him up to be an upstanding young fellow, just like you did me. I know you can do it, mum, in fact, I'm counting on you."

Elizabeth resorted to pleading and crying but to no avail, Jack's mind was made up. He let Christmas come and go and then on 5 March 1940, he joined the RAF.

After various academic tests, reading, writing and arithmetic; medical and dental examinations and a military haircut that was a shock to his system, he enlisted as Pilot U/T (under training) and was put on the reserve list, awaiting training.

After two months, he was instructed to report to Babbacombe, Torquay, in South Devon and was initiated into the ways of the RAF—kitting out, lectures, kit layout, inoculations and vaccinations, marching at 140 paces per minute and saluting. No time to look at the beautiful English countryside, no time to appreciate the beckoning beach and clear blue surf that he would just love to have a swim in.

Jack didn't exactly enjoy this introduction to military life, but he took it all in his stride and buckled down to learning all he could.

Meanwhile, Elizabeth accepted the fact that her little boy, her son was now a man and there was a child who needed her, albeit not one whom she previously had considered was acceptable in modern society, which is the way she had been thinking, such was her prejudice.

She was beginning to realise that her relationship with this innocent baby was teaching her a lot about herself and her capacity to love. She was thinking quite deeply about the effect that this child was having on her and was starting to see flaws in her own personality. Her colour prejudice was not based on any firm facts, just on cultural norms. The mixing of two cultures, two ethnic groups still bothered her and she realised there was absolutely no justification for the way she had been thinking.

As the days, weeks and months passed, she stopped looking at Harry as something different, he was just Harry, a baby, innocent, in need of love like any other child.

Two weeks later, Jack was posted to No. 3 ITW (Initial Training Wing) Cambridge. Here he learnt to march at 160 paces per minute. His group had daily lectures on aircraft recognition, mathematics, navigation and Morse Code (8 words per minute). Halfway through the expected course, Jack and his whole group were suddenly promoted to Leading Aircraftmen and posted to Gourock in Scotland.

At Gourock, the group boarded the liner, now troop carrier, the Duchess of Athlene; destination unknown. All the men were warned not to talk about their destination, which wasn't too difficult as they had no idea where they were headed anyway, but there was much speculation and nervous anticipation. Jack was thrilled once again to be out at sea. He loved being on the ocean and very much admired the sturdy liner with her two fat smoking funnels.

There were 800 troops on board the boat and no sooner had they set sail and were settling into a pleasant routine on board when the captain turned the boat round and returned to Scotland. The degaussing equipment (protection against mines) had failed. Once back in harbour, having no work or training for the group, the Air Force sent everyone home on leave, their first since joining up.

Elizabeth was thrilled to see Jack home and was proud to show him that Harry could now walk and at 18 months was a sturdy, happy toddler, into everything and learning something new every day.

Jack had only been home a few days when he received a telegram instructing him to return to Wilmslow; here he was told he had been selected for flying training in America. Once again he had to travel to Scotland, this time to embark on SS Stratheden, a tall, white, elegant liner which had Jack gasping when he first saw her tied up alongside. She was the most beautiful ship he had ever seen and best of all, he was to return to America in her.

Jack had loved being in America and retained all his fond memories of his life there, especially meeting and marrying Harriet. He hoped he would have a chance of visiting New York and maybe catching up with his aunt and uncle. They had been very good to him and he felt he owed them an apology for leaving without saying goodbye properly and without introducing them to Harriet.

However, it was not to be. Jack's group set out from Scotland in convoy, but after two days left the convoy and proceeded at full speed to St. John's Newfoundland. Jack loved being at sea again, the smell, the spray, the swell and motion of the ship, the excitement of being on the ocean filled his senses. He remembered his first journey out from England and he realised he hadn't lost that thrill and excitement of travelling towards the unknown. He also remembered his journey from America to England and how sick Harriet had been. He hadn't enjoyed the ocean at all on that trip and his memories brought tears to his eyes.

One of the other trainees, a red-headed spotty youth, nicknamed Ginger by everyone, came alongside Jack and tried to engage him in innocent conversation. When he saw the tears in Jack's eyes he immediately jumped to the wrong conclusion and nastily asked, "Oh, dear, are we missing our mummy then? Frightened to be at sea, are we?"

"Bugger off and mind your own business."

Ginger wouldn't let go of a chance to torment someone. He had been tormented, teased and bullied all his life and so, in turn, became a cowardly bully and enjoyed inflicting misery on anyone he could. He followed Jack around the deck, taunting him with cries of "Jack wants his mummy, Jack wants his mummy."

"I'm warning you, get off my back or I'll knock your teeth out."

Knowing that any violence would not be tolerated by the military personnel Ginger continued his taunting, "Jack's crying for his mummy, Jack's crying for his mummy."

Not able to stand the taunting any longer, Jack turned to his tormentor and punched him clean on the nose, causing a dreadful nosebleed. Unfortunately for the two, an officer happened to turn the corner and saw Jack hit the other trainee and Ginger retaliate by kicking Jack in the shins. The two boys were put on a charge and brought before their commanding officer for punishment.

As they were at sea and unable to return the trainees to England, the commanding officer decided to let the boys sort out their personal problems in the tried and tested way of the British. He also thought it would be a good diversion and entertainment for the other trainees and so ordered that the boys meet the next day in the ship's gymnasium for a boxing match to sort out their differences.

Jack was tall and skinny, on the other hand Ginger was short but stocky. Jack had led a soft life and had no need or knowledge of fighting, however the months of working in his mother's garden had given him some solid muscles. Ginger had only known street fighting and considered kicking, spitting, biting and the carrying of a knife to be the weapons of choice.

Once in the boxing ring, the officer in charge laid out the rules of boxing quite clearly. They were to follow the Marquis of Queensbury rules to the letter. Two by one minute rounds were being called for and both boys were given regulation boxing gloves. Neither had actually ever done any boxing and had only seen it on cinema newsreels.

The ship's crew and all the trainees congregated in the gymnasium around the boxing ring and started barracking for their favourite. Both boys were given last-minute instructions from their corners and the fight started.

Jack had no idea what to do and just jogged around the ring, weaving right and left, avoiding the flailing arms of Ginger. Ginger was keen to throw as many punches as he could but had no finesse and just kept throwing his arms wildly and futilely in front of him. Neither had actually landed a punch but got into one or two clinches, which forced the referee to pull the two apart.

By the end of the second round Ginger was exhausted, his arms felt like lead weights. He didn't realise it but his tired arms relaxed and lowered, just enough for Jack to see an opening and almost on the bell, Jack landed, yet again, a beautiful direct hit on Ginger's nose, which again started to bleed profusely.

The referee held up Jack's arm and declared him the winner. The two were told to shake hands and forget whatever it was that they had been arguing about. Jack was quite happy to do this and put the whole incident behind him, but not so Ginger. Under his breath, he swore to get even and Jack knew he could never turn his back on this boy; they were sworn enemies from that time on.

Once in St. John's Jack and his group were sent on to Toronto where they were given plain grey and navy blue suits which were meant to disguise them as civilians and they were all told to reply to any questions that they were Aeronautical Students and to pass themselves off as Americans. This was just plain stupid and impossible, as their English accents gave them away as soon as they opened their mouths.

While they were in Canada, there was a call to the base asking for help. Could they drive to a location in the forest to help with an emergency. At a nearby family campsite, in a wooded area, by the side of a fast-running river in the countryside, a child had gone missing. All the locals were out looking for her, to no avail and so the authorities decided to call in any other assistance that could be spared. The child had been put to bed at seven in the evening while the parents and other adults were having evening drinks and a BBQ.

When the parents returned to their tent, they discovered the five-year-old girl was missing. The parents were desperate and ran to all the tents, calling for their child. Everyone in the camp congregated in the centre and all the men volunteered to go out into the night with flashlights and whatever kind of torches they could muster. At midnight, most of the campers returned, dejected and worried as the child had not been found. The police were called, mountain rescue and other emergency services. It was agreed that the search would resume at first light.

No one knew whether the child had been taken by a wild animal or by a predatory human. There was no sign of a struggle, no one had heard the child cry out and there was no evidence that a wild animal had taken her. The parents, understandably, were beside themselves with worry and self-recrimination.

Jack searched that first day with other volunteer members of his group, thinking all the time how he would feel if it was Harry that had gone missing. He could barely imagine the anguish that the parents must be going through.

Four days went by with almost everyone in the area out searching and calling for the child. There was much speculation in the press and news teams arrived from Toronto and just got in the way, giving no help whatsoever. Chasing an interesting story seemed to be all that they were concerned about. Eventually, the search was called off.

It was a weekend and Jack and his group had been given two days' leave. Although they were all exhausted and thoroughly depressed, most followed Jack's lead and agreed to go back into the woods to look for the child. Two of the guys, though, Ginger and Cedric, had dates with the local girls and expressed their opinions that it was all a waste of time.

"Everyone," they said, "had been looking and it was obvious that the child had either fallen into the swollen river or been taken by a forest creature."

They didn't want to go back out again, chasing a lost cause. Jack swore at the boys and lectured them about selfishness and called them various names ranging from self-centred bastards to undisciplined woman chasers with no moral backbones. Ginger openly expressed his aversion to helping Jack in any way and ignoring such taunts the two turned their backs on the group and after expressing their views that it was a weekend and they had weekend passes, so didn't have to do anything they didn't want to do, they calmly walked away from the group.

Mike, one of the older guys, put his arm around Jack's shoulders and declared, "Bugger them, we don't need their help we can do this. We can at least give it another go before we give up. Let's try and work out what might have happened, everyone should have some input and then we'll decide the best course of action."

Jack and the group pondered on the problem and tried to think what might have happened. They dismissed the idea that a fellow camper might have taken the child, that would have been extremely difficult and in any case the police had checked every tent, vehicle and camper in the area. They dismissed also the idea that a wild creature had taken the child, although, goodness knows, from what everyone was telling them, there was no shortage of wild animals, from bears to cougars.

Jack tried to put himself into the mind of a five-year-old. What if the child had woken and needed to go to the toilet, the toilet block was a little way off from where her tent had been erected. What if she had seen one of the many woodland creatures that stayed around the campsite, squirrels, chipmunks, etc. She could have wandered off following a friendly critter and then got disorientated and just kept walking.

Before setting out again, Jack sat and discussed his reasoning with his group. One of the boys put forward a plausible theory. He stated that at seven in the evening, when the child went missing it was almost dark but not quite and one part of the evening sky would have been dark and the other part, in the west would have been lighter as the sun went down. Surely a five-year-old would head towards the light rather than the dark.

The group all agreed with this reasoning and so they headed off in the direction of the west. That way led them to a rough track that followed the river and by the side of the river were brambles and amongst the brambles were ripe blackberries, thimbleberries and huckleberries. Jack pointed out to his group of enthusiastic searchers that an intelligent child might well pick some berries and drink from the freshwater river and could therefore last for many days, assuming no humans or wild animals had attacked her.

How far a five-year-old could go was merely supposition but the parents at the beginning of the original search had declared that the child's shoes were missing and so presumably the child had put on shoes to go to the toilet block, if that was where she was headed. Jack and his group discussed the possibility that a five-year-old could actually survive on berries and water and sleeping rough for many days, especially as it was late summer and the weather had been exceptionally mild.

Jack and his group hiked, splayed out, but close enough together to keep in audible contact and trudged through the tracks, keeping close to the river for the whole of Saturday and most of Sunday morning. They were due to return to their camp on Sunday evening and were on the brink of turning back when one of the young trainees spotted a hunter's lodge. Really, a shack in the woods, some hundred metres from the river. He called to the others and they all converged, hopefully, on the wooden shack.

When the young group got to the shack, there was a huge surprise for everyone. Laid on a rough sacking bed was an old man with makeshift bandages on his right leg and dirty towels wrapped around his head. In the corner of the room was a little girl cuddling a friendly collie dog and not in the least worried about the sudden invasion of a dozen young men.

Jack immediately rushed up to the child and asked for her name. To his great relief, it was the child that they had all been looking for. Jack had tears in his eyes and hugged the child to him, which frightened her, but she was intelligent enough to know that she had been lost and asked Jack, "Where is my mummy?"

Jack assured the child that they would take her back to her mummy and daddy but first he had to talk to the old man.

Frank Sunderland, the old man, explained to Jack that a miracle had happened three days back. He had been setting traps and unfortunately tripped over and got caught in the trap himself. He had managed to extricate himself from the trap but couldn't walk or do anything but drag himself, bleeding and in agony, back to his shack.

He had laid there for a whole day before a little girl tentatively knocked on his door and came into his life. He was a religious man and claimed god had sent the child to look after him and for him to look after her. There was food in the cupboard and the child was able to fetch water from the river.

Together, the two survived and Frank explained that there was no way he could notify anyone that the child was safe with him, no phone, no neighbours, no visitors. He knew people would eventually come looking for the child, but frankly expected it would have been sooner than this. The child was in no danger and helped the old man; he of course gave shelter and comfort to the distraught child.

A rescue team was called and the old man was taken to the closest hospital. The child was returned to the grieving parents, who had all but given up hope of ever seeing their daughter again. Jack and his group were embraced with kisses, thanks and expressions of eternal gratitude from the parents and extended family. They refused to be interviewed by the press and returned, almost unsung heroes back to their base camp but with inner feelings of a job well done and self-satisfaction. The two that had refused to help and had abandoned the search were, as the English put it, "sent to Coventry." Persona non grata!

Jack's group was sent next to Georgia in the south where the locals welcomed them with open arms and all wanted to know how it was in England and how were the Londoners especially coping with all the threat of bombing, rationing and deprivation.

The journey south took five days and at each stop, the locals plied the happy travellers with candy, cookies and fruit. Jack and his fellow airmen thought this was the cushiest number. "If this is war," they laughed, "let's have more of it." Such was their youthful naivety.

The group arrived at Darr Aero Tech, Albany Georgia (a civilian flying school previously taken over by the U.S. Army Air Corps) and were immediately kitted out with khaki shirts and trousers but were instructed to wear civilian clothes when venturing into the nearby town.

Jack and his fellow English airmen had never experienced southern fried chicken, pumpkin pie, French fries (which they declared were really only thin chips), pecan nuts and iced tea, but were converts immediately to the American food and easy-going way of life; that is, if you were "white", however Jack was soon noticing the obvious restrictions for "coloureds".

The first thing that became obvious was that every time Jack and his group were walking on the footpath or sidewalk as the Americans called it, if a negro man or woman was coming towards them the negro would step off into the road to let the white boys pass by.

At first, Jack thought they were just being polite but when he questioned one of the American flyers, he was told that such behaviour was expected and sometimes there could be trouble if the negro didn't comply with this practice. Jack was appalled and couldn't recall anything like that happening in New York when he lived there previously. The English boys soon realised that life for the negroes was very different from that of the white population.

Segregation, they found out, was a rigid system that pervaded every aspect of life in Georgia and other towns in the south. Blacks and whites attended separate schools, used separate drink fountains, had separate public toilets, attended separate churches, rode the railways in separate sections. Public buses and theatres were well used by both blacks and whites, but the blacks had to sit at the back in a separate section.

The English boys found all this prohibition extremely disturbing, they had never experienced anything like it in England, however they realised that in actual fact there were very few coloured people in England. Jack was particularly angry at the segregation but was careful not to talk about his marriage to Harriet and the fact that she was coloured. He wasn't exactly ashamed of the fact but he didn't feel it was right to broadcast this information around, especially as Jack knew it was illegal for mixed marriages in the south. He dreaded to think what Ginger would make of information like that.

The one thing that set the English students apart from the Americans was the contempt by the Americans for the negro population. It seemed that it was so inbred into them that even their everyday speech involved putting down any person of colour and expecting absolute servitude and submission to their perceived "white supremacy". Jack and his co-workers found this aspect of American life very difficult to understand and to ignore, however, they were all astute enough to keep their thoughts to themselves.

Jack's first ever flight was an experience he would never forget. Firstly, for the euphoria he felt at being airborne and secondly, for the total horror at seeing just a little way in front of him, one of his fellow students who had recently soloed for the first time collide with a dual aircraft just ahead of him. The two planes crashed and caught fire. There were no survivors and suddenly the thrill of flying left Jack and his classmates, it wasn't fun anymore, it was serious and dangerous.

The military funeral, which was held at St. Paul's Church in Albany, cast a shadow and substantially dampened the enthusiasm of the young group.

While Jack and his group were training in Georgia, reports were coming in from Britain. In early September 1940, reports were coming in about the German Luftwaffe. Previously all raids had been targeting RAF airfields but now apparently Hitler put into action his plan to demoralise the population of Britain by firstly mass bombing London. An afternoon raid comprising 348 German bombers escorted by 617 fighters bombarded London for two solid hours. A second wave of attack followed and continued until 4.30 the following morning.

The newspapers and radio reported that London was almost destroyed, fires consumed much of the city, especially the east end and the dock areas. Residents who didn't have air-raid shelters were taking refuge in the underground stations. It was reported that over 150,000 people sheltered below ground during the night. Apparently, one air-raid shelter had accommodated 450 people and unfortunately received a direct hit.

Jack was beside himself with worry. He just wanted to know if his mother and son were safe. There was no way he could communicate: no one in Georgia could or would give any specific help in getting information to the British servicemen. Jack just felt so helpless and impotent. He wrote letter after letter to his mother but received no reply.

The mass bombings ended in 1941, with Jack still in America with no knowledge of his little family.

Jack and only half his group passed the rigorous course and by the end of December 1941, those who had passed were performing solo flights and were competent with all the service requirements, navigation skills and meteorological knowledge. Some of those who failed the course were given the chance to train as aircraft mechanics and ground support crew. Ginger was one of those who failed to obtain his "wings" but took on training as a ground support crew.

Jack and Ginger rarely met and when their paths did cross they simply ignored each other, that is, until an outbreak of flu at the station put many of the flyers and crew into the infirmary. Jack's normal ground crew were all taken ill and Ginger was temporarily assigned to service Jack's plane.

Instinct told Jack that Ginger had never got over their initial dislike of each other or the win that Jack had in the boxing ring. Jack was not happy to have his old enemy service his plane, there was absolutely no trust there at all and Jack did everything that he could to persuade his commanding officer to give him a different service mechanic.

Unfortunately, there were just insufficient ground crew available to be so choosy and so Jack had to rely on Ginger doing a good job and hoped that he wouldn't be so stupid as to actually sabotage Jack's plane.

Jack was scheduled to take a practise reconnaissance flight in the afternoon and feeling quite unnerved by the thought that Ginger might just be capable of sabotaging his plane, Jack had a sudden idea. He checked with his commanding officer and just before taking off, gave Ginger the order to board the plane to assist him. Ginger was confused, he wasn't supposed to go up with the pilots, that wasn't part of his job, but sometimes it was necessary if there was a suspected problem that a mechanic needed to be present to sort out.

Jack showed Ginger his written instructions and ordered Ginger to board the plane. He told Ginger there was a disturbing rattle in the fuselage that had Jack worried and he needed a mechanic to fly with him and to listen to the rattle to identify just where it was coming from. There was nothing to be seen on the outside of the plane and equally nothing that could be detected inside the plane. Just as Jack suspected, Ginger made an excuse before boarding and went to the rear of the plane and made some adjustment before climbing aboard. Jack now knew for sure that Ginger had planned some sort of malfunction.

With Ginger himself aboard, Jack knew he would be safe. There was no point in Jack reporting Ginger, nothing could be proved but thankfully Ginger was never again assigned to service Jack's plane while at that station and the two just ignored each other whenever their paths crossed.

Jack was offered the choice of accepting an RAF Commission, which meant staying in America and instructing future cadets or returning to England to take up the position of sergeant, with the hope of seeing real action instead of training other young cadets. He chose going home as he felt a real need to "do his bit" and see some action, but most important to him was finding out if his mother and Harry had survived the bombing.

By March 1942, Jack was on his way home. He was given a week's leave and made his way to London to see his mother and Harry. Jack couldn't believe his eyes when he saw all the damage and bomb sites as he travelled through London.

The devastation was incredible, houses and buildings were often only being held up by one wall and there were loose bricks and scaffolding everywhere. His heart quickened as he made his way home, praying that his mother and young son were still safe. Jack was not religious but, nevertheless, pleaded with god to have spared his mother and son. London and many other major cities had suffered from what had been named "the Blitz" which was shortened from the German name Blitzkrieg, meaning lightning war.

Jack caught a bus from the train station and as he got closer to his home his mind was in a turmoil, what if his home simply wasn't there anymore, what if his mother had been bombed out, where would his mother and son be now if that was the case? What if his mother and son had actually been killed, as many hundreds of others had, "but no," Jack consoled himself, "that couldn't be so, they, the authorities, would have told him. They knew where he was and would have contacted him."

Jack couldn't wait to get off the bus and once he did, he just ran down the road and round the bend. His home was still there. He sat on a low wall, with tears of relief and collected himself. He realised he was sweating profusely and his heart was racing, but slowly he calmed down and after a few moments walked down the road to his home. Again, he sent up a small prayer, "Thank you, god, thank you."

Elizabeth Singleton, Jack's mother, was delighted to see her son and chastised him for not letting her know he was coming home. Harry was asleep, having his afternoon nap but Jack couldn't wait for him to wake up, he picked up the child and smothered him with kisses. Poor Harry was first of all not used to such enthusiastic embraces and secondly was too young to recognise his father and so screamed and yelled for Elizabeth to rescue him from this noisy, exuberant stranger. Reluctantly Jack passed him over to Elizabeth, who rebuked him for being so unthinking.

"My goodness Jack, you're like a bull in a china shop. You can't just wake up a child and expect him to welcome you with open arms, you've frightened him."

"Oh, mum, you've no idea how worried I've been and I'm just so relieved that you are both OK. Why didn't you write and let me know you were safe?"

"For goodness' sake Jack, I wrote nearly every month. Don't tell me you didn't get my letters."

"Obviously not, mum, when I get back I'll put in a report and find out why we didn't get letters from home, but you are safe and I'm so relieved. Coming here, I couldn't help noticing all the devastation, how was it for you? Was it really frightening, did you go down to the underground to take cover? How did Harry react? Was he terrified?"

Jack couldn't stop hugging his mother and just kept telling her over and over how relieved he was that she was alright. "How was it then mum, can you talk about it?"

"Well, it was awful, son, worse than you can imagine. On that first night, we heard the sirens but were still taken by surprise. Later on, I'm ashamed to say we started to get used to the nightly bombings. They usually came just after dark. Once the sirens started, you could hear the planes overhead."

"Did you manage to get to the underground?"

"Well no, actually I always get claustrophobic in the underground so I reckoned we were safe enough in the house here. I would take Harry from his crib and we'd just hide under my bed. It was a squeeze but I reckon it's the safest place and luckily the house never got hit."

"Oh, for crying out loud, mum, are you crazy? You know, staying in the house was probably the most dangerous thing you could do. Why didn't you just bottle your fears and go down to the underground like everyone else? You were lucky, but I'm so cross with you for taking such a risk."

What Elizabeth Singleton didn't want Jack to know was that she still couldn't get over Harry being a half-caste and rather than her neighbours seeing the child, she decided to gamble with their lives and stay within the feeble protection of the house.

To change the subject, Elizabeth started to tell Jack all about the raids and her experiences.

"You know, Jack, we had the curtains drawn so that no light could escape but even so we could see the lights flashing through the curtain thickness. Harry was terrified for the first few raids and then I think he just accepted the noise and the ground shaking. Children don't know what bombing and fires are all about, they don't fear anything if you don't instil fear into them. He's a very trusting and docile child. The banging and booming of the heavy bombs eventually, I think, started to almost soothe him. I tried my best not to look or sound alarmed and I think he took this lead from me and didn't seem to be afraid at all.

"One night, the bombing was obviously a long way away and Harry was asleep under my bed so I made sure all the lights were out and tentatively opened the curtains to see the most incredible spectacle. The whole horizon of the city was lined with enormous fires, hundreds of them. It was indescribable, monstrous but at the same time, awe-inspiring. I was mesmerised.

"I could hear the fire engines, bells, emergency vehicles, ambulances and the sound of buildings collapsing. The flames were huge. They would die down for a while and then start up again. Planes were still flying overhead. I could see them but they were bombing the city and probably the docks. Nothing near us. The planes were dropping incendiary bombs, dozens and dozens. These started fires and were quickly put out I think but then started up again, it seemed the fires were jumping from one building to the next.

"The flames must have been fifty feet into the air or even higher; it was difficult to tell. The sky turned red, almost like a beautiful summer sunset, but this was no beautiful scene, it felt like we were living in a devil's lair, down in hell itself. There was the flashing of anti-aircraft shells bursting in the sky. Hardly any hitting the planes that were being picked out by spotlights.

"I could see some barrage balloons which were supposed to be silver, but the reflection of the fires had turned them into bright pink and red. It was all so surreal, so dramatically devastating but at the same time thrilling and disturbing. I should have been really frightened but I wasn't, I just stood at the window trying to absorb the enormity of what I was witnessing."

"Mum, I'm really cross with you. If there are any more raids, you have to promise me that you'll take Harry down to the underground. I mean it, promise me."

Chapter 10
More Training

Unfortunately for Jack, his training in America was deemed to be so valuable that he was sent to a Pilot Advanced Flying Unit in Gloucestershire and then on to flying instructors' school in Scotland.

At the end of May 1942, Jack was posted as an instructor to the No. 9 Elementary Flying Training School, engaged in assessing recruits for flying potential to be followed by elementary flight training. Jack was given a de Havilland Tiger Moth aircraft which he hated as the plane had an open cockpit and even in the summer it was cold in the air and miserable, nevertheless Jack felt he had good pupils who were keen and eager to learn.

By the end of November, he had progressed from Sergeant through Flight Sergeant and on to Warrant Officer. Jack was frustrated. It wasn't so much that he hated teaching and instructing but he still had a strong desire to see action and so put in for a transfer.

After much discussion, persuasion and arguing with his senior officer was eventually posted to No. 1 Group Support Unit at Swanton, in Norfolk for a conversion course onto Mosquito Mark 6 Fighter Bombers. There he "crewed-up" with a navigator, Sergeant Max Mulligan, a genial, good humoured stocky fellow with a mass of black curls and enormous eyebrows that danced as he laughed.

The pair immediately felt a bond of friendship that was cemented by many a pint of beer at the station bar. Max and Jack flew together for their first operational training run after five weeks research and study, concentrating on low level flying at night and day, air-to-ground and air-to-air gunnery, stealth bombing and "Gee Navigation," a form of radar. At last, Jack hoped he'd be seeing some action and he would be able to attack the Germans and at the same time defend his country.

After Christmas Max and Jack were posted to the 306 Polish Squadron at Epinoy, France, where their first task was to assist with the clearing of the runways. Snow had fallen and continued to fall with each day. Eventually the pair, as part of the 306 Squadron, were given the task to bomb and disrupt enemy transports. Apart from one daylight operation, all the other flights were at night. They were briefed before each flight by their Wing Commander and given details of patrol areas and enemy activity to be expected; bomb load to be carried and take off times.

After briefing, Max and Jack would plan their route and study a topographical map noting any high ground or major obstructions and any known flak area.

Jack couldn't have been happier. At last he was "doing his bit" even though he hadn't actually been shot at or in fact seen any other plane being shot at. It all seemed too easy, too comfortable, but that was to change.

In January 1943 Jack and Max were flying a Mosquito NS 844 in which they patrolled Siegburg, Puderback and Hagar and had their first chance to bomb enemy transport and after that a railway junction. They were jubilant as they realised their first real mission had been a runaway success.

Their next mission saw them at night cross enemy lines at 4,000 ft and were being fired on, for the first time, from the ground. They broke formation with the rest of the squadron and re-formed again as soon as possible.

In only a few minutes, Jack was being attacked with machine gun and cannon fire. There was an enemy transport which was being protected by a night fighter. It fired a long burst of cannon fire and although Jack took immediate violent evasive action, unfortunately, the plane was hit and the starboard engine caught fire.

Max operated the fire extinguisher and Jack "feathered" the propeller. A second burst of gunfire and the port engine caught fire. Jack throttled back and could tell that the fire had taken hold and was not being extinguished. Jack ordered Max to clip on his parachute and bale out. Max jettisoned the door and successfully abandoned the aircraft. The plane was now losing height rapidly. Jack struggled to get out of his seat but couldn't get his left leg past the control column. He pulled the seat pack of his parachute clear of the bucket seat, while at the same time trying to keep the plane steady and on an even keel.

With a great deal of difficulty, he reached the doorway and dived through the opening, pulling the ripcord as soon as he was clear of the aircraft, but there was no time for the parachute to fill with air. The plane flew on for a further half mile and Jack hit the trees on the hillside at the same time as the plane hit the ground further on.

Max watched the plane go down in a ball of flames and never saw if Jack had managed to bail out or not. The plane burst into a ball of fire on impact and Max assumed that Jack had just not managed to get out in time.

Chapter 11
Germany

Wilfreid Graff had been wounded and sent home from the front with shell shock, a broken arm, many lacerations and internal injuries from his shrapnel wounds. The doctors couldn't get all the shrapnel out from his chest cavity and he was told to stay in bed and basically move as little as possible, otherwise the shrapnel could move and seriously affect his internal organs, especially his heart.

Ida Graff was a solid, no-nonsense German woman; her beefy arms and solid body could do a day's work to equal any man's. Happy to be a farmer's wife, had married young but was now twenty-eight years old and had once been passionately in love with Wilfreid. She was distressed to see her proud, tall, athletic and once "farm work muscled" soldier husband so pathetically bedridden and reduced to the life of an invalid.

She loved him still but had no patience attending to his physical needs, cleaning his wounds, feeding, washing, shaving, toileting. He was in so much pain it kept them both awake each night and she needed her strength to run the farm that he had left to join Hitler's forces. All the men on the farm had been called to military service and only women were left to run the farms and factories.

Ida was not popular in their village, which was some five miles away. She regularly hitched their only horse to the small buggy and took her vegetables in to the marketplace to sell, but at such inflated prices that the locals felt incensed and blackmailed into paying the exorbitant prices. Ida had taken on the work of the farm herself with no assistance, but now with Wilfreid to look after, she felt overwhelmed with the workload. No one came to see her and there was no assistance from the government or the local council. She was alone and no one seemed to care if she was managing or not. They had no children and no close relatives.

It was winter; they had food stored and some vegetables still in the ground: potatoes, carrots, turnips, onions, swedes, beetroot and pumpkin, but no fuel for the fire or stove. Each day, Ida would take the horse and buggy out to the forest to collect firewood and to forage for mushrooms or wild berries. It was a harsh life but Ida was strong and had been managing quite well until Wilfreid had returned home sick and wounded.

It was at the beginning of February when Ida turned over in bed and felt her husband's cold, cold body next to hers. At first, she cuddled up to him, trying not to move him and exacerbate his pain, but in order to warm him up a little. He didn't respond and Ida asked if he was alright. The ominous silence told her that he was no longer with her. Wilfreid had passed away in the night and there was nothing she could do.

Ida knew she had loved her husband but she found it difficult to weep, to mourn for this shell of a man, a shadow of what he used to be, what he had once been. She grieved at losing the man she had loved before he left for the army, but this didn't seem to be the same man, this was an invalid and for the last few weeks had been a heavy burden that she felt she just couldn't cope with. Now she felt guilty that she couldn't grieve as she knew she should, but he was gone, the man she had known had left her some weeks earlier, she had been left with almost a stranger she barely recognised. She was sad, but couldn't cry.

Her first thought was how was she going to get a funeral organised, was that still possible with almost no men in the village? She knew there was no minister or pastor at the small Lutheran church, all the men, even the religious leaders, had left the area for Hitler's forces. She decided that she would bury him herself and mark his grave as best she could. There were no children or relatives to worry about and her main concern was the hard winter ground.

Ida took a pickaxe and a spade and chose the softest earth she could find and started to dig. It took her two days to get a hole large enough to give her husband a decent burial plot. The earth was frozen almost solid but she chose a patch which had been turned over in the autumn and she knew would be less compact than most other areas. She collected as many stones and rocks as she could, loaded them up onto the buggy and had the horse pull them back to the burial plot.

She had wrapped Wilfreid's body in a sheet and dragged him across the bedroom floor, through the kitchen to the back door. Once at the back door, she rolled him up in an old piece of carpet, tied a rope around the middle and around his feet and attached the rope to the horse. Carefully she led the well-trained horse, pulling his burden across the hardened earth to the field and at the hole in the ground she reverently rolled Wilfreid's body gently in. It was backbreaking work and in spite of the cold freezing weather, she was sweating profusely.

At last, the earth was piled up over his body, the rocks and stones layered over the mound and she fashioned a headstone from the smoothest rock she could find. Wood for the fire was too precious to waste on a cross. Ida was not religious but said a small prayer over him, regardless.

Chapter 12
Rescue or Capture

Jack had left it too late to parachute safely out of the plane, which hit the trees and exploded only half a mile away. He felt himself falling fast and realised that his parachute had opened, but not deployed properly. It was not strapped onto his body cleanly and his arms got tangled with the ropes, but he was helpless to do anything to rectify the situation.

It was midwinter and the snow had been falling for days. The hillside was covered with large trees, mainly conifers and beech trees. The snow had covered the trees and lay thick on the ground. As Jack hit the first layer of snow, he was fully conscious and expected to die instantly but was surprised when he found himself slipping through a thick covering of snow, ploughing through lush branches of fir trees to be caught up and suspended only about a yard and a half from the ground.

Although he hadn't had time to deploy his parachute correctly, it was still attached to him and now was attached to the branches above him. He was left dangling, his legs futilely thrashing the fresh air beneath him, like a pair of wet trousers hanging on the washing line. He felt quite stupid and ineffectual as he hung there, helpless. He might have been able to free himself had he been unhurt, but in crashing through the branches of the trees he had suffered many deep cuts and bruises and he was in agony from his shoulder which he correctly thought was probably dislocated and left arm which just didn't seem to be working at all.

Jack struggled, writhed and wriggled, all to no avail, he was trapped and couldn't free himself. It was cold, bitterly cold and he realised if he didn't free himself or get help, he would suffer from hypothermia and simply freeze to death. After two hours, he was desperate. He kept lapsing in and out of consciousness. He knew he was in Germany, didn't speak a word of German but, nevertheless, when he heard the soft rumbling of a horse and cart quite nearby he cried out for help. He realised he would be taken prisoner but he reasoned that would be infinitely better than freezing to death.

Ida had learnt to speak English in school and heard an English voice calling for help. She turned the horse towards the sound and, a little way off the track, was amazed to see an English airman suspended helpless, dangling from the trees. She had heard the plane go down a couple of hours back, but as it was well away from where she was at that moment, she just ignored it and got on with her firewood collecting.

Jack's face was covered in blood and his voice hoarse and rasping, but he was alive and obviously needed cutting down and rescuing. When foraging for wood, branches and wild berries, Ida always carried an axe, a pair of shears and a large hunting knife. She manoeuvred the horse and buggy to just under where Jack was dangling and managed to cut him free. He landed in the buggy with a scream of pain from his arm and promptly fainted.

Ida checked his body for any knife or gun and once satisfied that he carried no weapon, drove the buggy home in the falling snow. Jack regained consciousness and found himself looking into the blue eyes of a stern faced frau with a sandy coloured halo. At first he fancied he was in heaven but as his head cleared he realised this woman had her hair braided and wrapped around her head, giving all the appearance of a blond halo. She was washing his face with a facecloth and a basin of cold water. Jack blinked a few times and then ventured to speak to the woman. "Do you speak English?"

"Yah, yah I do. You are in a bad way, but I cut you down and now I will look after you. Do you speak German at all?"

"No, not a word. Thank you for cutting me down. Am I badly hurt? My arm is very painful, I think it could be broken and my shoulder feels as if it might be dislocated or something."

"Yah, it is, I think, broken but I will put a, how you say, board, on it."

"I think you mean a splint."

"Yah a splint. I will do that."

"Why are you helping me? Why aren't you turning me over to the German authorities, to the soldiers?"

"I am a German, not a Nazi, if I tell the soldiers you are here, they will take you to a prisoner of war camp and you will be treated very badly I think. I will keep you here until you are healed."

"Well, I do thank you for saving me but as my plane went down, won't the soldiers be looking for me."

"Yah," she smiled a wicked smile. "but I have a plan. My husband is dead and now you will be my husband."

Jack felt the hair rise up on the back of his neck and the thought of a German wife was appalling to him, but he was helpless. His arm, he felt, was probably broken, he was in pain from three deep cuts to his chest and stomach, it was midwinter, he didn't speak the language and the soldiers would be out looking for him. He couldn't think of any reason why he would or could reject her offer.

"How on earth are you going to pass me off as your husband and why would you do such a thing?"

"Yah, well, first of all my husband died only two weeks ago and no one knows that but me. I buried him on the farm in the field out there. He had returned from the front with a shattered arm and shrapnel in his body. He died when the shrapnel moved to his heart, I think. He was suffering from what you call shell shock and he couldn't walk or talk or do anything. If the soldiers come here looking for you, they will find only a man who resembles my husband. You will be shell-shocked and not able to speak or hear or do anything but look ahead, seeing no one. I have his papers and you are tall like him, I will bandage your face, chest and arm and they will understand that you are my husband."

When Ida tried to undress Jack to clean him up and attend to his arm, he just screamed out with pain. Eventually, taking it very slowly Ida eased Jack out of his thick flying jacket and then told him what he had already deduced for himself that his arm was broken and his shoulder had been dislocated, there was probably also a couple of broken ribs, but there was nothing she could do about that.

The cuts and abrasions were deep but Ida cleaned them up as best she could and stopped the bleeding. She was sure that he had broken his arm down by his wrist but the dislocation had to be attended to immediately. Ida was no nurse but knew enough about injuries to know that the shoulder and arm had to be readjusted. She told Jack to brace himself, she was going to have to pull his arm back out from its dislocation and hope it would slip back into the socket in place.

With Jack's swollen and extremely painful lower arm, Ida knew she couldn't pull on that part, but with all her strength pulled on his upper arm and when Jack screamed, she felt the bone slip back into place. Jack had fainted again and now Ida took advantage of his unconsciousness and put a makeshift splint on his wrist and forearm. She splinted his arm with the only straight, firm things she could find: two wooden spoons and a flat metal file wrapped in cloth. Ida was no nurse but did her best and hoped the break was a clean one and not any kind of compound fracture.

She put Jack's arm in a triangular support and bandaged his arm across his chest, releasing any pressure on the shoulder, but at the same time trying not to put too much pressure on his painful ribs. When he regained consciousness, Ida helped Jack take all his clothes off and helped him put on a pair of her husband's pyjamas and climb into bed. Jack screamed with each movement but Ida knew she had to get Jack's English clothes off and get him into German pyjamas.

When Jack felt around his neck, he realised his dog tags were gone. When he questioned Ida, she denied having taken them from his body when he was unconscious and Jack really didn't know if they had been ripped off in the fall through the trees. Either way, he was worried. If the soldiers ever did realise, he was an English airman, without dog tags he would be treated as a spy and executed immediately, that's what he had been told at base camp; "never lose your dog tags".

At least with his dog tags he would be taken to a prisoner of war camp, badly treated or not that would be preferable to being shot as a spy. Still, he didn't have them any more so there was nothing he could do.

Jack looked around the single roomed farmhouse and noted that what furniture there was appeared to be rough-hewn, homemade. The wooden, scrubbed table obviously served as a preparation area for meals as well as a dining room table. The large double bed was covered with an eiderdown made of many different coloured pieces of material and the rug on the floor in front of the open fire had a hand pegged, thick warm pile, looking like it had been put together with bits of knitted jumpers and jackets.

There was no cooker as such but there was a large pot on the open fire, already bubbling with something that smelt delicious.

The soldiers arrived the very next day looking for the pilot of the plane that was shot down. The wreckage showed that there were no bodies left on the plane. Max had been picked up some two miles west of where the plane went down. He was taken to Zwickau prisoner of war camp in the valley at the foot of the Erzgebirge mountains. He had reported to the senior officer there and given a statement about Jack and seeing the plane go down, but reported honestly that he hadn't seen Jack parachute from the plane and so assumed that Jack had perished in the fire.

That information was eventually passed on to the British authorities and, in due course, the terrible news was sent to Elizabeth Singleton, Jack's mother.

Elizabeth opened the front door and knew immediately what the telegram boy on his bicycle was there for. The boy knew also and just muttered, "Sorry Missis," as he handed over the telegram.

With calm reserve, Elizabeth walked through the hall and sat down at the kitchen table. She sat looking at the telegram for over an hour. While ever she didn't open the telegram, then Jack was still alive. She knew it was silly but she took her pen and pad and wrote Jack a letter, telling him all about Harry and what he was getting up to. She related all the past week's events and told him about what was in the shops and what was difficult to obtain. She kept the letter light-hearted and informative.

This was the longest letter Elizabeth had ever written to Jack. It made her feel close to him, keeping him alive. She looked around to see what else she could tell Jack about and decided to give him a long discourse about the flourishing garden, the vegetables and the fruit trees. She gabbled on in the letter about the different recipes that she was collecting and learning how to make different cakes and biscuits with little sugar or butter. She closed the letter with so many hugs and kisses and promises of what wonderful cakes she would cook for him when he returned home on his next leave.

Tears fell on the last few words and smudged the ink, but that couldn't be helped. She took an envelope, addressed it and licked the stamp. The telegram sat, unopened on the kitchen table all afternoon. She knew she would have to open it sooner or later, but if she didn't open it then Jack was still alive. She took Harry to the local post office and dropped the letter into the box. On the way home, she sat with Harry in the park and stayed out as long as she could. She reasoned that Jack was still alive, so long as she didn't open the telegram.

Elizabeth knew she was being silly and eventually had to take herself and Harry home. She fed Harry and put him to bed and then sat for a further hour before opening the telegram. Her hands were trembling as she slowly undid the envelope. The words just swam before her tear-filled eyes and simply read, "Regret to inform you that Jack Singleton is missing in action: plane shot down over Germany: presumed dead."

Chapter 13
Life on the Farm

Ida had thought out her plan and was pleased that it all seemed to be working out. She had burnt most of Jack's clothes that would burn but resorted to burying his leather flying jacket, as she realised that would be very difficult to burn. As predicted, the soldiers came within a few hours looking for the English airman. It was the most terrifying moment for Jack. He realised that if the soldiers discovered that he was the English flyer, then not only would his life be in great danger, but also Ida.

She was harbouring the enemy and he knew that wouldn't go down well with the authorities at all. When the soldiers came to the farmhouse, they just barged in without knocking. Ida had warned Jack not to say a word and not to look the soldiers in the eye. He was to stare, vacantly ahead, in front of him, without focussing on anything at all. Jack felt himself sweating and his heart was racing. He tried his best to keep a glazed look on his face and not to react to the brutal shouting and pushing of the soldiers.

As he didn't understand German, it was not too difficult to ignore the terrible threats that were being thrown at Ida. She carried off the charade with the ability of a seasoned actor, comparable to an Oscar award-winning performance.

They checked Wilfreid's identity and discharge papers and eventually, once satisfied that the mute invalid was indeed her husband, left and pestered Ida no more. They thoroughly searched the farm, fields and all the outbuildings; found nothing and so went looking for Jack further afield.

Jack's arm, deep cuts and the extremely painful ribs healed in a few weeks and while his arm had a strange bump in the middle of his forearm, it didn't appear to give him much trouble. The ribs had been the most painful but they were obviously healing and making life much easier as time went on. He was able to do things around the farm and was beginning to be a great help to the widow. He knew it was his duty to escape Germany and return to England but without the language and in the bitterly cold weather, he felt he was better placed to stay with Ida for the time being.

Ida was a crafty woman and once Jack was fit enough worked him as she would a field hand on the farm. She fed him and clothed him and got a good day's work out of him, seven days a week, nine hours every day.

Ida had been surviving war-torn Germany better than most widows and single women. She was capable and knew how to feed herself from the land and the river. Ida taught Jack how to set a trap or a snare for rabbits and how to catch the local fish in the river.

After two months, Jack informed Ida that, no matter what, he would take his chances and try to make his way back to England. Ida was worried. She had no intention of letting him go. She needed him on the farm and if he was captured by the German army, she knew she would be in a great deal of trouble for harbouring the enemy.

No, she couldn't let him go and in no uncertain terms told him that if he left her, she would inform the authorities and have him arrested. She told him that if he implicated her, she would simply say that he had forced her to lie and harbour him. He knew his chances of escaping Germany were slim, but it was his duty to return if he could. The problem of not knowing any German and without any money or transport, he realised he wouldn't get far, also he had lost his uniform, so if caught, he would surely be shot as a spy.

Jack could have killed her, she was, after all, the enemy, but Jack was no murderer and after all, he thought, she had saved his life. So he took the easy way out and decided to stay, just for a little longer. He was not to know how much longer that "stay" would turn out to be for and what consequences there would be for the delay in reuniting with his child and mother.

Hardly any of the village men had returned from the war. Many they knew had been killed and many more were reported "missing in action." Ida would take the horse and buggy into the village each week and discuss the war with the shopkeepers and other villagers. The general consensus was that the war was not going well for the Germans. Someone had a radio and could get foreign stations, including the BBC. Most people agreed Germany was in trouble and spreading their offences too wide.

Ida decided to relate bad news, false news, to Jack in an effort to keep him from absconding from her; she was constantly worried that he would run off in the night and leave her. She told him each time she returned from the village how it was being reported that England was suffering really badly, people were starving and were on the brink of surrender. She made up stories of political speeches being given by the British Prime Minister asking for calm but encouraging the British people to accept that defeat was inevitable.

Jack found it hard to believe, but without a newspaper or a radio to confirm what Ida was telling him, he was helpless to do anything but accept her lies. She wouldn't allow him to accompany her on her trips to the village. She realised many people would recognise that this man wasn't her husband. She advised Jack to keep working on the farm. He was safe there; well fed, had a good roof over his head and no worries.

Jack did have worries, though. He wanted to get home, to see his mother and his son; to report for duty, to fly again, but he was being fed propaganda that persuaded him to stay put.

The work on the farm was not so very difficult and at times, Jack felt guilty that he was quite enjoying the outdoor life. There was no livestock on the farm, the German army had commandeered what cows and goats there had been. They had taken all of Ida's chickens and ducks, leaving nothing but the vegetables on the ground. Jack and Ida often went down the valley to the river Zwickauer to fish for just about anything they could catch. Without meat, other than rabbit or proper bait, it was a difficult task but Jack would often dig up worms and these proved to be excellent bait for the local fish.

For almost three years, Ida kept up her efforts to keep Jack from running out on her. She valued the unpaid work he was putting into the farm and treated him decently. There was no physical attraction to each other from either side but they both had basic needs which were met on a dry, non-romantic, businesslike, emotionally detached fashion. As Ida put it, "Just an itch that needs to be scratched!"

Each week Ida would feed Jack lies which were getting more and more outlandish and difficult to comprehend. She told him how the British were starving and fighting each other to obtain basic needs. How London had been bombed continuously and virtually destroyed. She relentlessly fed him stories of how Germany had invaded England and how each city, in turn, was capitulating to the occupation of German troops.

Jack's only compensating good thoughts turned to remembering how his mother had insisted on getting in some chickens and growing her own fruit and vegetables. With the high wall surrounding their garden, Jack hoped that his mother was safe and able to feed herself and Harry. Ida's stories escalated to Germany starting to set up councils in each city.

Eventually, she related that Britain had surrendered unconditionally and Germany had taken over the British Parliament. Jack was beside himself with worry and distress but Ida kept up her barrage of bad news. She told how the British people were now virtually slaves, being forced to work for the German people and how German forces had taken control of all cities, factories, transport, hospitals, schools; in fact, every facet of civilised life in Britain was now under the control of Germany.

This charade went on until the beginning of 1946, when there was an incredible snowstorm and two days later a warm spell which caused some melting of the snow and a mini avalanche came down from the hillside, almost engulfing Ida's farm. Jack was in the far eastern field and Ida was alone in the barn.

As soon as Jack heard and saw the snow rushing down the hillside, he rushed to the farmhouse. The heavy snow had just reached the barn, which was on the western side of the farm and some fifty yards away from the house. The cascading snow had luckily stopped before engulfing the whole building. It had weakened the side of the building and part of the roof had caved in, trapping Ida.

Jack didn't know where Ida was and he ran through the house shouting and looking for her. He searched two of the outbuildings and eventually found Ida in the barn. She was unconscious and obviously badly hurt. Jack lifted the woman onto the buggy, covered her with blankets, put the horse into his traces and set off for the village. He had never been into the village and had no idea if they had a hospital or even how he was going to ask for help, but he was a decent man and knew he couldn't leave Ida without medical attention, even if it meant he would be arrested and sent back to England where things were obviously so very bad.

The road to the village was just a rough track really and Jack did his best not to bump Ida too much but there were lots of ruts in the uneven ground, which made it impossible to give the injured woman a smooth ride. Ida moaned out loud at each bump but there was nothing Jack could do to ease her pain or make the journey smoother.

Jack drove the horse and buggy through the village and saw nothing that resembled a hospital or even a first aid centre but he'd had the forethought to bring the German/English dictionary that was in Ida's desk and which she frequently used to help understand Jack and vice versa. He had been learning German under Ida's tutelage but realised that his English accent and lack of really good conversational German would give him away as soon as he spoke. He knew he could never pass himself off as a German and decided to play dumb.

He looked up the word doctor or physician and found the German word was "arzt" and that was what he was looking for. At the end of the main street was a small house, set back from the road, with a battered sign outside which read "ARZT".

Here he stopped and entered the office with some fear and trepidation. He didn't speak at all and just pointed to the outside, motioning for the receptionist to come out and see what was in the buggy. The young receptionist got the message and accompanied Jack to the front of the house, where it was obvious that Ida was in need of urgent medical attention. The girl disappeared into the surgery and came out a few minutes later with the doctor in tow. Together with Jack's assistance they took Ida into the examination room.

Jack left them to it and wandered, alone out of the surgery office and out into the world, to the world he hadn't been able to move around in for almost three years. He knew he was on dangerous ground and if found to be English, could be in a lot of trouble; what kind of trouble he wasn't sure, no one was pointing him out as a foreigner, the enemy. No one was chasing him. His clothes were German and he had fiery red hair, but even so, no one cast a second look at him, he just blended in with the other people in the village.

It felt strange knowing that no one knew he was English, so long as he didn't open his mouth, no one would take him for anything other than just another German villager. He'd had the forethought to put Wilfreid Graff's identity papers in his jacket pocket as a precaution but so far no one had challenged him to produce them.

He stopped at a small dusty bookshop, wandered around inside and was surprised to see two men in American military uniforms chatting amiably with the bookshop assistant, in English. They were asking for a guidebook to the area and seemed unconcerned that they were speaking English. Jack waited for the pair to leave the shop and then followed them out onto the street. He was confused but knew he had to approach them and try and find out what the situation was in either America or England.

His approach to these two was simple and later Jack was to reflect that he must have appeared to be almost stupid. His first line was simply, “Excuse me but you are American, are you not?”

“Holy Cow man, however did you guess?” They both laughed loudly.

“Well, I’ve been away and ill. Can you tell me how things are in England and America?”

“Gees man, America’s doing just fine. After we got the bomb dropped, Japan just caved in. They got what they deserved, I’m telling you man, it was awful but we had to do it.”

“Whatever are you talking about?” asked Jack. “What bomb?”

“Gees man, where’ve you been?”

“I told you I’ve been away and sick.”

“Well, we dropped the bomb, you know the atomic bomb. Well, two actually, one on Hiroshima and one on Nagasaki. That shook them up, I can tell you. Anyway, the Japanese surrendered on 15 August. Their surrender was signed on 2 September last year on the battleship USS Missouri. That ended the war and we can all breathe easier now. “Peace in our Time” as your Mr Chamberlain once said and hallelujah I’ll say to that.”

Jack was utterly confused. He had no idea what they were talking about. What kind of bomb was an atomic bomb and how could one bomb or even two finish a war and they were talking of Japan, not England. So he asked again, “What’s happening in Britain?”

“Hell’s bells man, where’ve you been, on the moon?”

“Please, just tell me how the people are coping in Britain?”

“Well, we were there on furlough just a month ago and they seemed to be getting back on their feet alright. I mean, they have strict rationing, so we help out where we can. We sometimes can take over nylons for the girls, they’ll do anything for a pair of nylons.”

The two laughed loudly. “They’ve started a rebuilding programme and are rehousing all those who were bombed out. You should see London and the docks, it’s a real mess, but they’re starting to get it all back into shape.”

Jack was desperately trying to comprehend what the two were telling him. It really didn’t fit in with what Ida had been feeding him. He couldn’t make sense of it all. “So what you’re telling me is that Britain is still a free country, even though they lost the war?”

"Jees man; what are you on about? Britain and her allies and mark my words, us, because we saved your asses, won the frigging war. You couldn't have done it without us."

"But when did the war actually end?"

"Oh, Christ, let me see. I think it was the 7, no 8 May last year. The allies accepted Germany's surrender about a week after Hitler committed suicide."

"Hitler committed suicide? Bloody hell! Bloody coward!"

"Yeh, he shot himself and his woman, what was her name; Eva Baun. Actually, I believe he married her just before he killed her."

"Bloody Hell!"

"Yeh, it was then parties all round, everyone went crazy. We were in Portsmouth at the time and I tell you, man, the English sure know how to party. Winston Churchill announced the victory in Europe and now they call it V.E. Day. Peace at last for everyone and I'll say again; hallelujah to that."

Chapter 14
War Time England

Even though she had promised Jack that she would take Harry and herself down to the underground when the sirens started, Elizabeth had no intention of doing so. She hated going underground, it was cold there and tiled, always reminding her of a public toilet and quite often it smelled like one too. She didn't want anything to do with her old friends, neighbours or anyone else. People were sleeping on the Tube platforms and singing to keep their spirits up, but this was not for Elizabeth. She preferred to keep herself and Harry separate.

She knew Harry would have to eventually be enrolled in the local school but Elizabeth decided it was too dangerous to journey out every day and so decided that when the time came, she would educate Harry herself. She was an intelligent woman and reasoned that she could teach him everything he needed to know, at least until he got to ten or eleven years of age.

She had started as soon as he could walk. Elizabeth started taking him once a week to different parts of London to see the famous buildings or to play in the various playgrounds, in order that he learn to mix with other children. She was well aware of the danger of isolating him from society and when in the different parks or gardens, encouraged him to mix with other people and their children so long as they were not people she knew.

Harry was a sociable toddler and a beautiful child. He learnt to babble, then chatter away to himself and eventually to speaking. Elizabeth refused to baby talk to him and only used the correct words. No gee gees, horsey or doggy. A horse is a horse and a dog is a dog. Every other aspect of the English language was dealt with in the same way. Harry learnt his alphabet from the few baby books Elizabeth could find in the markets or newsagents. Few, if any bookshops were open and toy shops were virtually non-existent. However, Elizabeth had her own way of teaching and devoted herself to this task.

She taught him the alphabet first and once he had mastered that, she held up simple articles in the house and spelt out their name, sticking a label on with the spelling for Harry to see. Cup was her first effort, shortly followed by a bat which she had found in Jack's old toy cupboard. She went through the house trying to find all the things that could be spelt with three simple letters: pen, box, tap, mug. She sounded out the spelling and Harry soon caught on. It was a game that both grandmother and grandson enjoyed playing. Before too long, Elizabeth progressed to putting letters together, vowels; ee and oo, as well as ch, sh and th.

By the time Harry was four years old, he could read and write very simple words. Elizabeth wrote him little stories and he loved trying to read the stories for himself. Life was progressing for these two in spite of the fact that Harry's father was believed to be dead and Elizabeth had no real idea how she was going to cope with a growing child, who would obviously need to go to school, eventually.

Life in London was not too difficult for Elizabeth and Harry. The blitz had not destroyed their home, as it had done to so many others. Food and clothing were rationed as were furniture and petrol, but Elizabeth had no need for these last two items.

Before the war, Britain had imported fifty-five million tons of food a month. Once the war had started, this figure dropped to twelve million. Rationing was introduced and Elizabeth found that while there was never an abundance of anything in the shops, she could manage quite well using the vegetables in her garden.

Harry's green ration book entitled him to a pint of milk every day and a double supply of eggs. The eggs Elizabeth didn't need as she had her chickens at home and so she decided to barter her eggs in exchange for meat. She wasn't sure how she could go about this and felt that at some point, that kind of exchange might well be illegal. It was a problem she worried about for three weeks before getting an idea. She went to her local library and asked if there was a section on "food for vegetarians," or "clubs or groups for vegetarians."

The librarian was puzzled at this request and pointed out, "Well I don't think anyone's interested in being a vegetarian in these times, except of course that woman over there. I was talking to her last week and she was telling me how much healthier she feels she is since she turned vegetarian."

That's all Elizabeth needed, a contact. She approached the woman and apologised for interrupting her reading, "Excuse me, sorry to interrupt you but I was wondering if you could help me."

"Oh, that's alright, I was just browsing. What can I do for you?"

"Well, I'm looking for a vegetarian and the librarian thinks you might be one, are you?"

"Yes, I am, but what's that got to do with anything?"

"Well, I and my grandson are not, we're meat eaters, but with rationing don't get much meat, like everyone else. I do have chickens though and they give us eggs. I was wondering if you might be willing to exchange your meat ration for my eggs?"

A deal was struck and they two agreed to meet every other week and exchange meat for eggs. It was a win/win situation and this arrangement continued until disaster struck.

Harry was a growing boy and at five and a half years old was healthy, intelligent and inquisitive about everything. Life would have been sweet except for Hitler's new round of terror that began raining on London.

The V1 was Hitler's new secret weapon. It was a winged but pilot-less sort of rocket propelled flying bomb. This was a serious threat to London and south-eastern England. The first V1 had fallen early June 1944 and three days later, the public were notified and given dire warnings. Elizabeth and all the other terrified Londoners didn't quite know what to make of the threat. They soon found out, though.

In that first month five hundred of the V1s had been fired with seventy-three hitting greater London and seventy-one hitting outside London. Eventually, there were over nine thousand fired against London during an eighty-day campaign.

Elizabeth could hear the whining of the engine of these bombs and then silence as the bomb ran out of fuel and descended with a deafening explosion. The dreaded wait and expectation from the engine cutting out to the explosion seemed to last forever. That time lapse was almost unbearable and Elizabeth found herself holding her breath, waiting for the noise and shaking of the house. Still, she didn't want to go down to the underground and there would never have been enough time, anyway. She still reasoned with herself that she was safer staying in her house and taking cover under the bed.

Most V1s were shot down by anti-aircraft fire and by RAF fighter interception however around two and a half thousand did hit London at a rate of fifty to a hundred a day in the June 1944.

As suddenly as it had started, the bombing seemed to finish. Everyone breathed a sigh of relief. The skies were clear for three months and life went on as usual. Elizabeth would meet up with Mary, her vegetarian friend and the eggs were exchanged for meat. The apples and pears were producing well but the plums were a great disappointment.

Elizabeth had been told by Albert, her gardening friend, that the Wickson plum trees needed Narrabeen for pollination. She had planted both but realised that they needed to be in flower at the same time in order for the bees to do their thing.

Unfortunately, the Narrabeen trees blossomed first with no sign of blossom from the Wicksons. The Wicksons produced their flowers some two months later, far too late to pollinate the Narrabeens. In five years there had been no plums and Elizabeth had been twice back to the gardening shop, only to be told the first time that Albert had been bombed out at home and had not returned to work. The second time the shop was simply not there anymore, it too had been bombed.

The three months of quiet were over and Elizabeth, with all Londoners, now faced an even more advanced weapon. The weary, battle scarred Londoners faced this new threat with typical stoicism. Londoners didn't even hear these new bombs, they were so fast. These bombs were the V2s; faster, more powerful than the V1s. In London, no defensive response was possible. English radar stations picked them up on their screens for a fifty-second window after launch, but their speed was far too great. Many bombs were being launched from occupied Holland and the V2s could hit London in five minutes.

One day, Elizabeth had taken Harry to Regent's Park when she heard the first of the V2s being dropped. A policemen directed her to the nearest air-raid shelter and she managed to get them both under cover just in time.

After two hours in the shelter, when all was quiet again, she ventured out and took the bus home, only to find that there was no home. Hitler had got her at last. She just stood there holding Harry's hand with her mouth agape, looking at the scene of devastation. Firemen, ambulances and Home Guard officers were running around putting out fires and generally trying to keep people away from the three houses that had been hit in Elizabeth's street.

Elizabeth had no idea what she was supposed to do. She had nothing but her handbag and the clothes she and Harry were wearing. A Home Guard patrolman chastised her for standing around gaping at the site and advised her, “There’s nothing to be seen here, missis. Go on, get along there. Go home.”

“That is my home.”

“Oh, sorry missis. You’d better report to the officer over there.”

Chapter 15
A New Life

Elizabeth and Harry were directed first to one agency and then to another. They were fed and clothed and given shelter. It was a bewildering time and Elizabeth was so glad that, although she had lost her home, at least she had her handbag and in it, her identity cards, bank book, a precious photograph of Jack and her ration books. Luckily, she was able to prove who they were and, after spending two weeks in a makeshift council camp, was sent to a village on the outskirts of London where temporary homes were being erected.

The accommodation, which was really only huts, left much to be desired but it was a roof over their heads. Essential food and clothing along with equipment was supplied, cooking utensils, bedding and toiletries. The semidetached huts were made of prefabricated curved asbestos with the framework and window frames made of steel. There were two very small bedrooms, the tiniest of kitchens and free gas and water. A bus route passed the village and they could get a connection to greater London.

There were only a few children in the village as most of the London children had been evacuated at the start of the war. They had been sent to country areas for safety but Elizabeth had never wanted Harry to be sent away as she felt he was far too young and she really needed him close to her. What few children there were in the "prefabs" were now enrolled in the local village school.

At last, Harry was mixing and learning with other children. He was proving to be a good student and well ahead of the other children. He could read and write, do simple arithmetic and had a good working knowledge of general geography. Elizabeth had taught him well, but realised that she couldn't have gone much further with his education as she was almost at the limit of what she herself knew.

Harry loved going shopping with his grandmother. His favourite shop was the "Co-op". This was a huge department store boasting three levels and a flamboyant ballroom on the top floor. It was a customer, profit sharing organisation which had departments dealing with clothing, bedding and furniture but the highlight for Harry was the groceries, meat and fish hall.

In the food hall there was sawdust on the floor, sometimes three or four inches deep. Harry and usually another child or two would sit on the floor and make roadways through the sawdust while he waited for Elizabeth to be served. If Elizabeth required butter, he would watch fascinated as the assistant would carve a small piece of butter from the giant slab and then pat the small portion into a smooth rectangular shape, wrap it in waxed paper and take the money and coupons from Elizabeth.

Then, the most magical thing happened. The assistant would put the money that Elizabeth had given him or her into a small suspended capsule, about the size of a can of beans and screw the top on and then put it into a sort of miniature cable car which would transport it across the food hall, above everyone's head, to an elevated cashier sitting in a lonely glass case, like some princess waiting to be rescued.

The assistant rang a bell to announce the capsule's despatch and once the cashier had put a receipt and any change back into the capsule, then it was despatched back to the assistant accompanied by another bell and the assistant would give Elizabeth her change and receipt.

As this procedure was the same for all customers, the sound of various bells going off was a source of joy and amusement for the child, in fact for all children entering the shop. Elizabeth would smile to herself as she indulged the child in this harmless play but outwardly always reprimanded him gently with the words, "My goodness gracious me, look at the mess you're in, you've got sawdust clinging to your trousers, on your jumper, everywhere." And would brush him down with much tut tutting.

Jack was never far from Elizabeth's mind. She grieved for her son but was determined to be a good grandmother to his child. She never forgot Jack's obsession with Australia and often wondered if she and Harry would have a better life if she pursued Jack's dream and went to live in that wild country "down under".

Elizabeth hated the communal living, there was no privacy, everyone knew everyone else's business and the women would congregate in small groups exchanging stories of despair and deprivation. They blamed the government and Hitler and "the reds" and anyone else they could think of for their situation. She was mortified one day as she was hanging her washing on the communal washing line, when one of the women asked her openly, “Does that coloured kid belong to you?”

Elizabeth ignored the woman and took her washing indoors. The very next day Harry came home from school and asked in all innocence, “Grandma, why do the kids at school call me nigger? What’s a nigger?”

Elizabeth had to think fast, she didn’t want to upset the child and at the same time she didn’t want to tell him any lies, but she felt she had to embellish just a little, to soften the blow. She wanted him to feel comfortable with who he was and who his parents were, well, his mother anyway.

“Well, Harry, I think it means a few things. First of all it means they like you, second I think it means you are a very clever boy and they wished they were as clever as you and thirdly it means you have coffee coloured skin which is a bit darker than their skin.”

“I don’t think they do like me and why is my skin different from their skin?”

“Well, that’s because your mother was born in America and she had dark skin. She was beautiful and your dad really loved her.”

“So, it’s alright having dark skin then?”

“Yes, of course, you are very lucky. It means you won’t get sun burnt if you stay out in the sun.”

“It doesn’t feel alright, I don’t think the other boys like me at all. They won’t let me play with them. Is that because I’m a nigger? Some boys call me a black carrot. Why do they do that? I’m not a carrot.”

“No, dear, they’re obviously not very nice children. You should be proud of who you are and who your mother was. They only call you a carrot because your hair is quite reddish. They are ignorant, stupid children and you shouldn’t take any notice of them.”

In her heart Elizabeth was saddened and stupidly she knew, ashamed. There was nothing she could do about it and she just had to hope that Harry was confident enough to put those taunts behind him. Her thoughts turned once more to Australia. Maybe if she could get away from this awful, stifling atmosphere, away from prejudice, away from hurtful taunts, maybe there was a better life out there in the colonies for herself and Harry.

Elizabeth stayed in that camp for twelve months before reading in the newspaper about the Australian Prime Minister Ben Chifley, who was visiting Britain to attend a conference. Apparently, he and his Minister of Immigration,

Arthur Calwell, were promoting mass immigration to Australia with the slogan, "populate or perish". They were calling on the British people to agree to either a free or an assisted passage to Australia to become "New Australians". They announced that they had an objective of raising the population in Australia to twenty million people.

Elizabeth was not religious but said a small prayer to her (as she thought) dead son. "Jack, I know this is what you would have wanted. I'm going to apply and see if I can't realise your ambition and get Harry and I off to Australia to see what you always wanted to see. I'll do it for you, son."

Chapter 16
Australia

It took another twelve months of interviews, medical and dental checks, vaccinations and many forms to be signed before news came through to Elizabeth that she and Harry had been accepted for an assisted passage to Australia. She told no one, not even Harry until the last day. Elizabeth was a very private person and didn't want to discuss her plans with anyone. She had no friends she needed to confide in, she didn't want anyone to make a fuss, she just wanted to get out of England with her grandson and start a new life.

Carrying only one small battered second hand suitcase, grandmother and grandson took the bus to Tilbury Docks where they were shepherded through a series of checks before being allowed to board the most beautiful ship either had ever seen. The RMS Orion Star of the Orient Steam Navigation Co. boasted a single large, majestic funnel already belching out white smoke. The deck was over five hundred feet long and looked as if it went on forever.

Elizabeth was disappointed that she wasn't allocated a private cabin for just the two of them, instead they had to share with two other mothers and three children, one just a baby. There was a small bathroom at the end of the cabin and everyone had a bunk bed to themselves. A cabin steward introduced himself and seemed to be a very helpful young man.

Everyone settled down, getting to know each other and putting their few clothes and belongings into the drawers and cupboards. The other women were all pretty angry at the forced separation from their husbands. None had realised that the men were to be housed in "male only" cabins, mostly four or six to a cabin. The women were allocated cabins for "women" or "women with children".

Two hours after boarding, an announcement was made to visitors over the loudspeaker for everyone who wasn't scheduled to travel to disembark as soon as possible as the ship was due to set sail. Elizabeth and Harry went up the many stairs to the top deck in order to wave goodbye to England. Many people were in tears, waving goodbye to friends and relatives.

Elizabeth had no one to wave goodbye to, but she and Harry waved as enthusiastically as everyone else, regardless. They watched the strong but quite tiny tugs manoeuvre the large hull of the ship, pushing it out into the middle of the water and eventually the tugs left as the liner made its own way. Harry wouldn't leave the railing until he could see England no more, only then was Elizabeth able to persuade him to go with her to explore what would be their home for the next few weeks.

They went through a series of sliding glass doors leading to enormous promenade decks where the layout for certain games had been painted on the wooden deck floor. Elizabeth recognised "shuffle board" and "hop scotch" but three others she didn't recognise at all.

They made their way to the official dining room, which was enormous, the largest room Elizabeth had ever seen. It was light and airy with tables set for eight people. There were starched white napkins at each setting and the cutlery and glasses sparkled in the unnatural bright light. The heat of the September day hadn't penetrated this room as it was air-conditioned and quite cool. All around the room were murals depicting dolphins, whales and all manner of sea creatures.

On everyone's bunk had been placed a letter of welcome and a news sheet informing them about everything that was to be happening that first day. Most important was the time for meals. Breakfast could be taken between seven and nine each morning; with casual, non-allocated seating. Lunch could be taken between noon and two but dinner was allocated to specific times. There were two sittings each evening and each passenger was allocated a seat at a specific table.

Elizabeth and Harry were scheduled to have their dinner at six thirty each evening and it appeared that the other mothers in their cabin were all scheduled to have their dinners at eight. The newsletter informed everyone that a prescribed lifeboat drill was to be held the first morning at ten sharp. Everyone must attend, children included.

The first night passed peacefully, everyone seemed to be exhausted from the journey and all the emotional goodbyes. The other women in the cabin had all travelled down to Tilbury from Yorkshire and were ready for bed as soon as dinner was over.

After dinner, Elizabeth and Harry walked around the deck, getting their bearings and getting used to the gentle undulations of the waves. They watched the sun go down in the west through a rosy cloud cover and Elizabeth felt suddenly at peace with the world. "Australia, here we come," she whispered to the waves and Harry copied her, laughing, "Australia, here we come."

Chapter 17
Repatriation

Jack was angry, really angry, probably more with himself than with Ida. "What an idiot I was to get sucked in to all her lies," he chided himself. "I should have known England wouldn't capitulate to Germany. I should have had more faith."

The more he thought about it, the more angry he got. He realised he had been manipulated and taken advantage of. He had wasted nearly three years working for Ida, with no pay, with no hope and no possibility of escaping back to England. "No, that's not right," he corrected himself. "I could have escaped and got back to England. I just got sucked in to all her lies. I'm just plain stupid."

Jack took the horse and buggy back to the farm with mixed emotions. He felt guilty at leaving Ida but at the same time he was really angry that she had taken advantage of him and kept him working on the farm under false pretences. Jack's main thoughts now were how to get home.

First of all he needed money and he knew that Ida had returned each week from the market and had disappeared into her bedroom, obviously with her takings and obviously had secreted her money somewhere. Jack decided to look for her stash of money, even though he reasoned it probably wouldn't be too much, nevertheless he felt he deserved to be paid for three years work and he was entitled to some, if not most of that money. It didn't take him long to find the tin box under her bed. There was plenty of money and he didn't bother to count it. He just took what he felt he deserved, had a meal, packed a small bag and went back to the horse, which was still harnessed to the buggy.

Jack took the horse and buggy into the village and left it outside the doctor's surgery. He treated himself to two beers and after which he went looking for the authorities and the way to get home.

Chapter 18
The Search

It was not an easy task getting back to England and it was even more difficult persuading the authorities that he hadn't been AWOL and he wasn't a deserter. He explained to the officers interviewing him about Ida and how he had believed all her lies. The officers were sceptical but had no option but to believe him and eventually gave him an honourable discharge. Jack's major trouble now was finding his mother and Harry.

His first mission on reaching England had been to go to the house and see if it was still standing. Jack was devastated with what he saw or more correctly, what he didn't see. His home was gone, it was now a pile of rubble the same as many hundreds of other bomb sites. He just sat on a low garden wall across from where his home used to be and stared vacantly at all the damage and the ruin.

Silent tears ran down his face and a grubby neighbour's child stopped his playing in the street and just stood staring at Jack, as if interested in why an adult was crying. Children of all ages now just accepted bomb sites as part of their lives, playgrounds made just for them. They had no real concept of the misery that those sites had caused.

Jack started making enquiries about the possible death or survival of his little family. The authorities confirmed to Jack that his mother had survived the bombing along with young Harry. Sifting through the official files, they were able to tell Jack that his mother and son had been sent to a new housing estate, temporary accommodation really, on the outskirts of London. Jack followed their directions and arrived at the prefabs only to be told that Elizabeth and Harry Singleton had left only a few weeks earlier.

No one in the little estate knew where Elizabeth had gone. The neighbours told Jack that Elizabeth had kept pretty much to herself and not socialised with the other families.

Jack went back to London and the street where they had lived before the war. He talked to those neighbours he could find, only to be told, what he already knew, that Elizabeth had been bombed out and no one knew where she had been relocated to. Jack asked if anyone had seen his mother since the bombings, but no one had.

Jack was in a lather of despair. "Where could she have gone? Where would she want to go?" Jack asked himself over and over and could never come up with a reasonable answer.

He checked every avenue he could think of: local libraries, Elizabeth had been an avid reader: local schools, Harry would be of school age now and should be attending a school of some sort: local councils, was Elizabeth on the electoral roll? Was Elizabeth receiving rate notices? All to no avail. Jack put notices in the newspapers and talked to the police, but no one seemed able to help him.

"They can't just disappear off the face of the earth." He kept telling himself. He went back to Martin's Bank, where he and his father had worked years before. He knew his mother had always had an account there and he spoke at length with the manager, firstly about his mother and secondly to enquire if there were any vacancies, as he now badly needed work.

Unfortunately, the manager who had been at the bank before the war had retired and now the new manager didn't know Jack at all. He was able to tell Jack that Elizabeth Singleton had closed off her bank account some months earlier and unfortunately had not left a forwarding address or any details as to where she was going to put her money. The manager also apologised to Jack for the fact that there were no vacancies now at the bank but wished Jack luck in his endeavours to find his mother and to secure a job.

Jack needed to work to earn a living and was eventually taken on by a small bank branch as a simple bank clerk. They wouldn't take into account his previous experience in international banking as they said he had been away from the industry for too long, but at least, as a bank clerk he had money to live on and at the weekends, time to continue looking for his mother and son.

Life went on for Jack and the weeks turned into months and the months into years. He never stopped looking for his mother but he was met with disappointment at every turn. He never gave up hope, but slowly he ran out of options.

Chapter 19
Getting to Australia

The first lifeboat drill was pandemonium. Everyone was instructed to wear their allocated life jackets, which were in the cabins. The children objected to the bulky, smelly objects being put over their heads and many were crying and being quite difficult. When people came out of their cabins, they were ushered along the corridors and up the stairs by the many crew members. Each cabin was allocated a lifeboat station but as no one had got their bearings, many went to the wrong place and there was much confusion.

The ship's crew were patient but the passengers were frustrated as most had never been on board a ship and everything was new and bewildering to them. Once the passengers were at the lifeboat stations, the crew did a head count and gave instructions as to the correct way to tie on the lifejackets.

Passengers were instructed as to the procedure in case "abandon ship" was called. The lifeboats looked huge and Elizabeth and Jack watched fascinated as the crew did a practise lifeboat launch. The wind started to blow and many people gave way to seasickness and needed to be escorted below decks. The whole drill took well over an hour and everyone was exhausted. The crew were frustrated trying to make themselves heard over the crying of many children, but kept calm and once the drill was over, ushered the passengers back to their cabins.

This drill was to take place each week and as the weeks passed, it became routine and quite boring. Everyone was instructed to attend every drill but towards the end of the trip only half the passengers turned up for the drill, very much to the frustration of the crew who had the unenviable task of going through the cabins routing out everyone, especially mothers with young children who had held back and refused to attend the drills.

The meals were good and solid with many choices. There were small cafes or bars around the various decks and snacks could be obtained at any time. There was a children's club and a nursery for babies. Harry had no desire to join the children's club and Elizabeth was glad for his company. She didn't particularly want to make close friends with the other women and preferred to keep herself and Harry separate and private. Harry was always good company for Elizabeth. He was an intelligent little boy and had a great sense of humour, always making jokes and keeping Elizabeth laughing.

Each morning there would be a bulletin of information and activities on board: a sort of daily newspaper which was delivered to each cabin. It usually started with "Nautical Hints":

We are navigating on our EASTerly and ENEsterly course between the 80th and 90th meridian of East longitudine and between the 42th and 41 of south latitude.

The depth of the sea in this zone is about 2000 ftms.

Weather forecast: fresh wind from north, sea moderate, sky cloudy, temperature steady.

Prior to receiving the daily bulletin, Elizabeth thought that all the passengers were the same but the bulletin showed that there were two classes on board, first class and tourist class. There was a different programme for each class and it wasn't long before the tourist class passengers learnt that there were areas they were not allowed to enter. The first-class passengers had their own promenade deck, dining room and recreation areas. This didn't bother Elizabeth at all as the boat was quite large enough to accommodate everyone and all their needs were adequately met.

The daily bulletin gave a rundown of events which changed from day to day. There were concerts, film shows, bingo, dancing, keep fit classes, deck games and intellectual talks by various speakers. Elizabeth had no idea what the first-class passengers were doing but after dinner each night she and Harry would go to the tourist class lounge where there would be dancing and music supplied by the resident "Orion Star Band."

This band was no group of virtuosos: at best they could play their own instruments, but jointly seemed to find it difficult to keep together. Elizabeth thought it was highly probable that they had only been brought together individually, not as an organised, professional band, but they did their best and seemed to manage reasonably well. The first hiccough for the band came when it was announced that there was to be a talent competition.

Many brave souls signed up for the event and most were passengers who fancied themselves as singers. They obviously told the band what song they wished to sing and the band did their best to provide backing for the competitors. It would have been better if the singers were given the option to sing "a capella" that is without music, but the band insisted on backing the poor singers. The band seemed always to be two beats behind or one beat in front and never in the right key for the singer's voice.

Either way, the poor performers were confused and put off and the whole show was a pitiful embarrassment for the competitors. Not all competitors were singers however. One brave soul put himself forward as a magician. He did two simple card tricks and ended his performance with a disappearing box. He was not very good and it was obvious to everyone that a large box was covering the smaller, disappearing box. A cheeky young boy had the audacity to call out, "It's under the big box."

The poor magician denied such a suggestion and fumbled his reappearance of the small box. A second child booed the poor man and pretty soon most people took up the chant "Rubbish! Rubbish!" The poor magician left the stage with a red face and much embarrassment. Eventually, the winner was a man who did bird impressions. His prize was a voucher for a free haircut by the ship's hairdresser.

There were many activities and competitions to keep the passengers amused and occupied. Elizabeth gave in to Harry one day by deciding to join the keep fit class. It was advertised in the daily newspaper that numbers had been low and they were trying a new approach, that is asking parents to come along with their children to join in.

Harry wanted to join in and persuaded his grandmother to take him along to the class. Elizabeth was no gymnast and felt embarrassed and stupid as she tried to follow the leader's instructions. Harry had good hand eye coordination and enjoyed going through the various exercises. The instructor tried to encourage the women, especially the older women, to "get in shape."

Elizabeth looked scornfully at the young man and declared, "Listen here, I am in good shape: round is a shape, isn't it?" Everyone had a laugh.

When the instructor asked the participants to keep their legs straight and touch their toes, Harry and most people had no problem, but Elizabeth just couldn't manage it. The instructor walked around the room encouraging those who were having difficulties. He stopped by Elizabeth and tried to coax her to try harder. "Go on, luv. You can do it."

"No, I can't. My legs are just too long and too far away from my arms."

"Come on, luv. Try harder you can do it."

Elizabeth was frustrated and angry and turned on the young fellow with the cutting words, "Listen young man, if god had wanted me to touch my toes, he wouldn't have put them so far away from my hands."

The class had a good laugh again and some of the older women applauded Elizabeth, who nodded appreciatively at them. The instructor rolled his eyes heavenwards.

The daily newspaper announced one day that there would be a fancy dress competition the very next day. Harry was all enthusiastic and very much wanted to participate. Elizabeth kept telling him over and over, "We have nothing to dress you up in. What could you go as? If you can think of anything, using just what we have, you can do it, but we don't have anything, do we?"

Tears rose to Harry's eyes. He didn't cry, but he was upset and tried hard to think about what he could possibly do in the way of a costume.

During dinner that night Elizabeth suddenly stopped chewing her meat and after swallowing hard declared: "I've got it."

"What have you got, grandma?"

"An idea. How would you like to have a terrible accident?"

"What? What do you mean? Why would I want to have an accident?"

"How about this for an idea? We go down to the medical centre and borrow a load of bandages and bandage you up with some mercurochrome for blood and you can go to the fancy dress competition as an accident victim?"

"Oh, great idea, can I have lots of blood, mercurochrome really looks like blood and maybe a broken arm or leg?"

"Yes, why not? We'll call in the medical centre as soon as we finish dinner."

The next morning was spent in feverish preparation, binding Harry into his costume. He had bandages around his head, with much red mercurochrome giving a really good impression of blood. Elizabeth had managed to borrow a splint and put Harry's arm into a bent position with much bandaging. His legs were bound and he limped realistically, getting into the part.

Elizabeth painted a large gash onto his face with eyeliner and lipstick. He looked dreadful but the child was ecstatic. The time came for all competitors to assemble on the top deck where the ship's captain was to judge the participants.

Most of the participants were adults but a few were children. There were pirates, a mermaid, an Indian sari clad woman, two tramps and various costumes which were difficult to interpret.

The captain made a great show of walking up and down the line of competitors and finally, much to Elizabeth's surprise, declared Harry the winner. He was given a small trophy, a replica of the ship, along with a box of chocolates. Harry was beside himself with pride and happiness. He refused to take off his costume and hobbled around all afternoon, showing off his trophy. Elizabeth had never seen the child so happy.

The highlight of the voyage was the "crossing the line" ceremony. Any adult crossing the equator for the first time is invited to take part in this traditional ceremony and everyone not taking part is invited to be the audience watching the spectacle. Elizabeth didn't want to take part but took Harry along for the day's celebrations.

According to tradition, anyone crossing the equator for the first time must pay homage to King Neptune and he, along with his queen, either accept the homage or sit in judgement and pass sentence on anyone whom they think needs punishing for misdemeanours. The ceremony is always performed by the side of the swimming pool as the punishments meted out sometimes get quite messy.

Many of the young adults signed up for participation and everyone else, first-class and tourist passengers, together crowded the lido deck to watch the proceedings.

It was a bright sunny day with a gentle breeze blowing. Everyone was in a happy mood and the ship's band played sea shanties as a prelude to the ceremony.

First off, all the participants were led from the lower deck to the upper deck roped together in a long line, all in their bathing costumes. Each in turn, the participants were made to kneel before King Neptune, pay homage and tell him how wonderful they thought he was and how grateful they were that the ship was being allowed to cross over his domain. The first two prisoners were allowed to go free after kissing the feet of King Neptune but the remainder of the prisoners were given sentences as punishment for their various crimes.

One poor soul was accused of spending too much money on board and so had his hands tied behind his back and was then told to fish out a coin, with his mouth, from the bottom of a dish which was filled with flour. He coughed and spluttered somewhat but finally got the coin. His hands were untied and he was then unceremoniously dumped into the swimming pool. Everyone had a good laugh.

Another participant was treated quite well, really. She was accused of eating too much and so also had her hands tied behind her back and was then presented with a very large layered cream cake and told to eat it. As she had no hands to manoeuvre the cake, she had to bend forwards and just put her mouth into it. The crew then pushed her whole face into the cake and everyone roared with laughter. The girl had her bonds released and, like the boy before her, was thrown into the swimming pool.

All the participants were treated similarly, all being accused of different crimes and given different punishments, most finishing up very messy and being thrown into the swimming pool.

It was a great day and everyone enjoyed it immensely except one family. The area around the pool was very crowded and a young boy, striving to get a better view of the proceedings decided, unseen by his parents, to climb one of the steel struts adjacent to the pool.

Unfortunately, as the ship rolled slightly, he lost his footing and fell to the hard deck. Immediately the child was taken, unconscious, below decks to the medical centre. The captain announced two days later that the boy had not recovered and that there was to be a burial at sea at 5 o'clock the next morning. Anyone wishing to attend the service and burial was welcome to meet on the rear deck.

The family, of course, was distraught. Like Elizabeth, they were on their way to a new life in Australia. It was the topic of conversation for everyone over the next few days and the public address system repeatedly requested that parents keep a special eye on their children.

There was another incident, almost a tragedy, when a small boy skidded across the wet deck and got caught up across a vertical strut which saved his life. There was a gap in the deck railing which was normally used for the gangplank when in port and this was covered by a horizontal chain and a vertical strut. If it hadn't been for this strut, the boy would have gone overboard, he was so small his little body fitted neatly into the space beneath the chain. It was another wakeup call for all parents. These particular parents were lucky.

Every day there would be a newssheet placed in each cabin, outlining the day's events. It was a great trip full of interesting recreational offerings by the ship's staff: quizzes, treasure hunts, whist drives, beetle drives and sporting competitions of every kind; swimming, table tennis, deck quoits and obstacle races.

The swimming competition was a particular challenge and on the day of the event, the wind had picked up and the sea had quite a swell. Many people congregated around the swimming pool to watch and were surprised to see the water sloshing forwards and backwards and from side to side. There would have been at least twelve to eighteen inches of water sloshing up and down the sides of the pool.

As the event got underway, the wind picked up and the pool water washed up and down even more and many times swept up and beyond the edge of the pool. It was a challenge for the competitors and gave everyone a laugh when one teenager was lifted up by the water and overshot the edge of the pool as he was turning and finished up floundering on the tiled surroundings, like a beached whale. No one got hurt and it was fun all round.

One of the competitions was to be a treasure hunt. Harry begged Elizabeth to put their names down as competitors. On the scheduled day, the competitors were all given a sheet with a list of things to collect. Some objects were easy to find, like a safety pin, a knitting needle or a postage stamp but others were almost impossible. One was a bus ticket and another a feather.

The whole treasure hunt took most of the day. There were signatures to collect from various crew members, items to collect from the dining room or the various bars, beer mats and serviettes. Harry and Elizabeth had a great time and the day passed very quickly. At the end of the competition, two teenagers won but Harry and Elizabeth came a creditable second.

Another of the competitions was for table tennis. There were two tables set up on the top deck and Harry had been practising with Elizabeth for the previous week, he felt confident that he could play as well as any other child. On the day of the table tennis competition, it was quite windy and with each gust, the flimsy light ball would get blown around, making it almost impossible to control. Harry was frustrated and angry when a girl beat him eighteen to twenty-one.

The wind had carried her serve out of his reach and he complained bitterly to Elizabeth, "It's not fair grandma, she didn't win fairly. I know I could have beaten her if it wasn't for the wind. It's just not fair."

Elizabeth sympathised but it was just beyond her control and consoled the child with an ice cream but he was not to be so easily consoled. He sulked for most of the day and she realised Harry had a real competitive streak in him that probably needed, at some time in the future to be channelled in the right direction.

Everyone seemed to be enjoying the trip immensely but Elizabeth, like so many immigrants was perpetually worried about what would happen when they docked in Australia, how was she going to manage, could they survive the hot weather, the incredible distances between towns and cities, the dangerous animals and creatures.

Jack, at almost eight years, could read quite well and had borrowed a book from the ship's library about Australia. Like many young boys, he was something of a tease and delighted in frightening Elizabeth with his lurid tales of dangerous creatures and dangerous places. The book he had been reading was all about "outback" life in Australia, telling tales of man-eating sharks, crocodiles, dry vast deserts, dangerous ocean rips, poisonous spiders, disease infested mosquitoes, dangerous wild dogs called dingoes, blue bottle stingers in the ocean and worst of all a tiny octopus which could kill you in a few minutes if one bit you.

Elizabeth declared she would never go swimming in the ocean and really didn't want Harry to do that either, but he just laughed at her. Life was full of promise and Harry couldn't wait, he was impatient and just wanted to get to Australia as quickly as he could and start this new life.

Chapter 20
Life in Australia

Like his father before him, Harry just loved the salt spray in his face, leaning over the ship's rail watching the retreating foaming frenzy of churned up water that the large propellers left in their wake. He desperately wanted to know all about his parents and frequently quizzed his grandmother about them. "What was my mother like? Why did my father go off to war? How did he die? Where are they both buried?"

Elizabeth did her best to answer all his questions and realised how much he was missing having parents, like normal children. She couldn't tell him much about his mother as she had never actually met her, but she did go on and on about Jack and how brave he was and how patriotic wanting to become a flier and always wanting to "do his bit" for his country.

She would tell him over and over, "It's because of men like your father that we won the war, that we are free and not German citizens bowing to bullies like Hitler. Brave men, men willing to sacrifice their lives so that we, those who are left, can live in peace. You should be very proud of your father, he was a great man."

Harry tried to understand but really, all he wanted was a father, with him, by his side, teaching him things, leading him through life. He watched wistfully at other children playing with their fathers, he watched fathers throwing balls to their boys, kicking a football or having fun in the pool.

He wanted a mother he could love, kiss, be cuddled by and spoiled. His grandmother did her best and was a good person, but was somewhat aloof, not cold but stiff. She loved the child but it just wasn't in her to kiss and cuddle him, she wasn't that sort of woman. She gave Harry the one photograph that she still had of Jack and Harry cherished that photo. Everything that they had possessed had been burnt in the fire that consumed their house when it was bombed. Still, Harry was happy enough and loved his grandmother.

Elizabeth had never had to go out to work and had no clear idea what she would do and how she could find employment once she got to Australia, but trusted that something would work out for her and Harry. The boat docked in Fremantle Harbour and those passengers disembarking there were ushered through the enormous customs shed and had their baggage, passports and other documents checked. Once through all the formalities, they were led to a special bus which took them straight to the migrant hostel. The weather was hot and grandmother and grandson were sweating profusely.

Once at the hostel, they were given an air-conditioned room to themselves and a tour around the remainder of the hostel. Their room was spacious enough, with a wardrobe and three sets of drawers. It had a tiled floor, which kept the room cool and a small refrigerator for keeping drinks cold. There was a communal dining room, communal showers, toilets and a small shop. It was all very clean and while somewhat sparse, still comfortable enough.

The officer in charge interviewed Elizabeth and explained how the system worked. They would be fed at the nominated times and there was clothing available if they needed it. There was a bus which went into town four times a day and would ferry Harry to school and Elizabeth into the centre of town, where she was expected to look for work.

Harry found that he was at least a year ahead of the other children in his class for basic subjects; reading, writing and arithmetic, but was way far behind with history, basic science, rules of sport and generally socialising with his peers. At the local school, the teachers were used to new migrants and made allowances for all sorts of difficulties that such children encountered. At least this child could speak English, many of the migrant children were from non-English-speaking countries, Italy, Greece, Germany etc. and it took them at least two years to catch up to the other pupils.

Harry had no knowledge of the local customs, children's games, street language and general geography or knowledge of Fremantle and Perth. He was a smart child though and quickly learnt to fit in and was accepted by his peers. No one seemed to notice that his skin was a different colour to other children, no one was bothered, mainly because there were so many children from different countries, some Asian, some European and so many with different coloured skin.

Harry settled down into a comfortable routine of school in the day time, relating all his news of the day's events with his grandmother in the evenings and seeing the various sights of Fremantle and the larger city of Perth at the weekends. Perth was only a bus ride away and Harry just loved the busy hustle and bustle of the large metropolis.

He enjoyed riding the trolley buses in Perth and was always highly amused when the trolley bus went round a corner too fast and the two long metal arms that connected the bus to the electric cables would sometimes come off and the driver, knowing full well that he was providing entertainment to his passengers, would have to get out and fix it.

Elizabeth made appointments during the week with various employment agencies but no one seemed to want to employ her. She had no qualifications, no experience and wasn't even young and attractive enough for consideration as a simple receptionist. Weeks went by and she scoured the newspapers every day, hoping that someone might want a middle-aged grandmother with a child.

The supervisor at the hostel asked her to step into his office one day. He knew that Elizabeth was looking for work and he was always doing his best to find work for the immigrants in his care. He told Elizabeth that he knew of a farmer down south, who had recently lost his wife and was looking for someone to help out on the farm. Not to do any farm work as such but to do the cooking for the farmer and his three employees, to be the housekeeper really, which would involve cleaning and laundry.

The farmer didn't mind having a child in the house and there was the local village school that Harry could attend which was serviced by a school bus which picked up various children from the neighbouring farms. He wanted to know if Elizabeth would be interested in this kind of work. He explained that there wouldn't be much of a wage in it, but there was a private bedroom and bathroom for Elizabeth and Harry and, of course, they would take their meals with the farmer and his workers.

Elizabeth talked it over with Harry and the following day agreed to meet up with the farmer for an interview. Harry was excited at the prospect of living on a farm as he had never experienced anything of an outdoor kind of life. He knew nothing of cattle, horses, sheep but was enthusiastic and wanted to try out anything new. Elizabeth realised this was probably the best offer of employment she would ever get and although had never worked for a living before certainly knew how to cook, clean, wash and iron. It was work she knew she would be able to do.

Elizabeth and Harry were to meet the farmer at a small café on the outskirts of Fremantle. Samuel Briggs turned out to be a tall, tanned, rough Australian with a well-trained trusty red kelpie dog at his heels. Sam had lost his wife to a ten-year battle with breast cancer. He had suffered almost as much as she had, just watching her, the love of his life withering away before his eyes. The doctors did all they could, but it just wasn't enough.

Sam's rough exterior belied a soft-spoken gentleman. He wore the most battered Akubra pulled down hard on his head of thinning hair, almost covering his permanently creased eyes, shielding them from the harsh Australian sun. His jacket, trousers and thick boots were all covered in the cloying, staining red dust and bore witness to the fact he was a working farmer and not in any way given to "dressing up" or "putting on a show". Not like some of the "gentlemen farmers" that Elizabeth remembered had frequented the golf club back home in England.

Sam was straightforward and greeted Elizabeth and Harry with hearty handshakes. Elizabeth liked the look of him and felt straightaway that he was a trustworthy, hardworking farmer who would command respect from his workers. Harry and Rusty, the dog, fell in love with each other immediately. While the grownups talked, Harry and Rusty played a game of 'pull' with a piece of rope that was attached to Rusty's collar.

Samuel Briggs asked them both to call him simply Sam and explained what was to be expected of a housekeeper and cook. He acknowledged that the wages were poor but that Elizabeth and Harry would have their own room and would be looked on as family. There were three other farm workers and everyone was treated as an equal, even Ben, who was an "Abbo". Neither Elizabeth nor Harry knew what an "Abbo" was and were too polite to ask the question.

It was agreed that Elizabeth would be taken on and Sam organised for a car to pick up Elizabeth and Harry the following weekend and transport them, some two hundred miles up north to the farm.

Chapter 21
Life on the Farm—in Australia

At 6 o'clock in the morning, Elizabeth was woken by a loud knocking on her bedroom door and was informed that a vehicle was waiting for them. She had said her goodbyes the night before to the few friends she had made at the hostel. She and Harry were excited and at the same time a little apprehensive about what lay ahead of them.

Their chauffeur turned out to be a very black Ben who regaled the two on their long journey with stories of his people and life in outback Australia. Harry was fascinated with the man and asked bluntly, "So Ben, are you an 'Abbo' then?"

Ben laughed at Elizabeth, who rebuked the child for being so rude. "Aghh, no worries, missis. Yes, young fella, I'm an 'Abbo' that's short for Aboriginal. We were the first people here, before the white man came. My people have been here for over forty thousand years. Think on that young fella."

The journey up to the farm was an eye opener for Harry and Elizabeth. They had never seen such an arid land in some places and almost floodplains in others. Many fields were dry and parched with pitifully thin sheep doing their best to survive the obviously harsh conditions. On the other hand, there were many fields full of fat, healthy sheep and well-rounded, contented cows. It was obvious to Elizabeth that there were some good farmers on good pasture land and some not-so-good farmers on quite poor barren land. Elizabeth and Harry learnt to call the fields' paddocks.

As they passed paddocks, hundreds of noisy cockatoos squawked at them and flew across the path of the vehicle, much to the annoyance of their driver. Ben pointed out many features of the landscape as they drove north. He named the different birds and many of the trees. Harry was thrilled when Ben stopped the car to allow a father emu to cross the road with his seven baby emus following him. Harry asked why it was a father and not the mother looking after the babies.

Ben confessed he didn't know why, just that it's only the father that looks after the babies.

Further on, Ben stopped the car again for Harry to see his first kangaroo. There was a paddock with half a dozen or so 'roos' quite close to the road. Ben pointed out that two of the kangaroos were mothers and had baby joeys in their pouches.

Just to prove a point, one of the mothers leant forward and, to Harry's amazement, tipped a joey out of her pouch. The baby jumped around for a few moments and then climbed back into his mother's pouch, head first and left one long leg hanging out of the pouch, as if there was no more room inside or even if he had sort of forgotten it was not yet in the pouch, Harry was beside himself laughing, it was the funniest thing he had ever seen. Ben told them how farmers are often referred to as "cockies".

Harry looked quizzically at Ben and asked, "Do you mean cockies, as in short for cockatoos?"

"Yes, young fella, you see, when the first settlers came out here from England, there were so many of them and they were white and we Abbos thought they looked like a flock of cockatoos, so that's why we call them cockies."

"Do they mind?"

"No, I don't think so. It's not an insult."

The homestead was situated at the end of the three hundred feet long driveway, through three different gates which had to be unlocked and locked again as they passed through. Harry was quick to learn and eager to help by jumping out of the car and unlocking and locking each gate. There were sheep in the paddock and a large dam. A densely wooded area was on the eastern side of the house and many large eucalyptus trees lined the driveway and surrounded the homestead, as Ben explained, "The trees keep the house cool in summer and help break the wind in winter."

There were many outhouses, barns, stables and various sheds. Ben pointed out each one as they passed by and eventually he pulled the car to a standstill outside the main house. He carried their few belongings in and showed them their rooms and around the house. No one else was around and he instructed them to make themselves at home. Dinner, he announced, would be at 6 o'clock as usual and with that he took off, putting the car under a lean-to carport and promptly disappeared, leaving Elizabeth and Harry slightly bewildered.

Elizabeth was in a quandary: she didn't know if she was supposed to get dinner ready, with what and for how many. As it was 1 o'clock in the afternoon and she and Harry had not eaten anything since breakfast, they were quite hungry. It didn't appear that Ben was coming back for any lunch and so, after unpacking their few belongings, Elizabeth and Harry explored the house and the kitchen. They found an abundance of food in the large fridge: eggs, bacon, cheeses, fruit and vegetables.

The freezer part of the fridge was packed solid with frozen meat and Elizabeth explored the walk-in pantry to take stock of what kind of provisions there were there. She had a good examination of the cooker and the stock of pots and pans. She was satisfied that there was just about everything that she would need to cook for a household of six people. The house was simply furnished with the essentials but nothing too fancy. It was obviously a working farm and not a holiday hotel.

Elizabeth decided to roll up her sleeves and get to work, whether she was meant to or not. She found half a loaf of bread and made a sandwich for herself and Harry before shooing him out of the kitchen so that she could start preparing dinner.

Harry needed no second bidding, he was keen to get out of the house and go exploring. No one seemed to be around and Harry took note of all the various vehicles that were stored in the largest shed, tractors, harvesters and many contraptions that were totally foreign to him. There were farm implements and tools hung up on all the walls of the shed and one barn was full of straw or was it hay, he didn't know the difference. There were sacks of seeds and fertilisers; containers of chemicals, petrol and kerosene. Harry had never seen anything like it all and was fascinated, but astute enough not to touch anything.

He wandered out to the closest paddock and there encountered two friendly horses which came over to see him and he knew just enough about horses to know that they liked fresh grass and he enjoyed pulling up tufts of grass from the adjacent paddock to feed to them. There was a mesh wire enclosure and a small wooden arrangement, which was obviously a chicken coop.

Harry examined the back flap and discovered three warm eggs. He carried the eggs carefully back to the farmhouse and gave them over to Elizabeth. She was delighted to note that there were chickens on the property and as she looked out of the kitchen window, she could see there was a vegetable garden also. As Elizabeth had cared for her veggie patch and chickens at home in England, this was all something she could relate to and decided to ask Sam if she could be responsible for these items which would be her and Harry's contribution to the running of the farm.

At about 5 o'clock in the evening, Harry spotted a cloud of dust and the sound of horses trotting coming towards him over the rim of the nearest small hill. He had been out in the sun for well over an hour and was feeling quite hot but was glad to see through the dust the figures of four men coming towards him on horseback. Sam with Rusty at his heels were the first to greet the boy and introduced him to the other men, "See you got here then, young Harry, here's Dick and Mort, you've already met Ben."

The men swung down from their horses and, after shaking Harry's hand, led the horses off to the back of the barn before taking off the saddles, bridles and such. All the men disappeared except Sam, who led Harry back to the house where the most delicious smell was wafting towards them. He greeted Elizabeth with a good welcoming handshake and declared that whatever it was cooking, he hoped she had prepared a lot as he was starving and knew the men were too.

Elizabeth's instincts had been right. She had just jumped right in and set to work. Ben had said dinner should be at six and she had organised the meal to be ready for that time. She had found her way around the kitchen and discovered where all the cutlery and crockery were and the table was set out ready for the meal.

At precisely six, all the men converged on the main house, clean and showered and Sam introduced Dick and Mort to Elizabeth. Unannounced, they all took immediately to calling her Liz except Ben, who insisted on calling her "missis."

Elizabeth had found vegetables and plenty of eggs in the pantry and had made a green salad to complement two separate flans, one mostly bacon and the other mostly vegetables, just in case someone might be a vegetarian. It was a simple meal but Elizabeth knew she could make a flan and if there was any leftover, it would serve for someone's lunch the next day.

The men fell upon the meal with relish and politely declared it the best meal they had eaten in months. Elizabeth didn't know if they were just being kind or really did enjoy the meal, but Sam looked as if he was really happy with the meal and he was what Elizabeth was most concerned about. He had employed her and she wanted to make a good impression.

That meal, as every other meal from then onwards, was in no way a quiet affair. The talk around the table mostly centred on the day's work, the weather forecast, the animals, the crops. There was never a lapse, never a pause for silence; always something new to discuss, to be decided. Harry spent the meal feeding titbits under the table to Rusty and as soon as the meal was over asked if he could take Rusty outside. Harry and Rusty played for an hour with Harry throwing an old ball and Rusty retrieving it, wet and soggy with saliva. As the sun went down, Elizabeth called Harry in and instructed him to get ready for bed.

At that first meal, everyone had wanted to talk to Elizabeth about England. How had she fared in the war, how was everyone else in England coping with rationing and housing.

Eventually, the men talked to Harry and Sam informed him that the school bus would pick him up on Monday morning at seven and would drop him back off at the farm at five in the evening. He apologised for it being such a long day but the bus had to pick up and drop off other children from the outlying farms and there was only one school and one bus to service a very large area.

Chapter 22
Back in England

Jack never gave up looking for or hoping to find his mother. He had to work and so his time was limited but he spent each weekend visiting parks, the zoo, the river; places that he thought his mother might take Harry. He visited all the tourist spots, The Tower, Changing of the Guards, Trooping of the Colour.

Anywhere that might be an attraction for a child. He had written to the Education Department to ask if they had any record of a Harry Singleton being enrolled in a school, but he never had any success. He made friends with a girl at work and explained what he was trying to do. She advised him to just "give it up!" but he couldn't, it was his mission in life now, he felt he just had to find his mother and son, he couldn't just give it up: but time was passing and he was no closer to finding them.

He thought his mother might just keep in touch with Allan and Amy in New York and so he wrote to them, enquiring if she had kept in touch. He got a reply back two weeks later explaining that they had not had any correspondence from Elizabeth since the death of George, Jack's father. They had assumed that she was still living in the same house in London.

One night, as he lay tossing and turning, not able to sleep, he tried to put himself into his mother's shoes, "What would mum do, where would she take Harry and why would she take him anywhere other than London?" He talked to himself and asked the same question over and over and eventually a thought struck him.

"Oh, what an idiot I am, she'll want him to know his family. She'd take him back to America. Of course, that's where she'd go."

He jumped out of bed and paced up and down, then took a notepad and wrote down all the places he could remember that Harriet had told him about, where most of her family were, where her old friends were. He was excited now, just thinking that this might be the answer he was looking for. He reasoned his mother was getting old and had no one to take on the responsibility of Harry if she got sick or simply couldn't provide for him. He knew his mother had cleared her savings account.

"Of course," he said to himself, "She'll have taken out her money to get herself and Harry to America. Why didn't I think of that before?"

At first, he reasoned that if she had travelled to America, she would have contacted Alan and Amy, but then remembered that she was embarrassed that Harry was a half-caste, maybe for this reason she hadn't contacted her brother and sister-in-law.

It took only a few days to apply for annual leave at work and then to organise his trip to New York. He booked a British Overseas Airways Corporation flight going from London through Shannon, Gander and finally landing in New York. Jack had never flown in a commercial plane before and was interested in the Lockheed Constellation.

He spoke to the young stewardess and after some discussion about his flying experiences in the war, she agreed to ask the pilot if Jack could visit the cockpit and see for himself the complicated workings of the large airplane. Jack was much impressed and wondered if he might, at some time in the future, sign on for further training and change from banker to pilot. He still had a love of flying but decided to put it to the back of his mind, his first task was to find Harry and his mother.

Jack felt really guilty that he had never kept in touch with Harriet's family and had no idea how he would be able to find them. He knew her family had lived in Washington DC but he'd lost the address. He didn't know if they would have electoral rolls in Washington or even if negroes were allowed to vote. He also didn't know if her family would have had a telephone. Did they still live in Washington, maybe not, he really didn't know.

He tried to think how his mother would have approached the problem; how she would get information about Harriet's family. Maybe she was a better detective than he was proving to be. He did, however, remember that Harriet had worked for Charles Houston at the National Association for the Advancement of Coloured People (NAACP) in New York. He decided that would be his first port of call, they must have records of her home address and family details.

At fifty-two years of age, Charles Houston was a very busy civil rights lawyer, but agreed to see Jack at short notice. Jack found him to be a serious but gentle, large stocky man with a receding hairline and not a trace of a smile on his face. He shook Jack's hand vigorously and asked how he may help.

Jack explained his mission and hoped that Mr Houston may be able to help him locate Harriet's family. Charles Houston was shocked to hear that Harriet had died in childbirth and agreed to break out the records and get to see if he could find details of her background. He explained that he remembered Harriet very fondly and went on to say that she had been a good worker and how upset they all were in the office when she decided to leave them. He also was sorry to relate to Jack that as far as he knew no Elizabeth Singleton had contacted his office or made any enquiries about Harriet Watkins.

After a short wait one of the secretaries in the office brought out a file marked "Personnel" showing Harriet's details when she first joined the group. It gave a home address in Washington DC and her next of kin being May Watkins, the mother.

Jack thanked them profusely and left the office with enthusiastic hope in his heart. He immediately took a bus to Washington to find May Watkins and hoped and prayed that his mother had done the same thing. He had no idea how his mother would have got any information about May Watkins, but he knew his mother was a smart woman and maybe she had succeeded where he, so far, had failed.

Jack took the bus to Washington and checked into a small hotel in the centre of town. The next morning, after a hearty breakfast, he quizzed the owner of the hotel as to the whereabouts of Jackson Road. The owner had no idea where Jackson Road was and after quizzing some of the negro kitchen staff found that it was in an area on the outskirts of town, an area not really suitable for a single white male to go wandering around on his own, especially after dark. Jack heeded the owner's advice and agreed to take along one of the kitchen hands, a very large, well-muscled negro as a companion/bodyguard.

When Jack and his companion drove up Jackson Road in the hired taxi, they drew the attention of many residents who were just sitting around on their doorsteps watching the world go by. There didn't appear to be any numbers on the houses or on the letterboxes, none that he could see anyway and so it was necessary for Jack to ask if anyone knew of May Watkins.

Three youths verbally abused Jack and obviously were not going to help at all so Jervis, Jack's temporary companion, offered to do the asking and told Jack to stay in the taxi out of the way. Further down the road, Jervis had better luck and was directed to number twenty-eight Jackson Road, which had to be counted down from the corner to find the right number.

May Watkins turned out to be a white-haired, mountainous negress, almost as fat as she was tall. She had her "mutton leg" arms folded defensively across her enormous bosom and asked Jervis unceremoniously, "Whatcha want?"

Jervis deferred to Jack and left Jack to do the talking. May Watkins was none too friendly and wanted to know why Jack was looking for a young boy called Harry Singleton. Jack tried to explain why he was there and was sensible enough not to let May Watkins know that he was the man who had taken Harriet away to London, that he was the one who had married Harriet, that he was the father of her grandchild: his instincts told him that she may box his ears or worse.

May Watkins assured Jack that no one had brought a child to her door, no elderly English woman, no one. Jack tried to quiz the neighbours but May Watkins told him in no uncertain terms to get his "skinny white ass" away from her house and back to where he came from. As he and his companion climbed back into the taxi, three grubby children started pelting them with stones and two shirtless wrinkled old men swore at them and spit on the ground.

It was not a pleasant experience and Jack couldn't wait to get back to the safety of the hotel. He was dejected, depressed and now out of options. He had no idea what he was going to do. He spent the next day in bed. After that, he decided he might as well do some sightseeing before heading back to England, to work, to trying to live the rest of his life with his regrets and without his son.

Jack was the most uninterested tourist doing the sights of New York. He visited all the famous landmarks and heard the tour guide's words, but none of it sank in. He'd seen it all before anyway, when he lived in New York. He was in a deep depression and moved in and out of his hotel like an automaton. He knew he should visit his aunt and uncle and eventually rang them and arranged to call in on them.

Aunt Amy made a big fuss of Jack and had prepared a meal of gigantic proportions for his "homecoming". There was the largest serving of spare ribs for everyone and Amy had made pumpkin pie, which she remembered Jack had loved so much. Uncle Alan was far more reserved and immediately remonstrated with Jack for not visiting them before he left for his return trip to England some years earlier.

Both Alan and Amy were so sympathetic to Jack's plight and tried to offer advice for finding Elizabeth and Harry. They forgave Jack for not introducing them to Harriet but understandably were a little miffed that the social conventions had not been served at that time. Jack's visit lasted only a few days and he was feeling so depressed that he made his excuses and moved out of their home and into a hotel.

For two days he just sat in his hotel room feeling sorry for himself and finally decided that it was all a futile exercise and he might as well go somewhere he hadn't been before while he still had some leave left. He wandered listlessly into the closest travel agency and asked where a flight, within the continent might be going the next day. The question amused the young man in the agency as he answered bemused, "Well, sir, we have over a hundred different flights leaving New York tomorrow, where would you like to go?"

"I really don't care."

Somewhat taken aback the assistant checked his screen and then, with a friendly smile informed Jack, "Well, sir, as you are willing to travel at such short notice we have a special offer for a flight to Mexico City, leaving at 3.00 in the afternoon. That would be American Airlines Flight 157. It's bound for Mexico City with an intermediate stopover at Washington, DC National Airport and then a routine stopover at Love Field in Dallas, Texas. We've had a cancellation and I can get you on that flight if you wish."

"Yes, no problem. Book that for me, please."

The flight left LaGuardia Airport on time, bound for Mexico City and was a blur to Jack for the first two hours. He had noted that the plane was a DC-6 with the title *Flagship of South Carolina*. He sat for the most part with his eyes closed, not really caring where he was going. A passenger sat down next to him and he never even acknowledged her presence.

Eventually, he opened his lacklustre eyes and noted that the plane was flying in and out of huge thick cumulous clouds and it was truly a spectacle that even in his jaded depressed state, he couldn't help marvelling at. As a pilot, he had flown through so many cloud formations but these thick fluffy mountains seemed so awesome that it was a different experience.

He started to actually enjoy the breathtaking vista, which took his mind off his miseries for a short while and lifted his spirits somewhat. He hadn't even noticed the woman who was sat next to him, he had been so preoccupied in his own misery, but eventually he heard a soft gentle voice next to him openly express what his mind was thinking, "Honestly, 'majestic' is the only word I can think of to describe those monstrous clouds, it's wonderful, isn't it?"

"Wonderful, yes, truly awesome."

Jack turned and, for the first time, looked at the woman and smiled at their mutual admiration for the spectacle. "I'm sorry," apologised Jack. "Look, I've been a pilot and seen this phenomenon many times, would you like to exchange seats and you can have a better view through the window then?"

"Oh, would you? That would be marvellous. This is my first flight. I wanted to book a window seat but they were all taken."

Jack gallantly stood up and exchanged seats with the woman. As they brushed past each other, Jack couldn't help breathing in the subtle floral perfume she was wearing. She thanked him graciously and proceeded to keep her nose from almost touching the window as she watched the plane fly through, sometimes over and sometimes under the cottonwool mountains.

Jack took advantage of the attention that his fellow passenger was giving to the outside journey through the clouds to have a look at the woman. He noted the soft blonde curls and beautifully manicured fingernails. He could only see the back of her head but noted that she was quite small in stature but of slim build and wore simple but obviously expensive clothes. He realised she'd had an English accent and he was intrigued as to why this pleasant woman was travelling alone.

Eventually, one of the two air hostesses introduced herself as Josephine and offered a drink from the trolley for the two. Jack ordered a beer and his fellow passenger ordered a glass of wine. Eventually, lunch was served and the woman turned her attention from the window to the meal.

"What have we got here then, this looks interesting?" she commented as she poked her fork at the pasta and then proceeded to introduce herself and chatted quite naturally, with no reserve whatsoever.

"My name's Alice. Did you say you had been a pilot? How come you're not flying this plane then?"

"Hi, my name's Jack and I'm not a commercial pilot, I was a fighter pilot in the war."

"Oh, right, do I hear an English accent? Were you in the RAF then?"

"Yes, but I did the majority of my training in America. I really loved America."

"So have you just been on holiday in the U.S. or was this a business trip?"

"Oh, it's a long story I'd rather not go into."

"Oh, sorry for prying, but we have a few hours to pass, if you want to talk, I'm a very good listener."

"Thanks but I really don't want to talk about it. So, are you going to Mexico for a holiday?"

"Yes and no, it's work really, a job waiting for me. For the first time, I've been able to throw off the shackles of parental authority and am going to meet up with a friend of my cousin who has promised me a job in Mexico City, as the subeditor of a fashion magazine. I'm thrilled to bits and can't wait to get started." The two chatted easily over lunch and discussed the in-flight magazine that Alice had studied when she first boarded the plane.

The flight for the next half hour was uneventful until one of the outboard engines on the left wing began backfiring and obviously running quite roughly. Jack could feel the crew reducing power and noted that the engine had been closed down. He knew enough about planes to feel the feathering of the propeller and realised all was not well.

Alice and all the other passengers also realised something was wrong but the flight attendants were quick to reassure everyone that engine failures were not unusual and they could easily fly on to their destination with only one engine out of action and the remaining three being perfectly adequate.

The captain announced over the loudspeaker that they were having a slight problem but that they would change to another airplane upon arrival at Dallas.

As the plane approached Dallas airspace, Captain Claude alerted air traffic control that they were flying on three engines. It was not seen as a major problem and the flight was given permission to enter the incoming traffic pattern at Love Field.

Jack noted that the weather was clear with good visibility and reassured Alice that the plane could fly and land quite easily with only three engines working. Everyone felt the lowering of the flaps and the deployment of the landing gear. There didn't appear to be any major problem and the flight attendants relaxed as they took their seats, feeling the pilot making a right-hand turn to land on runway 36.

However, the airplane came out of the turn slightly to the left of the runway, forcing the pilot to make an "S" turn to correct their course and align the DC-6 with the runway centreline.

Inexplicably, the plane shook and its airspeed dropped alarmingly. Most of the passengers gasped at the unexpected shaking and Alice immediately grabbed

Jack's hand for comfort and reassurance. Jack himself wasn't feeling too comfortable as the left wing dropped and the plane began to turn to the left. He instinctively knew the flight crew was experiencing some kind of difficulty, apart and separate from the loss of one engine.

He spoke softly and controlled as he held on to Alice's frantic grip and explained that this was not unusual and for her not to worry. He himself, however, was quite worried but there was nothing he could do and was as helpless as any other passenger. Jack's experience in planes gave him the awareness and knowledge of what was probably happening in the cockpit as he sensed the captain applying full throttle and probably applying the booster pump to increase the fuel flow to the three remaining engines.

Jack noted that the flight crew were applying full right aileron, obviously in an attempt to raise the dropping left wing and he realised that the captain was also re-raising the landing gear, apparently intending to circle the airport and attempt another landing or go-around. Jack knew what he would do if he were flying the plane, he thought the flaps should be raised to assist the aborting of the first attempt at landing, but he was not too sure if things would be the same in this DC-6 as the much smaller fighter planes that he had flown in the war.

Jack was sensitive to the sound of the engine and the feel of the movement as he realised the RPM was dropping and he could feel the feathering of the prop as the captain was trying to reduce the drag helping the airplane accelerate and climb. Jack looked across the aisle and realised that a second engine had failed and the plane was now struggling on the remaining two engines. He could see through the window that the flaps were down and could feel that the plane was not accelerating.

A go-around was going to be extremely difficult and Jack held his breath as the plane continued to drop, headed on a path that would be crossing a runway, probably not on a straight, intended course.

Some passengers were praying and some were crying. Alice clung onto Jack and kept asking, "Are we going down? Are we going to crash?"

"We'll be fine, truly. The captain knows what he's doing. We'll be fine."

Jack didn't feel fine though, he knew they were in trouble, he could tell the captain was trying to raise the airplane's nose but realised it was a futile attempt to climb and knew the plane was about to stall.

The plane stalled and hit the runway tail-first. It skidded off the left side of the runway, trampolining into the air as it crashed into a stationary smaller plane, which burst into flames upon impact. The DC-6 crashed through a hangar and immediately burst into flames. The momentum of the crash sent Jack's plane careering, on fire, further along the ground, breaking into many pieces as it skidded sideways, coming to rest after hitting a small office block.

The fuselage opened up like a can of beans and the emergency doors opened up over what part of the wings were left intact. The captain and flight crew were in the cockpit section of the airplane, which had broken free from the main fuselage and they were able to scramble to safety before the ensuing fire engulfed them. Passengers were scrambling to get out of the plane.

Alice was in a state of shock and just froze in her seat. Jack tried to get her to follow him but she just didn't seem able to move. A large hole in the forward fuselage was allowing passengers to escape before the fire from the rear reached them.

Jack shouted at her as he undid her seatbelt but she was unresponsive. Her eyes were unblinking, glazed and wide. He resorted to physically lifting her out of her seat and carrying her like a baby out onto the wing. The flames were licking at his heels and the smoke was blinding and choking him so he simply threw Alice away from the plane as far as he could and then jumped out into the unknown to save himself.

Jack lost consciousness and was rescued by fire officers. He was taken to the local hospital and treated for smoke inhalation, minor burns and a broken leg. As soon as he was able, he asked after Alice and was told that she too was suffering from smoke inhalation and had two broken legs. Of the forty-five people aboard the DC-6 fifteen passengers escaped as well as the flight crew. The two flight attendants and the remaining passengers perished in the intensive fire, which ravaged the broken plane.

Jack had to spend a week in the hospital under observation with his leg in a plaster cast. Three days after the crash, Jack was able to visit Alice in another part of the hospital and was surprised to see an elderly man embracing Alice as she lay helpless with both her legs in plaster casts and elevated, looking very uncomfortable. He asked if it was an awkward time to visit and was welcomed into the private room with much enthusiasm. "No, no, come in."

Alice introduced Jack to the elderly man, called Ernest, who turned out to be her father. Both Alice and Ernest thanked Jack profusely for getting her out of the plane and saving her life. Ernest kept shaking Jack's hand and patting him on the back. Jack asked Ernest how he had got there so fast and where had he come from.

"Oh, I was at home in London when the hospital rang me shortly after the crash and I caught the first plane out here. Alice tells me you were a hero and risked your own life to save her. We are so very grateful, really truly grateful."

"Oh, I only did what anyone would have done. I mean, I couldn't just leave her there, could I?"

"Well, we are very grateful." Jack withdrew his hand, rubbing it from such excessive shaking and went around the bed to sit on the spare seat facing Alice.

The three discussed the crash and the possible reasons for it. Ernest volunteered his views, "There'll be a hearing, I think, in the not too distant future and they'll find out just what went wrong and what actually happened. Do you remember any of it, Jack? Alice tells me you were a fighter pilot in the war; do you have any opinion as to what went wrong?"

"Well, I don't really know, of course. I was only a passenger, but I think the crash could have been avoided if the captain had held the plane straight and level after he made that sharp turn to the runway. He maybe should have raised the flaps and climbed to a safe altitude to circle the airport and make a second attempt at a landing. The weather was good, visibility was normal. Maybe they ran out of fuel. I really don't know. They will find out whenever there's an airplane crash, there's always an investigation. I'm just so glad that you were not too badly hurt, Alice and I'm really sorry for dropping you over the edge of the wing, but the smoke was so thick I just couldn't see anything at all."

"Oh, please don't apologise. I'm just so very grateful that you got me out. You could have left me there, but you didn't, you risked your own safety and I'll always be in your debt."

"No, no, please don't think like that. I only did what anyone in the same circumstances would have done."

Ernest reached into his inside pocket and took out his cheque book. "Look, Jack, I really am grateful to you for saving my daughter's life. I'm not short of a bob or two and I'd like to show you my appreciation."

"No, no, please, you don't have to do that. I don't need a reward, I'm just grateful that Alice is alive and will make a full recovery."

"Look, Jack, this is not England, it's not a welfare state and unless you are well heeled, this stay in hospital will be very expensive. The very least I can do is to pay for your hospital care. I come from a wealthy family so it's no problem for me. Please let me cover your hospital expenses. Both Alice and I really want to do this for you."

"Well, I must admit I don't have much money, so if it's what you really want to do and can readily afford it, then, OK, why not? Thank you. You're both very kind and thoughtful."

Jack stayed in hospital for eight days under observation as his lungs had been compromised with the heat and smoke but as he was young and fit, he was told that he would make a full recovery once his leg had healed. He visited Alice in her private room every day and was beginning to have quite strong feelings for her. He sort of remembered someone famous or was it an old Indian folktale that stated, "if you save someone's life then you are forever responsible for them."

That's how Jack felt about Alice. At the end of his hospital stay, he visited Alice to say his temporary farewells, but to also ask if he could keep in touch. He very much wanted to see her again, he felt he was falling in love, but had to return to England, to work and to his quest to try and find his mother and son.

On this his last visit, Jack was surprised as he entered her room to see Alice in a deep embrace with a young man.

"Oh, sorry, I didn't mean to interrupt." His face coloured and he felt a wave of jealous nausea rise. Who could this man be who was kissing the girl he was falling in love with.

"Oh, Jack, come in. I want you to meet Gerald. Gerald, this is Jack the hero who saved my life."

Gerald rose from the bed where he had been kissing Alice and took Jack's hand, shaking it vigorously, saying, "So pleased to meet you Jack, Alice and Ernest have been telling me all about you and how you saved our girl. We are all so grateful."

Jack was embarrassed and couldn't quite work out who this young man was, Alice had never spoken about a Gerald, but Jack realised he really didn't know much about Alice, anyway.

"Please, I only did what anyone would have done."

"No, I understand you were quite the hero." Alice looked from one man to the other and then, blushing slightly, held up her left hand for Jack to see. "Look Jack, look at my ring. Gerald has just proposed and we are engaged. You know, we're going to be married."

Jack was shocked and surprised and mumbled his congratulations before saying his goodbyes. He couldn't get out of the room fast enough. He had been so close to making an utter fool of himself. He walked out of the hospital cursing and calling himself all sorts of stupid names for being so naïve.

"How could you fall for the woman? You didn't know anything about her." He chastised himself.

"You idiot. You were about to pour your heart out to her, god, I bet she would have laughed in your face. Idiot. You stupid idiot. Go home, back to where you belong, forget her, she was obviously never for you."

Chapter 23
Harry's Education

Harry's first day at school was different from anything he had encountered in England. There were 16 children of all ages in the one roomed school. There were only two teachers, a married couple, Mr and Mrs Stone. Mrs Stone taught the younger children and Mr Stone the older ones. Mrs Stone was a gentle, caring motherly type who would sit the younger children on her knee as she led them through their reading and other various lessons.

Mr Stone, on the other hand, was a strict but fair disciplinarian who stood no nonsense. It was Mr Stone who took the older boys for what was called PE or physical education. Under his careful eye, the boys learnt cricket, football and swimming. The tiny school had no sports field of its own but used the town's parkland oval for its football and cricket. Swimming was carried out in the shallows of the local river, when it wasn't in the flood or when it wasn't too low in the dry summer.

There were rules that Harry had to learn, what to do and when to do it, where to go and where not to go. He made friends immediately with a very black Aboriginal boy called Buddy. It was Buddy who was charged with teaching Harry how to line up each morning before entering the school, how to find his file from the cupboard. How to check the toilet seat to make sure no redbacks lurked there.

Harry already knew what a redback was from his reading of dangerous creatures on the boat. He learnt to stamp around in any long grass to scare away snakes and not to eat any berries that he wasn't familiar with. One thing that did surprise Harry was the singing of the National Anthem each morning. He was familiar with and sang with gusto the familiar "God Save the King".

He asked Buddy, "How come you sing the English National Anthem, when you're all Australians?"

"I dunno, ask Mrs Stone." Mrs Stone explained to Harry how Australia was part of the Commonwealth and so part of Britain. "Britain's king is our king too."

Harry was only eight years old and was initially put in the care of Mrs Stone but after only two days was elevated to the "big boys group". His reading, writing and arithmetic were way beyond his peers but in all the other subjects he was definitely behind and so joined the younger group for geography, history and social sciences.

Although he was a good student Harry couldn't wait to get out of the confines of the classroom and was learning the intricacies of the various sports. He was shocked and embarrassed when asked to kick the football. The football was nothing like he had ever seen before, it was oval and not round and when he did try to kick it, the ball shot off at an angle.

The other boys laughed at him but Mr Stone appreciated that Harry had never seen such a ball and so patiently took the boy to one side and guided him through the exercise. The boys were playing a scaled-down version of Australian Rules Football and Harry had no idea what it was all about. He was tall for his age though and once he had learnt how to pass the ball, tackle and kick he could hold his own. The rules seemed complicated to him but he was a quick learner and Buddy helped and guided him through the game.

Harry had never been swimming, Elizabeth hated the water and had never taken him to the local baths in England. Harry didn't even know that he couldn't swim. When Mr Stone took the boys down to the river, they all jumped in from the small jetty and swam up and down having a whale of a time.

Harry stood tentatively at the end of the jetty platform and, eventually, one of the boys playfully pushed him in. Harry hadn't the faintest idea what to do. He flapped his arms in panic and lost his footing on the sandy bottom. The water closed in over his head and he knew he couldn't hold his breath any longer, he was drowning and no one was taking any notice. Buddy was the first to realise Harry was under the water and not coming up.

By this time, the slight current had taken Harry into the middle of the river and into quite deep water. Buddy dived down and caught Harry by his hair, pulled him up and dragged him back to the edge of the river. Mr Stone was frantic as he pounded Harry's chest. Almost at once, Harry vomited a large amount of river water and then looked into the very frightened face of his teacher. All the boys were out of the water now and crowding around to watch the spectacle to see if Harry had actually drowned.

One of the boys asked unceremoniously, “Is he dead?”

Mr Stone curtly addressed them, “What are you lot gawping at? Get back into the water, nothing to be seen here.”

The boys all returned to their play except Buddy, who stood watching as Harry tentatively stood up with a few coughs and splutters. Mr Stone took the two boys to one side and instructed Buddy to watch over Harry and to teach him how to swim.

Harry, however, refused to go back into the water and from that moment was terrified of swimming and at every river visit refused to go into the water. He never did learn to swim and always adamantly refused to go near the water, even to paddle at the edge. Mr Stone felt so guilty at his assumption that the new boy Harry could swim that although he tried to gently coax Harry into the water left him alone when he realised the boy had been traumatised and never pushed him into learning how to swim again.

As he confessed to his wife that evening, “My god, Maggie, the boy could have drowned. I would have been to blame. It was all my fault, I just assumed he could swim. I’ll never make that mistake again.”

The incident brought Harry and Buddy close together as friends. Harry knew Buddy had saved his life and felt he owed him a debt of gratitude and kept telling him, “I owe you one, mate, really I do.”

Buddy would just shrug his shoulders and mumble, “Naw, it’s nothing.”

Mr Stone’s real passion was actually for cricket. He taught the boys the rudiments of the game and lectured them eternally about the greatness of “The Don”. He mixed the PE in with social science and made every boy aware of the hero of their country, Don Bradman.

Harry had no idea who Don Bradman was but soon learnt that cricket was expected to be in the blood of every Australian male and the great man’s statistics, scoring and playing matches, were all an essential part of a boy’s education. Mr Stone would lecture them unceasingly about what he called “the greatest batsman who ever lived and the greatest cricketer of all time”.

They were told all about the Don’s test debut in 1928 and were made to memorise all the details of the great man. Mr Stone would shoot questions at random and expect the boys to know the answers immediately, “Where was the Don born, Smith?”

“Cootamundra, sir.”

“Where’s that Fenshaw?”

"New South Wales, sir,"

"Was the Don a right-handed batsman or left-handed, Jones?"

"Right-handed, sir."

"How tall was he, Robbins?"

"5 ft 7, sir."

"Singleton, are you paying attention?"

"Yes, sir."

"Well, make some notes and remember this, the Don scored 254 runs against England in 1930 at Lords and in that same year scored 334 at Headingly. Got that?"

"Yes, sir."

"Well, remember it, no cricketer has ever done that before and you should be glad that you aren't in England any more. Learn to be proud that you're now an Australian."

"Oh, I am, sir."

"Fisher, what was the Don's score at the MCG in 1932?"

"Sir, it was 103 not out."

"Quite right, well done."

Mr Stone was a fanatic and tried his best to instil that enthusiasm into his pupils. He had the boys listen to the radio, following the commentary when a match was being played and he cut out newspaper clippings about the great man and pasted them onto the back wall of the classroom. He organised games of cricket every day in the summer and Aussie football in the winter, but it was the cricket that he loved the best.

Harry was learning to love the sport too and being a tall boy was taught to concentrate on bowling and bowling as fast as he could. He tried holding the ball in slightly different ways and under Mr Stone's tutelage, was beginning to show real promise as a fast bowler.

Chapter 24
Harry from Eight to Twelve

Life on the farm was never dull. After school and at the weekends, Harry was allowed to help Elizabeth with the chickens and with the veggie patch but he really wanted to get out and help the men in the paddocks. Sam took a real liking to the boy and selected one of the horses, a very quiet mare and started to teach Harry how to ride. Harry loved the horse and Mort showed him how to take care of the animal, its feet, its coat and food.

All the equipment needed to be taken care of and Harry was shown how to oil the leather, take apart all the pieces of tack and put it all back together again. He was taught to saddle up and get the horse to take the bridle. It was all a steep learning curve, but Harry wanted to get involved and Sam encouraged him in every way. Mort showed Harry how to take hold of a horse's lower leg and lift it to care for the horse's feet and showed him some rudimentary shoeing. Harry had a go and made a good job of his first effort.

Sam nodded his head in approval and complemented Harry, saying, "Well done, young fella, I can see you'll make a first-class farrier."

"No, I'm not in the first class anymore. I'm in the third class at school now."

Sam laughed and explained to the boy, "No, I don't mean at school, if someone says you're first class, it means you are really good at something."

"Oh, alright."

Harry got on well with the other men on the farm. The boys often referred to Dick as "Dick the quick," as he was super-fast when shearing the sheep. He showed Harry how to cut the wool from the sheep and spread it out on the shearer's table, but Harry was too small and not strong enough to use the shears. He vowed, though, that he would help with the shearing when he was older.

It was agreed by all that Mort was the best horseman and had an uncanny knack of being able to handle even the most difficult of the horses. He would talk to the horses and no matter how wild the horse might have been, once Mort had spent a few hours with the beast, it came to him with no trouble at all. Sam had never liked the heartless way most farmers broke in a wild horse and so he used Mort and his magic with the new horses, taming them and teaching them how to respond to commands and to come when called. It was Mort who taught Harry most of what he needed to know when around and riding his horse.

Ben, the Aboriginal, was Harry's favourite amongst the men and everyone had a good laugh one day when Ben's hat flew off in the wind and landed in the dam. Ben loved his Akubra and immediately jumped off his horse and shimmied down the steep side of the dam to retrieve his hat.

Once in the water, he caught the very wet hat and pulled it down hard on his head. Going down a steep sided dam is easy but Ben found that getting up the sandy side was near impossible. Every time he pulled himself up a few feet, the sand would give way and he would tumble back down into the water.

Sam and Harry sat on their horses laughing and shouting encouragement to poor Ben. Eventually Mort could see that Ben was becoming quite exhausted and frustrated and decided it was time for the fun to stop and for Ben to be pulled out. Mort had a coil of rope around the pommel of his saddle and just threw Ben into the line. It was an easy matter then for Mort to keep the end of the rope tight around the saddle pommel and for Ben to pull himself up the steep sandy slope. Everyone but Ben was laughing and they never let him forget the incident.

For Ben, one of the worst aspects of the whole affair was the awful realisation that the four black lumps on his bare legs was not mud but leaches. Blood sucking leaches. He knew they wouldn't really hurt him, but he hated leaches and pulled them off as quickly as he could. He'd been attacked by the creatures many times before and seen leaches on other people; his whole body shook with revulsion each time he thought about them. He took many a ribbing about his wet hat retrieval, giving everyone a good laugh for weeks thereafter.

Life on the farm was paradise for Harry; at last he had a man in his life. Sam was the father figure he could look up to, someone, other than his grandmother who cared about him, who was helping him to grow up. He had a dog who, when not working on the farm with Sam and the other men, followed him everywhere and, although it was very much frowned upon by Sam, crept into Harry's bed at night.

There was a small river near the farm and in February Sam took Elizabeth and Harry down to the river for a picnic and to show Harry how to catch marron. Neither Elizabeth nor Harry had ever heard of marron and so it was a completely new experience for them both. Sam explained that the marron are pretty much like a small English lobster and the only way to catch them was to lasso them from behind.

It seemed silly to Harry but after a few goes with a long rod looped at one end with thin wire and a slip knot, he got the hang of it and caught three good sized marron.

Sam taught Harry how to avoid getting bitten by the aggressive creatures and Harry watched in fascination as the black marron fought with each other in the bucket. Sam caught nine and declared the afternoon a raging success. He showed Elizabeth how to cook the marron once back at the farm. Both Harry and Elizabeth were surprised to note the very black marron, once in the boiling water, changed to a brilliant red. Everyone had a real feast for the evening meal and the boys congratulated Harry on his first marron catch.

Elizabeth was as happy as Harry. The work at the homestead was not what she really considered work at all. It was only an extension of what she had been doing in England. She loved cooking and the men treated her with respect and never failed to compliment her on the evening's meal.

Every week, Sam would take Elizabeth into town to buy in supplies and more often than not they would have lunch in the small café on the main road. Harry was frequently left at home playing with Rusty or riding his horse with the other men. It was an idyllic existence and Elizabeth was not only happy for herself but for Harry too, she could see how he was developing and was proud of his progress with the horses and his willingness to help around the farm.

Harry had been eight years old when they first came to the farm and the years started to pass very quickly. Harry embraced the life on the farm and one year passed, then another and in no time at all, Harry was celebrating his twelfth birthday.

Elizabeth made him a special cake decorated with a cricket wicket, bat and red ball. Harry enjoyed his cricket, even though it was a small school and was just sorry that they could never get a proper game, they just didn't have the numbers.

His next love was his horse. He had progressed from the gentle mare and was now riding a spirited gelding called Jerimiah. He was allowed to ride with the men mending fences and checking on the stock but he had not been allowed to assist with the annual mustering. That work was just too dangerous and itinerant workers were mostly used to help with this seasonal chore.

Sam decided one day that the farm needed another shed and so bought in the appropriate materials. The boys, as he called them, had put up sheds before and knew how to fit the corrugated sheets together. He called Harry over to witness how a team of men can put up a shed in just one day. He wouldn't let Harry help as he thought the boy would only get in the way, but Harry was keen to help and did just a bit of fetching and carrying, which was all he was allowed to do.

The men put up the vertical struts first and as they started fitting the sheets together, the wind came up the valley behind them. It took them all by surprise and by the time four large sheets had been erected Sam realised it was going to be too difficult a job to complete with the wind getting worse by the minute.

Mort and Ben were holding one large sheet in position when Dick shouted that he couldn't hold his end. They all realised that the situation was impossible and on Sam's command they all left the half built shed and ran to safety, just as the wind took the large sheets and scattered them around the paddock. The boys all laughed but Sam had been seriously afraid that someone may have been hurt. He was shaken and resolved to be far more careful and aware of the weather pattern before he would attempt such a thing again. Harry learnt quite a lot from that experience.

In fact, Harry was learning something new every day. School work was no problem and life on the farm was easy-going. Elizabeth was a good cook and housekeeper. Harry had his own room and got on well with the other men, especially with Sam.

What Harry didn't know was how much Sam and Elizabeth were beginning to have real feelings for one another. Neither was what Sam called "spring chickens" but they still had urges and romantic notions.

As they were living under the same roof, it was impossible not to feel the attraction that they had for each other and it was only at the weekends, on their shopping trips that they were able to openly discuss their feelings. Sam would order lunch and they would sit facing each other, holding hands across the table. It was a new sensation for Elizabeth and she was starting to feel like a young woman again.

They never overtly showed their feelings for each other in front of either Harry or the other men but decided to wait a while before declaring any intentions. Elizabeth needed to know that any romance between her and Sam would not upset Harry. She was in unknown territory and didn't know how Harry would feel about the situation. She decided to bring up the subject with Harry one evening when Sam was out tending one of the sick cows.

"Harry, do you like Sam?"

"Yes, grandma, he's great. He's going to let me help with the muster next year."

"Well, that's nice. I guess I like him too. Quite a lot, actually." Harry shot her a quizzical look and then a sly smile crossed his twelve-year-old face.

"What's a lot, grandma? Do you want to kiss him and stuff?"

"Well, I just like him. Would that bother you?"

"No, it wouldn't bother me, but you're a bit old for that sort of stuff, aren't you? I mean, kissing and all that stuff." He openly shuddered at the thought and they both laughed.

"Oh, you're never too old to like someone. But we'll see."

For Elizabeth, that was a big hurdle. As far as she could tell, Harry wouldn't be offended or hurt if she took up with Sam seriously. She talked it over with Sam and they discussed how the future might work out for them both. He wanted to ask Elizabeth to marry him and couldn't think of a good "where and when". He wanted it to be special and decided to wait a while before "popping the question".

The following weekend, he left Elizabeth in the local butcher's shop and went looking for the jewellers. He never said anything to Elizabeth but chose a small diamond ring surrounded by six small Australian opals. He was no judge of jewellery and just chose what he could afford and what he thought Elizabeth might like. He kept the small box in his top pocket and decided to wait for the opportune moment to ask her the all-important question.

It was August and the South-Western Agricultural Show was advertised for September. Sam and the boys decided to enter one of their Marino Rams into the wool section competition. It was to be a big event and the show was really all about farm machinery and animals but alongside the main showground were stalls selling craft work, ice cream, candy floss and various lotions and potions.

There was also a funfair, or as Ben called it, Side Show Alley and Harry couldn't wait to go and see everything. He had never been to a fairground and had only read about it in children's books. He desperately wanted to go on the roller coaster and the Helter-Skelter. He'd seen those in various books but never in real life.

When the men, Sam, Elizabeth and Harry arrived at the show, Dick and Mort took the Merino ram out from the back of the trailer and took him off to the animal section. Harry begged Elizabeth to give him some money so that he could go to the fairground on his own. Elizabeth gave him some money and many warnings; "Don't get lost, don't wander off, meet us back in the animal section, don't make yourself sick with ice cream." And all the other advice she could think of.

Sam just laughed at her and slipping Harry some more coins chided her, "For goodness' sake, let the boy go and enjoy himself. He'll be just fine." Sam had an agenda of his own and actually wanted to get rid of Harry for a while.

Harry wandered off on his own and after treating himself to an enormous cloud of pink candy floss on a stick, quickly followed by a large chocolate covered ice cream, stood watching the Dodgem cars. He had never seen such small cars and was amazed at the way people were all banging into each other. There was loud music playing and everyone seemed to be enjoying themselves, even though they were all crashing into each other. It just seemed so bizarre to him. Eventually, Ben saw Harry and decided to join him watching the Dodgems.

After a while Ben asked, "Well, young fella, do you want to have a go?"

"No, I can't drive a car like that and everyone's crashing into everyone else."

Ben laughed, "That's what you're supposed to do, well not really, you're supposed to dodge out of the way, that's why they call them the Dodgems. Come on, we'll have a go, you can ride with me, there's room for two."

Harry's first ride on a Dodgem was an experience he never forgot. The pair were bumped and jostled and at first Harry was terrified, but as he relaxed, getting used to the game, he started to really enjoy the ride. He started giving Ben instructions as to which way to go when someone was getting too close. "Turn right, that red car's going to get us, no turn left, there's another car coming for us. Get him in front, quick, go quicker."

At the end of the ride, Harry was flushed and excited. "Can we go again, but this time I want to do it myself?"

Ben laughed and so paid for the two to have another go, but in separate cars. Now the real fun began. Harry did his best to chase Ben and another couple of young boys but they kept running away from him until he got himself stuck in a corner of the arena and then they turned on him and bumped and jostled him so much he thought his head might just fall off. They were all having so much fun, but the operator came over and told Ben to leave Harry alone and back off until

Harry's car could be rescued and restarted. Harry was frustrated he wanted to attack and not be attacked, but realised it was all in the fun of the ride.

At the end of the ride, Ben declared himself a champion of the Dodgems and offered to treat them both to a well-deserved ice cream. Harry didn't like to tell him that he'd already had one ice cream, but it didn't really matter, he loved ice cream and was grateful for the second delicious treat.

The two protagonists wandered around the fairground trying their hand at almost everything that presented itself. Ben showed Harry how to shoot a rifle on the rifle range and how to throw three balls at the coconut shy. Harry was fascinated at the turning heads of clowns where one had to put ping-pong balls down the open mouths of the clowns and try to get the balls to fall into the outside lanes of the receiving board. It was all a wonderland for Harry.

Eventually, he recognised a Helter-Skelter and decided that's where he wanted to go next. Ben refused to go on the slide as he stated, "It's really only for kids, but you go, I'll wait here for you."

After the Dodgem cars, the Helter-Skelter seemed tame but Harry was happy that he had given it a try. Ben wanted to go on the roller coaster and so the pair went looking for that ride. Harry was shocked by the speed of the ride as they approached, watching people whizzing around in front of them. The riders were screaming and didn't really look as if they were enjoying the ride at all. Ben said it would be fun though. "Are you up for it, young fella?"

"Oh, I guess so," answered Harry somewhat slowly, he wasn't actually too sure that it was the fun that Ben swore it would be, but he was determined to be brave though and try everything.

The ride was incredibly fast to Harry's way of thinking and not only did the cars go fast round and round but they also went up and down, up and down. It was not long before the two ice creams and candy floss started to make themselves felt. Harry's head was being thrown around with the momentum of the ride and he could feel his stomach starting to object to the violent motion. He couldn't wait for the ride to stop and after getting out of the car as quickly as he could, he dashed to the side of the park and lost all his ice cream and candy floss. Ben just laughed as poor Harry's stomach emptied itself of its contents.

At the funfair, there was a large Ferris wheel and Sam wanted to take Elizabeth on it. He had a private chat with the operator before paying the man twice the asking price for the ride. Elizabeth giggled like a schoolgirl and declared she had not only never ridden on a Ferris wheel but had never even been to a funfair. Sam was sweating and nervous. He had prepared a speech and was trying to remember his words. The wheel started to go around and Elizabeth felt excited but a little sick with the soft swaying motion of the chair.

Once the wheel had been round the full circle three times, it suddenly stopped with Sam and Elizabeth right at the top. The chair swayed in the gentle breeze and suddenly Sam put his arm around Elizabeth and in a voice he didn't recognise as his own croaked out the words, "Elizabeth, I've learnt to love you and your grandson. Will you marry me?"

"Oh, Sam Briggs," she teased him, "I'll have to think about that," she paused for effect as his face fell and then went on, "well I've thought about it, yes, OK I will."

Sam fumbled, with his big rough farmer's hands in his pocket for the little box and when he found it he took the ring out and tried to put it on Elizabeth's finger, unfortunately the wheel operator started up the motor again at that moment and the sudden movement made Elizabeth jump.

The ring shot out of Sam's hand and disappeared out of the chair and flew down below them. It was then panic. Sam appealed to the operator and to some of the locals to help him find the ring. Many people volunteered trying to find it among the grass and weeds below the wheel. The wheel operator was none too happy, as he couldn't operate the wheel while so many people were searching the grass for the ring.

Eventually, a small child found it and everyone cheered. The wheel operator was happy that he could get his wheel operating again. The small child was rewarded with a stick of candy floss and Sam was much relieved to be able to put the ring on Elizabeth's finger and to seal the deal with an embarrassing public kiss and gentle embrace.

When Sam and Elizabeth met up with Harry and the other men at the animal section there were two great reasons for celebration. The first reason was that Sam's Merino ram had won first place in the fine wool section. The boys were overjoyed and had photographs taken with the ram and held aloft the large blue rosette and sash. Sam told the group that he and Elizabeth had some more good news to tell them. Mort was the first to guess and took Elizabeth's left hand to check out the ring.

Harry couldn't stop laughing and told everyone around that, "I'm going to have a grandfather. Guess what? I'm going to have a grandfather."

It was a great afternoon and evening of celebrations. Sam brought in some wine, beer and soft drinks and Elizabeth baked a special cake. Everyone was almost delirious with the success of the day and all went to bed that night with smiles on their faces.

For the first time also, once Harry had gone to bed, Elizabeth gave in to Sam's pleading and left her own room to join her future husband in his bed. Middle-aged lovemaking was not the vigorous physical exercise carried out with wild abandonment that both had experienced when younger. This was a night of warm gentle passion cementing their newfound love and respect for each other.

Over the next few months, Sam and Elizabeth discussed the future and how things might work out for them. Sam wanted to adopt Harry and they included him in all their discussions. Harry just loved the big burly farmer and he loved being on the farm, helping out wherever he could, learning all about the stock, the horses, the machinery. He was now allowed to drive the tractor, pulling behind various farm implements. Everyone was happy and life was sweet. Harry had never known his real father and now he had a father figure in his life and he looked up to the man who actually wanted to adopt him.

A wedding was being planned for the autumn and Harry and Elizabeth couldn't have been happier. Australia was everything she thought Jack, her lost son, would have wanted it to be.

Chapter 25
Back to Work for Jack

Jack arrived back in England with the weather reflecting his mood. It was raining, cold and dismal. His broken leg was healing and he was getting around on crutches. His heart was not in his work and his depression was apparent to all around him. He talked to Mollie Robbins, a motherly middle-aged accountant who was worried about him.

She assumed that the broken leg was making him so depressed. She also knew why he had flown to America and had hoped that he would find what he was looking for, but as he explained to her, it was a hopelessly wasted journey. Jack didn't tell Mollie or anyone else about the airplane accident, he didn't want her to make a fuss and told his boss that his search in America had just taken a lot longer than he had imagined it would and the fall that broke his leg had kept him longer that he intended as well.

Mollie tried to cheer him up by inviting him to her house for dinner, for him to meet her jolly husband and three grown-up children, but Jack kept putting her off, he really didn't feel like socialising. Once his leg had healed completely, he went back to playing basketball and three times a week joined some good friends at the local YMCA hall.

Jack was by now an "A" grade player and competed with his team, winning many competitions. It was only this outlet that gave him any joy in life at all. Back at work after a successful weekend's basketball game, Mollie asked Jack how his team had fared. "Oh, we did alright, but I only play the game to keep fit."

He was still slightly depressed and didn't want to admit that he actually enjoyed playing the game. Mollie realised he was a little down in the mouth and answered him with a wry smile, "You know, Jack, some famous person once said, 'sport is like sex, it has an inherently good basic application but that's not why we do it.' And I think you don't just do it to keep fit. Admit it, you actually enjoy playing basketball."

"Oh, I suppose so."

Work at the bank was boring and he was seriously thinking of giving it up and going back to flying. The airplane crash had significantly affected him, far more than he had thought at the time. He kept going over and over in his mind what could have happened in the cockpit and what he would have done in the same circumstances. Would he have been able to fly the commercial plane better, would he be able to accept the responsibility for so many other people's lives.

He was started to get itchy feet again and was seriously thinking of going back to flying, probably not as a fighter pilot, but as a commercial pilot. It would mean at least a year of training, probably more. He resolved to find out more about the possibilities.

The following week, on a particularly cold day, Jack could not go to work as he had the flu and was really ill in bed. His landlady brought him some breakfast and a copy of the local newspaper. Listlessly, Jack started reading the news about the imminent Korean War and it was at this point that he really started to live again.

He knew that the Korean peninsula had been divided into North and South, with the North being occupied by troops from the Soviet Union and the South, below the 38th parallel, being occupied by troops from the United States. Although both rival countries tried initially to use diplomacy to reunite the divided nation, it was the Northern faction that tried to do so with military force. Troops from the Soviet backed North Korean Army crossed the 38th parallel on 25 June beginning what the paper called Korea's new Civil War.

Jack sat up and read with great interest now how the United Nations were calling for all hostilities to end and North Korea to withdraw to the 38th parallel. He went on to read how the Australian Prime Minister Robert Menzies was offering military assistance to the United Nations and Jack, remembering the thrill he had when he was flying, thought this might be his opportunity to get back into the air.

He went on to read that the Australian Government was calling for any British men who had prior military experience in World War Two to enlist in the Australian forces for three years with one year of overseas service in Korea. The unit would be called the K-Force and at the end of their enlistment, personnel recruited in Great Britain could elect to be discharged in Australia or returned to the United Kingdom. Apparently, any previous military experience would be taken into account with a view to rapid promotion and would facilitate almost immediate deployment to Korea.

It was amazing how quickly Jack recovered from the flu, once he had a new purpose to life, something to get enthusiastic over. Five days later, Jack was on the steps of Australia House in London requesting an appointment to see the recruiting officer with a view to joining the Royal Australian Air Force. It was a mere formality, a foregone conclusion really that Jack would be accepted as his flying record was produced from the RAF with glowing commendations.

Leaving London was no hardship for Jack. Mollie organised a farewell party at work and the bank presented him with a silver engraved beer mug. It was all very touching but Jack really couldn't wait to get away from the office and get on the plane to go to Australia. It was what he had dreamt about and wanted from being quite a young man, a child, in fact. At last it was happening, he was actually flying off to Australia.

Jack was sent to the RAAF College and Pilot Training Centre at Point Cook, southwest of Melbourne, Australia, on the shores of Port Phillip Bay. He revelled in the sights he could see from his training flights. Often he would fly over Swan and Duck Islands and gaze with awe at the pink lakes below where sea water was being fed into shallow pools and allowed to evaporate. The dried salt was then harvested from the floor of the lagoons, all new and interesting for Jack. Often too the trainees would fly over Cheetham wetlands twelve miles southwest of Melbourne where they often encountered ducks, geese and even sea eagles flying alongside their planes.

On the few occasions when Jack's group had a few hours off, he would go walking along the edges of the wetlands and was amazed at the profusion of wildlife living or visiting there. He recognised sandpipers, snipes, oyster catchers and plovers. He didn't see but could distinctly hear a curlew. It reminded him of home in England but he wasn't homesick, he was exactly where he wanted to be.

After six gruelling weeks of revised training, Jack joined the No. 77 Squadron RAAF as LAC or Leading Aircraftman. Now he was living. He was so proud of his insignia with its one chevron and the word "Australia" beneath. He felt at last that he "belonged" and that he now had something important to do, a mission in life other than looking for his mother and Harry.

He did his best to put his quest for looking for his mother and Harry behind him and concentrate on the task ahead.

Following his training, Jack's unit was quickly despatched to Korea, where they became the first United Nations air unit to enter the war, primarily in ground support, combat air patrol and escort missions. It was October 1950 and Jack was only 34 years of age. He felt he was in his prime and able to take on the many sorties his squadron were expected to undertake. Most of the men in his squadron were younger than Jack but the esprit de corps was tangible from the outset and age didn't matter. Everyone had a job to do and was learning how to do it to the best of his ability. They all relied on each other for support and cooperation.

One day as Jack was making his way across the tarmac to his airplane he couldn't help overhearing the two flyers in front of him sharing a joke. One had a laugh so distinct that Jack felt a wave of nostalgic nausea waft over him and then a realisation that this wasn't just a similarity, it was in fact a real memory, a very familiar laugh. He shouted out to the two above the noise of an aircraft engine warming up.

"Blood Hell! I don't believe it. If I'm not mistaken, that's the voice of my old navigator, Max Bloody Mulligan."

Max turned around slowly and put his gear on the ground, shaking his head in disbelief, whispered, "No, it can't be, you're supposed to be dead. I saw your plane go down. Oh, Jesus, Jack, is it really you?"

The two fell into a very unmanly embrace with tears in their eyes. They kept pulling back from the bear hugs and looking at each other and then hugging again and again. They both had a sortie to complete and it was take off time. A quick promise to meet up later in the mess and the two had to go to their separate planes. Jack found it very difficult to concentrate on the bridge raid but when it was over, he made his way as quickly as he could to the mess hall.

The night was spent in catching up on each other's story, drinking to each other's health, laughing and crying. Max told Jack, "You know, after I was released from the prisoner of war camp and repatriated, I spent a few weeks in hospital recovering and then I went looking for your mother. I had your address but when I got there, I'm sorry to tell you but it was just a bomb site.

"I don't know anything about who, if anyone, survived. The authorities wouldn't or couldn't tell me anything, as I wasn't related. I'm sorry, I just wanted to let your mother know that I saw you go down and I was convinced that you would have died immediately and not really suffered. I thought she might have wanted to hear that. I never saw you parachute out. It's a miracle that you survived."

Jack related all that had happened to him, much to Max's utter amazement.

Max told Jack how he had decided to become a flyer instead of just a navigator and had received his initial training in Scotland before seeing the same newspaper article that Jack had read and he remembered that his old friend Jack had constantly talked about his obsession with Australia and so decided to apply for a position in Australia to help fight in the Korean War. "I joined up to honour your memory, you old fraud and now, how dare you still be alive."

They both laughed and kept slapping each other on the back as they got more and more drunk.

The other flyers left the pair alone as there was obviously a lot of history between the two and the emotional joy of the meeting, mixed with many drinks left the two wallowing in maudlin reminiscence.

Chapter 26
January 1951 in Australia

At twelve years of age, Harry was settled and contented. He had a dog who adored him, even though strictly speaking it was Sam's dog and a working dog at that, but when not out in the paddocks with Sam, he was all Harry's.

Harry got on well with his friends at school and Mr Stone was forever encouraging the boys to develop their cricket. He organised interschool competitions and at the weekends would often drive his team up to Perth to meet with the larger schools there. They generally had to rope in some substitute boys, as the little country school never had enough players. Mr Stone was proud of his boys, they never actually won a match but more often than not would give the opposition a good run for their money. Harry was proving to be an excellent bowler and could hold his own at batting too.

On the home front, Harry was now allowed to help the men with the mustering and getting the cattle to market. He could drive the tractor and rode his horse with confidence. Sam was proud of the boy and he and Liz were looking forward to the wedding, being planned for April. Life was sweet and everyone was happy.

It had not been an excessively hot and dry summer but rainfall was well below average and had been so since the previous August. The forests were drier than would normally be the case and Sam was worried: a dry summer could mean trouble on many fronts. Lack of water was never good for farmers, the stock suffered, the crops suffered and home and vegetable gardens needed to restrict their use of the precious life giving commodity.

Far to the north in the Pilbara region, a tropical cyclone had formed and was moving down the north-west coast of Western Australia. There were reports on the radio of hurricane-force winds demolishing buildings along the way and a storm surge flooding coastal areas. The strong high pressure system east of the cyclone was causing hot north-easterly winds to develop and for three days the temperature had been rising to over one hundred and four degrees.

Dry thunderstorms were predicted and Sam knew this could be a major problem if they hit the region where the farm was located. He decided he would take the men across to the western edge of the farm to check on the stock there and to do some repairs on the fence line. Harry was at school and Elizabeth was home doing the laundry and preparing vegetables for the evening meal.

Elizabeth heard the thunder first and looked out of the kitchen window to see the trees bending in the hot wind. She could see lightening in the distance to the east but took little notice of it, not realising the danger that such conditions could pose.

On the eastern side of the homestead were many eucalyptus trees and beyond that, a pine plantation. A valley or dip in the land obscured much of the pine plantation from Elizabeth and she was never aware of the danger as the lightning flashes came closer and closer to the property. One jagged fork hit the base of a small pine tree and immediately it burst into flames. No one saw this happen and as the flames spread from one tree to the next, a full-blown bush fire of incredible strength was gaining ground and fast approaching the farm.

Elizabeth saw nothing and heard nothing until she suddenly started to smell smoke. She dashed to the cooker thinking that her roast was burning, but no it was fine. Only then did she look out of the window and saw the red glow on the ground and the orange flames leaping heavenwards and leaning over in the wind. Now she heard the noise and instinctively knew the danger she was in. "What to do, what to do?" she talked aloud to herself. "Get the garden hose and play it on the vegetables, no play it on the house."

Now it was getting hot, very hot. Elizabeth started to panic. She had never experienced anything like this at all, not even in war-torn London. She played the water hose on herself and then went around the back of the property to find the truck. The men had taken it and there were only horses left in the paddock at the side of the house.

Elizabeth had never learnt to ride and had no idea how to catch a horse or saddle it up. The horses knew the danger and were now whinnying and cantering around the paddock. Elizabeth didn't know what to do for the best but thought that she should open the gate and let the horses out and after that, would run back to the house and take refuge there. She could feel the radiant heat and was terrified but thought that if she drenched a towel or two and laid down low in the kitchen with the towels over her she would be fine.

Sam and the farmhands only noticed the smoke as it came over a ridge and only then realised that the farmhouse was in the path of the bushfire. Sam sent the men to open all the farm gates and then told them to get into town and warn the people there. He whistled for Rusty and took the truck and drove as quickly as he could back to the farmhouse to get Elizabeth. When he got to within a few hundred feet of the farmhouse, he actually couldn't see anything, the smoke was incredibly thick and started to choke him. He knew he should turn back and get to safety but he had learnt to love Elizabeth and was desperate to save her.

He drove through the thick smoke with his windows closed but still the smoke entered the car and was both blinding and choking him. He was yelling for Elizabeth as he pulled the car to a standstill. The outbuildings, barns, machine sheds and the house were all ablaze. As Sam got out of the car, he tried to take a few steps but he couldn't breathe and collapsed in a brave but tortured failed attempt. Rusty was barking frantically, but he too succumbed to the smoke.

Chapter 27
Jack and Max

It was an exciting time but not an easy time. The squadron was sent out on missions to bomb various installations as well as meeting the enemy in the air, where they met with great opposition. Their planes were not as manoeuvrable as the Russian planes and Jack as well as his comrades, struggle to hold their own, barely managing to avoid being shot down.

Only a few months into their support deployment the 77 Squadron was withdrawn to Pusan in response to the Communist forces counter attack. Puson United States Air Force Base was adjacent to the Suyeong River in Haeundae District, Busan, South Korea and from there Jack's group could attack many bridges across the river and especially the railway bridges, with little opposition from the enemy. It was an easy assignment but that was not to last.

Jack's squadron ranged far and wide over the Korean peninsula, providing crucial support in relieving some of the pressure on ground troops and providing cover for the advancing United States Eighth Army as well as making their own attacks on North Korean forces. Their hundreds of bombing attacks disrupted immensely the progress of the enemy ground forces. Their foremost targets for air attack included railway lines, roads, military installations and any heavy vehicles seen on the ground.

Initially, Jack's squadron were given propeller-driven P-51 Mustang fighters, remnants from the Second World War. The weapons that these aircraft carried and used were bombs, rockets, machine-guns and napalm. Jack and Max would sit in the mess hall each evening that they weren't flying and discuss at length the morality of using such weapons, which they knew would affect the local population as well as military installations.

They were keen to meet the enemy in the sky but were guilt-ridden about the collateral damage that was being done to the people of North Korea. Jack kept casting his mind back to his mother and young son who were also victims of war.

Their home had been bombed and Jack could only imagine what devastation and grief this had caused his mother, not to mention relocation and upheaval of the life they had known. Jack could only reflect that it must be similar for the people of North Korea; innocent villagers being bombed and traumatised.

At times, the weather was just as hazardous to pilots as flying under attack. Taking off was difficult in winter; thick ice and snow had to be removed each morning and in the event of having to ditch in the sea they were warned that the pilots' immersion suits gave them only a few minutes to be rescued before the freezing water temperature would give them hypothermia and they would die quite quickly.

Conversely, the summer heat caused its own problems. Many times the runway bitumen would melt and hamper the wheels of the aircraft during take-off and landing, also the summer heat haze could extend into the atmosphere up to well over one thousand yards, cutting visibility to a mere two miles or less.

One near tragedy happened when Jack's plane got almost stuck to the ground, due to the sticky tarmac and the wheels were so sluggish to turn that his take-off had to be aborted almost causing him to crash into a parked vehicle close to the runway and causing a following plane to almost run up the back of Jack's plane.

Jack's Wing Commander was not amused and thereafter ruled that all planes should be seen to leave the ground before the next plane was allowed to set off down the runway. Jack's team mates ribbed him unmercifully about the incident, saying that he was eating too much and getting so heavy that his plane wouldn't and couldn't take off. Jack was good natured though and with a shrug of his shoulders took it all in his stride.

Jack's squadron and the rest of the United Nations combined forces' airpower was superior to North Korea's, but then the entry of the Chinese into the war made the situation in the air quite complicated. The Chinese too had airpower and it appeared that they had superior aircraft; MiG-15 jet fighters. It was at this stage, in 1951, that the commanders on the ground decided that 77 Squadron needed to switch from flying Mustangs to Meteor jets. All the pilots were thrilled to get the news and couldn't wait to be sent to Japan, where they were to re-equip with Gloster Meteor Jet Fighters.

Max was familiar with the Meteors, having experience of them in Scotland and lauded their capabilities to the group. His enthusiasm was infective and the men were keen to try out these new planes. "You'll see mate," he told Jack,

“We’ll show the little yellow devils and the reds how to fight a real war, in the air.”

The 77 Squadron returned to action with these new aircraft in July, where they met with greater success against the Soviet MiG pilots. However, the MiGs were still far superior to the Meteor. Max and Jack both had near misses as enemy fire tore into their separate planes. They arrived back at the airfield with holes in the fuselage and in the wings and counted themselves lucky that they had not been actually shot down.

For many weeks, following heavy losses from MiG-15 fighters, the squadron were only allowed to operate in the ground attack role until called upon to join the American forces flying over Sunchon. For Max and Jack, it was a humiliating and frustrating time. They felt they were wasting their time only covering ground attack, but that was to change.

The Battle of Sunchon was an air battle fought near the city of Sunchon on 1 December 1951. 12 Gloster Meteor jets of Jack’s squadron were attacked by almost 50 Chinese MiGs. Despite the Meteors having inferior manoeuvrability to the Soviet built MiGs, the Australian pilots managed to score their first hits on enemy aircraft.

Although the Australians lost 3 aircraft, they were able to report that they had taken out 10 enemy MiGs. There was much celebration and the Australians, as Jack found out, could and did drink copious amounts of beer, not the warm English beer but the freezing cold American beer.

Chapter 28
Alone

The school was evacuated and all the children were taken to the local community hall for safety. Many of the students had experienced the effects of bush fires in previous summers but none of the fires had been really serious. None of the children were really worried and for Harry, it was a totally new experience. He had no idea what a real bush fire looked like. His childish idea of a fire was based on backyard bonfires on Guy Fawkes night in England. He was even excited at the thought of a fire coming close to the little town; something novel and new. Nothing could have prepared him for what he was about to find out.

At first there was a sharp pungent smell and then a cloud of thin smoke. There was no fire to be seen but Mr Stone was experienced enough to know the danger and took all the children and some of the townsfolk into the community hall. The adults were worried but Mr and Mrs Stone kept up a barrage of games for the children to play and diverted their attention away from the worried looks of the adults. They could all hear the fire engine bells and much shouting from the firemen outside but the games kept them occupied and the danger soon passed. Apparently, the fire had been contained and it was safe for the children to return to the school and then to their homes.

The Chief Fire Officer did, however, speak to Mr Stone and told him that Buddy and Harry's homes had been destroyed. Mr Stone asked the two boys to stay behind, as he needed to talk to them. Still, the boys didn't suspect anything untoward in this request and happily sat down with a glass of milk supplied by Mrs Stone to wait for what Mr Stone had to say.

At this point Ben, the Aboriginal from the farm, came into the schoolroom looking very dirty and dishevelled. He was crying and went straight over to Harry and folded the boy into a gentle embrace, saying, "I'm sorry kid, we did everything we could, really we did, I'm really sorry."

Harry had no idea what Ben was on about and felt very uncomfortable being at the end of such an emotional embrace.

It was Mrs Stone who, eventually, gently told the two boys that their parents, family and homes had all been lost in the fire. Buddy lost his parents, two uncles and an older brother. Harry had lost his grandmother, Sam and his beloved dog.

The two boys just sat and stared at Mrs Stone, hearing what she was saying but not really aware of what it meant to their lives. Neither of them cried, it was just too much of a shock and the implications had not really penetrated their comprehension or understanding. The Chief Fire Officer asked Mr and Mrs Stone if they would keep the two boys at their home until arrangements could be made for their welfare. It was agreed that the boys stay with Mr and Mrs Stone overnight.

Buddy had relations who came to collect him two days after the fire and that was the last that Harry ever saw of Buddy. Harry had no one. He had no idea what would happen to him and he was just too miserable to ask questions. The next few days were a blur to him, he was numb and couldn't think of anything except his pain at losing his only relative, the only person who truly loved him; his only father figure, Sam who had actually wanted to adopt him and lastly at losing Rusty.

He tried hard not to think about how they all died, what they would have felt, how would Rusty have acted, would he have been scared, did he die in pain? It was all just too much and Harry just sat staring at the wall vacantly, he was lost in a world of his own and Mrs Stone was worried. Harry was not eating and not talking to anyone, he had disconnected and disengaged from everyone and everything around him. After two days she called in the doctor who said the child just needed time to assimilate the terrible news and accept the situation; no pills or potions could do that for him.

The local council contacted the Children's Welfare Society and it was agreed that a home should be found for Harry, but meanwhile, he would be taken into the custody of the closest orphanage. Mr and Mrs Stone offered to keep the boy but the authorities stated that Harry was now a ward of the court and would need to go to an orphanage. Harry didn't care what happened to him, not that anyone asked for his opinion: he just sat impassive as adults around him discussed his welfare and future.

Chapter 29
Life in the Orphanage

At the end of that week, a large car came to pick up Harry and transported him to his new home, a religious order two hours' drive away from the school. This religious order was no haven for Harry or for any other orphan, this was every child's worst nightmare.

As the car drove up a long driveway, Harry looked out of the car window to see an enormous red brick, three-storey building surrounded by trees and paddocks. In the paddocks, many boys were tending something that looked like potatoes or turnips, Harry couldn't tell. The children were ranging in age from about six to fourteen; they were all hatless and the sun was blazing down upon them.

No one smiled or waved a greeting and the car deposited Harry on the steps of the large imposing building. He had no bag or personal effects and stood on the steps, not quite knowing what to do or where to go. The car left him as two monks dressed in long brown cassocks came out of the main door and greeted him none too kindly with the words, "So you're here at last, took your time. Another mouth to feed, another soul for us to save. Singleton aren't you? Well, come along Singleton, we'll show you where you'll eat and sleep. Don't hang about, look lively."

With that, Harry followed the two into the building, through a dark and dingy hallway and up two flights of stairs to a large dormitory. There were sixteen beds in the dormitory, eight on one side and eight on the other. He was instructed as to which bed he had been allocated and at the end of the room Harry was shown where the bathroom was and the showers. He was instructed to have a shower and put on the clothes that were placed on his bed.

The monk stood and watched as Harry started to take off his clothes, preparing to shower. Harry was now thirteen and acutely embarrassed. He turned to the monk and stated as politely as he could, “I can manage on my own now thank you.”

The monk stood impassively, saying nothing, watching. Harry took the towel which was draped over a rail at the end of his bed and wrapped it around himself before proceeding to the showers. Still, the monk stood and watched him. Harry finished his ablutions and returned to his bed, where he dressed in the clothes laid out for him. He was instructed to put his old clothes in a bin at the end of the room and following that was silently escorted downstairs to where the other boys were just entering the hallway.

The boys were unnaturally quiet, it seemed to Harry and keeping their eyes downcast, all disappeared upstairs, presumably to shower prior to having their evening meal. Each monk had a leather thong about two inches wide by two feet long in his hand and occasionally beat the thong against the wall making a disturbingly loud crack as the boys proceeded up the stairs. Harry was told to take a seat at one of the long tables and after twenty minutes or so the other boys came down and took their places too at the tables. Four boys laid out cutlery and crockery, along with glasses of water and two boys carried in large pots containing the evening meal.

The monk at the head of each table ladled out what looked like potato and pea mash but smelled like cabbage. When Harry received his ration he was not very thrilled with what he saw. It was just a large dollop of mash accompanied by a dry slice of brown bread. He was so hungry he started to eat his food straight away and was immediately sorry as he felt a powerful cuff to the side of his head and a loud rebuke from one of the monks who was walking up and down the line of seats.

“What do you think you’re doing boy, where’s your thanks to god for this gift?”

“Sorry, sir.”

“You will be sorry. Everyone now says Grace.”

“Thank you, Lord, for the fruits of our labour and for the nourishment of our minds and body.”

The rest of the meal was taken in silence. Harry was instructed by the monk to assist with the clearing of the tables, followed by his share of doing the dishes. Harry didn’t mind doing his share of the chores but was so tired he couldn’t wait to go to bed.

Once in the dormitory, the boys undressed for bed and crowded around Harry, wanting to know who he was and where he came from. They were curious to know how and why he came to be sent to the orphanage. When they found out he was English, they all wanted to know about England and the war. Eventually, a monk came to turn off the lights and, looking round the room, selected one of the boys, seemingly at random, to follow him. Once the lights were out, Harry ventured a question to the boy next to him, "What's your name and why was that boy taken out of the room?"

"Shhhhhh, you're not supposed to talk after lights out, but my name's Ross."

"OK Ross, but why was that boy taken out of the room; is he coming back?"

"Yes, he'll be back later on and you mustn't ask questions like that, it's a kind of secret, the monks say it's giving penance to the Lord."

"What?"

"Well, that's what they call it. We're not allowed to talk about it, you're not to say a word." Harry was perplexed but being so tired, just fell asleep and worried about it no more that night.

The following day started as the sun came up. The monk came into the dormitory shouting for everyone to get up. After getting dressed, the boys filed downstairs to the dining room where they were presented with a bowl of porridge and a glass of milk. There was no sugar in the porridge and Harry shuddered at the bitterness of the cereal and asked the boy sitting next to him, "Are we allowed to have some sugar?"

"No, we never get sugar, but you'll get used to having your porridge without it. It's not so bad."

After the meal had been cleared away the boys were sent across the hallway and were split into two groups; the younger boys to the right and the older boys, which included Harry to the left. These were the two schoolrooms. School consisted of four lessons only: reading, writing, basic arithmetic and bible study. One hour each, followed by lunch in the dining room. After lunch, the boys were instructed to return to the dormitory to change into their work clothes.

The afternoons were spent doing farm work; some boys in the vegetable fields and some tending stock or the chickens. Harry was instructed to help in the vegetable field, pulling out weeds and piling the earth up around some unknown plants. It was not difficult work but Harry's body was not used to bending over so much and before too long his muscles were aching like an old man's. One of the monks came over to Harry when he saw the boy taking a rest, "What do you think this is nigger, a holiday camp? Get on with it."

In his innocence, Harry corrected the monk with the observation, "I'm not a nigger, sir."

Whack! Down came the strap across Harry's aching back, "If I say you're a nigger then you're a nigger or is it you're an Abbo?"

"No sir, I'm not an Abbo either." Another whack!

"Don't answer me back, Nigger."

With that, Harry was thereafter referred to by the monks as "that red-headed nigger" and there was nothing Harry could do about it. He actually didn't mind all that much, it was just that he knew he wasn't one, just as he knew he wasn't Aboriginal either. Harry remembered well his grandmother's words of advice, "Listen Harry, people who call you names aren't really hurting you unless you allow yourself to feel hurt. The more they think they are hurting you, the more they will do it. Just try to ignore people who try to hurt you. Remember, it's only words and words can't really hurt you."

School work was no problem and once he got used to it neither was the outdoor farm work. What bothered Harry was the strict discipline and desperately unhappy atmosphere. Mr Stone at the school had been fairly strict, but never unfair and he always encouraged the boys with their sport. There was no sport here. No one smiled or laughed. The monks were austere and unbending. The strap was used liberally and everyone was terrified of the nightly callout for one unhappy boy. Harry had not been called out of a night and still didn't know why or what the callout meant.

Each night, whichever boy had been called out would usually come back sniffling and crying. Eventually he could stand it no longer and realised that his turn was coming and really wanted to know what it was all about. Ross was called this particular night and when he returned Harry was awake and waiting for him. "What happened Ross?"

"Nothing, go to sleep."

"No, I need to know."

"I'm telling you, don't ask questions and don't talk about it, just go to sleep. Your turn will come." Harry was worried now, his common sense told him things were not right, something terrible was happening.

In the morning, he noticed that Ross had blood on his pyjama bottoms; now he was really worried, scared, in fact. Once out in the paddock that afternoon, he had the chance to question Ross again about what happens in the night. What Ross told him, Harry could hardly believe. Ross was in tears as he related the abuse but made Harry promise not to say anything, it would only mean a whole lot of trouble for them both, in fact for everyone.

Harry was tall for his age at thirteen and intelligent enough to know that he couldn't stop any adult from tormenting him or physically attacking him, so he decided he wasn't going to hang around and allow himself to be abused. No, he had to do something. Running away seemed to be the only option for him. He waited that night until lights were out and all was quiet and carefully, in stockinged feet, he cautiously crept downstairs and tried to get out of the front door.

Unfortunately for him, one of the monks, Father Septus, happened to be leaving the kitchen area and saw Harry at the front door trying to get out. Immediately Harry was pounced upon and dragged into the kitchen for questioning. "What are you doing, Nigger?"

"Nothing, sir."

"Nothing? Where do you think you're going?"

"Nowhere, sir."

"You're right about that, Nigger, you're not going anywhere."

With that, the monk took hold of Harry's ear and forcibly yanked him up the stairs, not back to the dormitory but to the monk's private room. Once there, Father Septus told Harry to remove his pyjama bottoms and bend over the table. Harry was horrified, was this what Ross had been telling him about?

The monk went across the room and picked up the leather thong that always accompanied him. Harry closed his eyes and screamed as the leather thong bit into his bare buttocks, over and over again. Eventually, when his arm got tired, the monk kicked the almost unconscious boy, who by this time was just a crumpled whimpering heap on the floor and shouted at him to get back to his bed. Harry crawled and stumbled back to bed, vowing vengeance with hatred in his heart.

The next few days were torture for Harry. Although he wasn't beaten any more, he was in agony sitting in the schoolroom trying to do his lessons and it was even worse working in the vegetable patch in the afternoons. The skin and muscles across his buttocks felt as if they were on fire, but he was too scared to complain.

Father Septus had been the third son of his very religious parents and been promised to the church since childhood. The church was not his calling, but his perceived "duty." A family promise, a commitment that he had to honour. He'd had the natural longings for love, a wife, children, a family of his own, but that was all denied to him.

His was a life of commitment, sacrifice, frustration and bitter resentment. He had been bullied at school and abused by the clergy when he was an altar boy. His whole life had been one miserable episode, followed by another. His only relief from his misery was in the repeating that behaviour and heaping misery, revengeful misery, on others, helpless, defenceless children. He knew no other way. He took his frustrations out on these poor dependant souls. He had no compassion and any sins he considered he may have committed were absolved and washed away in the confessional box.

The next night Ross was surprised to be called out again: twice in one week was unusual and the poor child whimpered as he obediently followed Father Septus out of the dormitory. When he came back to bed, Harry was waiting to question him but Ross was unable to talk and just cried himself to sleep.

After school on the following afternoon, Ross was assigned to the barn to clean it out and set traps for the mice. No other boy was helping him and the monks were busy elsewhere.

The barn was a two-storey affair going from the ground floor to the storage area. Only half the upper floor was built as a storage area and not the whole area and so a long ladder gave access to the upper area and wooden beams held up that first floor. Much farmyard equipment was stored in the barn alongside coils of wire and rope. There were also some leather bridles and various pieces of harnessing equipment.

Ross was in despair and desperation, he could take the abuse no longer and just wanted to be left alone. He couldn't see a way out and just wanted it all to end. He looked at the sturdiest of the leather bridles. He unhooked it from its stand and carried it up the ladder to the first floor. He unclipped the buckle and wrapped it around one of the wooden supports and with deliberate care, he wound the remaining strap around his own neck.

Without any hesitation or thought just walked out from the upper floor into space. He made no noise and swung gently to and fro until one of the older boys came into the barn and shouted for help. It was too late, of course.

None of the monks discussed what happened to Ross, but the one boy who had found him told all the other boys. There was no funeral as far as Harry could see. Ross was not mentioned except one young boy was incautious enough to ask of Father Septus, "Where is Ross, sir?" The leather strap came down across the boy's legs.

"Mind your own business. Get back to work."

The following week was supposed to be a celebration for the monks, it was their Founding Father's Day and the boys were to be taken on an excursion to the coast as a special treat. A bus had been organised and three monks were taking all the boys to the beach for the day.

The younger boys were taken by two monks for games on the beach and the one monk, Father Septus decided to take the older boys for a trek along the cliff tops.

The revenge that was burning in Harry's heart was almost as painful as the bruising that had been on his bottom. He saw an opportunity and without really any premeditation or thinking about the situation, held back from the group and carefully just leant over the edge of the cliff face and then started to yell to Father Septus to come and see.

Father Septus instructed the remainder of his group to keep walking and impatiently walked back to where Harry was leaning over the edge of the cliff and demanded curtly, "What is it, Nigger? What are you shouting at?"

"Look sir, a body, someone's fallen over the edge of the cliff."

The monk leant out over the cliff edge, demanding, "Where? I can't see anybody."

"There, sir, look, just below us."

As Father Septus leant precariously over the edge, it was a simple matter for Harry to just give him a hefty push. There was no hesitation, no time for thought. The monk screamed as he went over the edge to his death and landed on the rocks, some thirty feet below.

As he went over, Harry shouted at him, "That's for me and for Ross, you bastard."

Harry only had to tell people that Father Septus had lost his footing in a moment of distraction, tripped over a stone and fell to his death.

Harry had no conscience, no remorse, no regrets, no guilt; his enemy was gone and good riddance.

Chapter 30
Romance in Korea

In November 1951, the 77 Squadron were given a Presidential Unit Citation from Syngmann Rhee President of the Republic of Korea. The unit had lined up on the tarmac and saluted smartly as a formal group of dignitaries inspected the troops. A march past with all flags flying preceded a celebratory dinner of mammoth proportions, only eclipsed by the enormous amount of beer consumed.

The MASH (Mobile Army Surgical Hospital) unit was only situated a few miles south of where Jack and Max were stationed and all the personnel from that American unit were invited to the party, particularly the nurses. Many nurses were needed to care for the sick and wounded back at their hospital and so could not attend, but quite a few did manage to get away for a few hours. An American Army band was invited to play for the night and the allied forces partied hard. Everyone was feeling the anxieties of the war and a large party was just what was needed to relieve the pressure of the fighting.

Jack was no dancer but Max really enjoyed "tripping the light fantastic." He had learnt to dance at an early age and enjoyed showing off his jitterbugging, if he could find a partner who could keep up with him. As soon as Jack saw the girls coming into the room, he spotted her. "That's her, Max, that's the one for me."

"Wow, that didn't take long. Which one are you talking about?"

"The one in the red dress, with the short blonde curls. That Max, believe me, is the future Mrs Singleton."

"Are you mad? You haven't even spoken to her."

"I know, believe me, I just know. Bye, good luck to you, I'm off to claim her." He was smitten and before anyone else could grab her he approached and asked blatantly, "Hello, are you a nurse? I think I'm sick. Can you help me?"

"You don't look sick to me."

"Oh, I am, take pity on a poor airman. Feel my forehead I think I'm running a fever."

The girl laughed, "What's your name, soldier?"

"Jack Singleton and what's your name?"

"Madelaine Green, Nurse Madelaine Green"

"Well, Nurse Madelaine Green, would you care to dance with a very sick airman?" Jack had no idea how to dance and that fact became obvious immediately. He stumbled and trod on her toes. He had no finesse, no timing and the fast music did nothing for him at all. Madelaine stopped Jack after only three or four steps and announced, "You can't dance, can you?"

"Guilty as charged, Ma'am, but if you let me buy you a drink, I can tell you all about my many other good qualities."

The two left the dance floor and proceeded to the bar where Jack bought Madelaine a lager and lime, after which she quizzed him, "Alright, Jack Singleton you have two minutes to convince me that you have other good qualities, not counting your not-so-brilliant dancing."

"Well, I'm a sucker for blonde curls and nurses in red dresses."

Max cut in on their conversation with, "Excuse me you two but I'm a friend of Jack's and I have a real need to dance and I mean really dance, do you sweet lady or any of your friends know how to jitterbug?"

Madelaine looked Max up and down and then informed him smartly, "Listen Limey, we're American and so jitterbugging is in our blood, we can jitterbug before we can walk. Hang on a moment, I'll see what I can do."

With that, Madelaine turned to Jack and excused herself for a moment, before taking a couple of steps to the side to have a quick chat to a pretty redhead and after a brief moment brought her over to meet Max and Jack. "This is my friend Gladys and she'd love to show you how to jitterbug."

Max's eyes shone as he introduced himself, "Hi, gorgeous, my name's Max and this poor excuse for a man, cos' he can't dance, is Jack."

With that, he took Gladys onto the dance floor to show the world what he was made of. He made such a spectacle that at the end of the dance, poor Gladys was puffing and panting with exertion but had a very happy smile on her face. Everyone applauded the pair and many patted Max on the back as they made their way to the bar for a cool drink. Meanwhile, Jack and Madelaine were getting acquainted and Jack decided to have a little fun with the girl.

"Do you know, Madelaine, that I can kiss you on the lips and you wouldn't feel a thing, you wouldn't feel my lips touching your lips at all?"

"You're crazy; if I was dumb enough to let you kiss me, I certainly would feel it."

"Well, here's an American five-dollar note that says you wouldn't."

"You're on. That's five dollars if I feel your lips, right?"

"Right."

With that, Jack leant forward and planted a soft, delicate kiss straight on Madelaine's lips. She jumped back and declared loudly, "I felt it, I felt it, I win the five dollars."

"Yes, yes, you do and it was worth every cent."

Madelaine had a big smile on her face as she declared, "Oh, Jack, whatever your name is, you tricked me, you devil." The pair laughed and drank and fell in love.

It was quite difficult for Jack and Madelaine as well as Max and Gladys to meet up, the separate units hardly ever met socially, but the two pairs corresponded regularly and occasionally managed to meet when the fighting was at a low ebb and all was quiet. The deployment of the Australian Air Force continued until the end of July 1953, when hostilities ceased.

During that time, Jack and Madelaine were corresponding every day and it was agreed that after the war and after Madelaine had been repatriated to America that she and Gladys would endeavour to emigrate to Australia to be with the two boys.

By the end of the Australian participation, it was reported that the No. 77 Squadron had destroyed an incredible amount of infrastructure in North Korea, in total some 3,700 buildings, 408 vehicles, 16 bridges and 98 railway carriages. Overriding these successes was the sickening and heartbreaking knowledge that over 40 RAAF personnel had been killed, 30 of them in action and the rest in accidents either in the air or on the ground. Seven were taken prisoner. The Chinese managed to shoot down 22 Mustangs and 44 Meteors during the Australian's 18,872 individual sorties.

Max and Jack always felt so guilty at the thought of the Korean population who had suffered so much and who were, in most cases, innocent victims of all this aggression. There was little they could do other than discuss endlessly the futility of war and the dreadful unnecessary loss of life, but the two had always followed orders and conducted themselves with commendable skill and bravery.

Jack's squadron was rewarded with many diplomatic citations and their excellent reputation played a prominent role in the signing of the ANZUS pact.

Chapter 31
Making a Life in Australia

The Korean War ended on 27 July 1953 and it was six more months before both Madelaine and Gladys were granted permission to emigrate to Australia. The two nurses had been great friends during their time in Korea and agreed to stay close, regardless of how their individual romances worked out with Jack and Max.

It had been agreed that the girls would travel to Sydney, which seemed far more attractive to the two than any other city and rent an apartment together. Although they liked the boys very much, they were sensible enough to realise that life in "civvy street" would be very different to life in the forces. They all needed time to really get to know each other.

The two girls found a small apartment and were taken on as registered nurses by the main city hospital. It was only a short walk to the centre of town from the hospital and most days, the two girls would go sightseeing in their time off. They would have lunch in the shade of the famous bridge or sit under the huge eucalypts in Hyde Park.

Their apartment was at Bondi Beach and each morning and evening the pair would travel to or from work on the green and yellow boats ferrying them across the harbour. It was an exciting time for them and Australia was everything they hoped it would be. Sydney was a vibrant, thriving city, so multicultural, so different to anything they had ever experienced before.

Max wanted to stay flying and so applied for extensive training for his commercial pilot's licence. Jack didn't particularly want to go back to banking but a position in international banking in central Sydney was offered to him and as they say, "It was too good an offer to refuse". The salary was so much more than he knew he would be able to earn flying for a living and the hours were far more congenial.

Neither Max nor Jack had relatives in Australia and so, like the girls decided to share an apartment. It was only a matter of time before the two couples realised that there could be a much better living arrangement for them all.

After only three months, Max moved out of the boy's apartment and moved in with Gladys and Madelaine moved out of the girl's apartment and moved in with Jack. Everyone was happy and the two couples met up with each other each weekend or whenever work permitted. Sometimes the girls had to take the night shift and sometimes Max was away training out in the country areas. Jack was the only one with stable working hours and so became the organiser of the weekly meetings and social events.

Their first real party was scheduled for the end of November and was for the girls who, being American of course, wanted to celebrate Thanksgiving Day. Jack had lived in America and so knew roughly what to do. He ordered a turkey and bought some cranberry sauce in a jar. He came home loaded with fresh vegetables and a cookery book. He was determined to do a good job with the turkey and wanted to impress Madelaine with his culinary knowledge, even though he actually knew nothing about cooking, especially cooking a turkey. He bought a dozen bottles of Australian wine, some local beer and made a fair attempt at a pumpkin pie.

Madelaine came home from work at 6 o'clock and was amazed at the beautifully laid out table; a tiny posy of roses in the centre of the table, wine glasses, linen napkins, candles; the lot. "My goodness me, Jack Singleton, I didn't know you had it in you. What a lovely surprise! The table looks amazing and that smell, mmmmmmm something delicious cooking, I think."

Max and Gladys arrived at 7 o'clock and the party officially got underway.

Everyone was having a super time until Gladys halfway through the meal asked if they could continue her family's tradition of taking it in turns to state what they were each most thankful for.

Madelaine went first, asking everyone to hold hands around the table. She lowered her head and proceeded with a reverent, "Thank you, Lord, for giving me the love of Jack Singleton and for these friends around the table, my life has never been sweeter, thank you."

Max went next without the reference to the Almighty, "Well, I'm grateful for the peace that now seems to have settled upon the world and for Jack and I coming out of the Korean War, in fact all of us coming out of the war, in fact two wars unscathed."

"Here, here," they all murmured.

Gladys, like Madelaine, was somewhat religious and thanked the Lord with her head bowed, "Thank you god for my family and friends, for our good health and for the fruits of thy bounty. Mostly though, thank you for allowing me to find Max, who, as I think you must know, is the love of my life."

Jack was last and took his time collecting his thoughts. He looked intently at Madelaine and slowly closed his eyes as he declared his love for Madelaine and then surprised them all by stating that he wasn't entirely happy with his life. Madelaine was the first to ask, with tears in her eyes, "Whatever do you mean, Jack? I thought you were happy here with me?"

"Oh, please don't understand, darling. I am more than happy with you. I love you dearly but I haven't been open with you. What I need to tell you, in fact all of you, is not a secret, it's just something I never got around to telling you. I think it's really time I offloaded my conscience. It just never come up in conversation and it seemed over the months to have little relevance to our lives, but I've been thinking about it and dwelling on the subject for the last few days. I've never really discussed it with anyone as it was too upsetting but now I feel I should get it out in the open and this is as good an opportunity as I have so far had."

"For god's sake, Jack, you're killing me! Whatever is it? Are you an arch criminal or something?"

Madelaine was on her feet and her hands gripped the back of a chair, making her knuckles white. "I'm sorry Madelaine, really I am. I should have told you but the truth is, I've been married before."

Madelaine's mouth fell open and her eyes widened with shock and disbelief. "What?"

Gladys was the first to swallow the news and declare, "Is that it?"

My god, I thought you were going to tell us you were an escaped convict or a drug dealer.

"Is that all? You've been married before? Not such a big deal. I thought you were going to confess to something awful. So, were you divorced?"

Madelaine was in tears as Jack left the table and went to comfort her. "I'm sorry, Madelaine, I know I should have told you when we first met, but somehow I just couldn't broach the subject. It's all too upsetting. It's been laying heavy on my conscience."

Madelaine dabbed a wet handkerchief to her eyes and looked Jack straight in the eyes. "So, are you divorced or are you still married? And why is it so upsetting and why couldn't you have told me before?"

"No, my darling."

"Don't 'my darling' me, just tell me the truth. Are you still married, Jack Singleton?"

"No, I'm not married. My wife died in childbirth fourteen, no fifteen years ago."

"Oh. I'm sorry," she paused as she took in that information, thought about it for a moment and then continued, "I suppose I'm sorry your wife died but I'm still pretty mad at you for not telling me before, but why is it still so upsetting for you, do you still grieve for her? Do you still love her?"

"No, you don't understand. I'm not unhappy because my wife died. I'm unhappy because although she died in childbirth, our son was born healthy; I have a son somewhere. I'm unhappy because I want my son, I want to see my son, to know my son."

There was stunned silence around the table and it was Max who broke the silence with so many questions, "A child, a son, Hell's bells, whatever next? Well, where is he? Where is your son?"

Jack just shrugged his shoulders in reply. Max continued, "Well, have you tried looking for him? Well, I mean, I assume you've tried looking for him. Who did you leave him with, who has the care of him? What happened to him?"

Jack held Madelaine's hands in front of him as he explained, "You see, Harry, that's his name, was born just at the beginning of the war in Europe and I was in the Air Force when he was a baby. My father had died the same week that my wife died and as I had to 'do my bit' for the war effort, my mother took care of the child. I went home on leave a couple of times and she was fine with the child, but after the war I returned to London only to find that one of Hitler's bombs had made a direct hit on the house."

Gladys interrupted, "So did they die, then?"

"No, they survived."

"Were they hurt, injured?"

"No, I made a lot of enquiries and apparently my mother and Harry escaped the bombing and survived. They were rehoused on the outskirts of London in what was known as 'prefabs', just temporary housing. By the time I got to the place, after the war ended, they had moved on. Believe me, I tried everything I could think of to try and locate them. I went to the local council, to the local church where we used to live, to so many schools in London because Harry should have been going to school.

"I went to the not so local churches, those near to where my mother had been rehoused. I talked to old neighbours and to those who had known my mother in the 'prefabs' but no one knew where she had gone. I even went to Somerset House in London, that's where all the deaths, marriages and births are recorded. They could see that Harry had been registered at birth but as far as the records were showing, neither my mother nor Harry had died. So I can only assume that they are still alive and that's what is making me so unhappy. I want my child, I want to know my son. I want to know where he is and how he is."

"So why are you here in Australia? Why aren't you still in England looking for them?"

"Well, I guess I just gave up. I mean, how long can you go on beating your head against a brick wall? I'm talking here of a few years and remember, the war was over and so I had to work. I felt really guilty giving up on my quest, but eventually I saw an ad. in the paper for joining the Australian Air Force and, well, it just seemed the right thing to do. I couldn't waste the rest of my life chasing a dream, a lost cause."

Madelaine put her arms around Jack and declared, "Well, Jack Singleton, I'm still mad at you for not telling me, but I suppose I sort of understand now."

Jack's confession had put a damper on the whole evening and eventually Max and Gladys went home, discussing all the way the funny turn of events.

That first Christmas in Australia was a revelation for all four. The boys had been brought up in England, where Christmas was always cold. Madelaine came from Seattle and Gladys had been brought up in Olympia, the capital of Washington State and about two hours' drive from Seattle. Both girls, like the boys, had celebrated Christmas in cold weather, more often than not with snow on the ground.

An Australian summer was a shock to the system. It was hot, very hot and the mere thought of cooking a turkey and all the traditional food was ludicrous. All four agreed that they would spend Christmas day together and Jack volunteered to produce an Australian Christmas.

He shopped around and discovered that he couldn't find holly or mistletoe to decorate the apartment and so settled for homemade paper chains. He managed to buy a very miserable excuse for a Christmas tree. It was nothing like the trees back home. It was not a tree at all really, just a large branch of some sort of pine, but it had to do and he and Madelaine did their best to decorate it.

He had made friends at the bank with one or two of the women there and they all advised him to shop for locally caught fresh seafood. It seemed absurd to Jack to be serving seafood on Christmas day, but Madelaine agreed with him that "when in Rome do as the Romans do."

When Max and Gladys arrived Christmas morning, the first thing they noticed, hanging just inside the hallway a large bouquet of eucalyptus branches with tiny white balls of sodden cotton wool attached. "Whatever is all that?" queried Gladys.

"Mistletoe" sang out Jack, loud and clear. "And you all know what you're supposed to do with mistletoe. Well, it's not real mistletoe but it's the best that I could do. I don't think they have real mistletoe in Australia." There followed much laughing, kissing and hugging.

The four all exchanged gifts and started the celebrations by opening a bottle of what was supposed to be champagne. They all knew it wasn't really champagne but it was the best that could be done. They all joked around as the radio played Christmas songs and carols that all related to the snow and jingle bells, snowmen and frost. It just seemed ludicrous to them as they sweated through the heat of the summer day.

Gladys apologised but had to announce that she had been asked to fill in at work later that afternoon to cover for a nurse who had suddenly developed the flu. "Honestly, I don't think for a moment anyone could possibly get the flu in this weather, she's just 'pulling a fast one'. It's really not fair, but what can you do? I have to go in."

It was a blow but everyone just shrugged their shoulders and accepted what they couldn't change.

The meal consisted of prawns, fish, scallops and crayfish, accompanied by a green salad. None of them had eaten scallops or crayfish before and so it was a real treat and something different for them. The man in the fish shop had instructed Madelaine and Jack how to prepare everything and it all turned out really well. After dinner, Gladys gave her apologies and left for the hospital.

The evening was spent telling jokes and playing cards. They all had a little too much to drink but were happy enough, except for the fact that Gladys wasn't able to stay with them. Max caught the bus for home later in the evening. He wasn't expecting Gladys to be home until six or seven the next morning but at 3 o'clock there was a knock on his door.

When he opened the door, he was surprised to see two policemen looking very solemn. Immediately he felt a wave of nausea and asked in a faltering voice, "Good evening, I mean good morning. What can I do for you?"

"Sorry to get you up, sir, but are you Max Mulligan?"

"Oh, god, what's wrong? Yes, I'm Max Mulligan."

"Can we come in? We have some bad news for you." Max felt his knees go weak as he led the two officers into his lounge room.

"Is it Gladys? What's happened? Just tell me quickly."

"I'm sorry, sir, but there has been an incident at the hospital. Two young hoodlums got drunk and assaulted each other, which led them to being taken to the hospital. Nurse Gladys Johnson was attending to one of them when he took exception to her trying to stitch him up and he pulled out a knife and stabbed her."

"Oh, god, is she alright? Was she badly hurt?"

"We're really sorry, sir, but the knife hit an artery and the nurse lost a lot of blood; she just couldn't be saved. We're really sorry."

Chapter 32
Escape

Even though Father Septus was no longer a threat to either Harry or the other boys, there were other monks who were just as abusive. Septus was only one of many and the boys were terrified of every single one of them. They all carried the feared strap and used it liberally, following any slight infraction of the strict rules.

Harry was still determined to run away and hatched a plan in his mind. He decided that the next time he was working in the turnip field he would try to escape as he realised that particular field must be fairly close to a road. Previously, he had heard vehicles not far away, behind a coppice of trees and bushes and determined that if he could work his way around the field so that he was close to the bushes, he might just be able to slip away unnoticed.

There was obviously a road not far away and he might be able to hitch a lift somewhere. His chance came three days later. After an hour slowly working his way around the field Harry was able to get close to the bushes and after checking that the monk in charge was not looking his way he just dived into the bushes and crept on his hands and knees through the undergrowth, hoping that he wouldn't meet up with any snakes or terrifyingly large spiders.

Once clear of the bushes and trees, Harry ran as fast as he could and, after covering only a couple of hundred yards or so, came to the side of a country road. He was familiar with the practise of "thumbing a lift", although he'd never done it himself and after two farm vehicles passed him by, a large transport van stopped and the driver asked him where he was headed. Harry had no idea where he was and where he could possibly be headed but, trying to be believable, simply stated, "Oh, just about ten miles up the road."

"OK, young fella, hop in." Harry needed no second bidding. He gratefully climbed into the cabin and sank back into his seat, hoping that none of the monks would be close to the road and be able to see him.

After a mile or so, the driver introduced himself as Alf and asked Harry where he was headed again and how come he was out on the road alone. Harry made up a story about how he had decided to leave the farm he was working at and try his hand in the big city. Alf looked at the boy quizzically and asked, "So how old are you, Harry?"

"Err, I was seventeen, just a few weeks back," lied Harry. He knew he was tall for his age and hoped his, as yet unshaved chin wouldn't give him away. "So where are you driving to, Alf?"

"I'm a long distance driver and I'm taking this load of furniture to Sydney. The folks who own it all are moving house and I'm just the removalist. I like Sydney. Have you ever been there?"

"No, but isn't that where the famous bridge is?"

"Oh, yes Sydney Harbour Bridge or the 'coat hanger', as some people call it."

"Why?"

"Well, it's sort of shaped like a coat hanger. It doesn't look very big in pictures, but close up it's huge."

Harry sat nervously watching the scenery pass by and couldn't help but keep glancing into the side mirror, half expecting the monks to be coming after him. After ten minutes or so the van had covered about ten miles and again Alf asked, "So, where do you want me to drop you off?"

"Oh, not for a long time yet."

Alf was not stupid and realised that it was highly probable that Harry was a runaway, however if the boy really was seventeen then he had every right to run away from whatever it was that he didn't like. Alf didn't feel it was his duty to pry and left Harry alone for the next hour. Eventually, Alf had to stop for a meal and invited Harry to join him. "Come along, young Harry, let's get some tucker."

"No thanks, I'm not hungry."

Harry was actually very hungry but hadn't any money and didn't want Alf to feel sorry for him or to spend his money, but Alf quickly summed up the situation and, being a kindly soul, insisted. "Come on, young Harry, it's my treat. I'm grateful for the company. You know, driving long distances on your own is very boring. I'll buy us a meal if you talk to me and keep me awake."

"Well, if you're sure?"

"Of course, come on, they serve great fish and chips here."

Once the meal was served Harry tried not to eat too fast, but he was ravenously hungry and the fish and chips were just delicious. "My, Oh, my! For someone who says they're not hungry, you did very well, young fella. I reckon you would have eaten that plate if that waitress hadn't taken it away from you."

Harry laughed. "I guess I was more hungry than I thought I was. Thank you."

"So how long do you think it will take you to drive to Sydney, Alf?"

"Well, to be perfectly honest, Harry, I've never driven there before. I've been by ship once or twice but this is something different for me. Have you ever heard of the Nullabor Plain?"

"No, is it an airplane of some sort?"

"No, it's a place, well sort of. You see, to drive from Perth, which is in Western Australia, you have to cross a vast desert called the Nullabor Plain. Half way across is the Western Australian border limit and on the other side is the South Australian border and then some four or five thousand miles further on is Sydney."

"So, are you going to drive through a desert?"

"Yes, I hope to. Not many people have driven across but I want to do long haulage trips over there where there are more people and a better chance for me to start a little business, doing this long haulage. You see, I'm not married. I was, but my wife left me for another man. I don't have a family or anything so this is my chance to start a new life."

"OK, I understand, but isn't it dangerous driving through a desert?"

"Yes I guess so, but it's not a desert like the Sahara, it's not all sand and sand dunes, it's more like, well, just a rough track, really. They keep talking about making it into a proper road but I guess that costs a lot of money and believe me it's a long, long way. There aren't any trees, well not many anyway, on this track and that's why it's called the Nullabor. Nullabor is an Aboriginal name meaning no trees."

"Can I come with you?"

"Oh, crickey, all the way?"

"Yes, why not, although I don't have any money or anything really, but I can talk to you and keep you company, like you said." Alf scratched his head and, chewing on his lip, pulled over for a toilet break before answering.

"Tell me young Harry and mind, tell me the truth. Are you running away and is anyone looking for you?"

Harry decided to trust Alf, he seemed a decent sort and so told Alf most of what had happened to him, leaving out the part where he pushed Father Septus over the cliff. He told him of the cruel beatings and the hard work in the paddocks that was expected of him and all the other children.

He explained that as an orphanage the monks were taking in children who had no parents, children who had no one to defend them, no one to care for them. Harry couldn't repeat to Alf what Ross had told him, the things that happened when a boy was called out of the dormitory at night. He could hardly believe it himself and was sure Alf would never believe him and so decided to keep quiet about that side of things.

"Well, if you're sure no one is going to come looking for you, then I guess we could do the trip together, but if you come, you have to take the good with the bad. No whingeing. It might be quite difficult and tough. And whether you're running away or not, what are you going to do when you get over to Sydney? Have you thought this thing through? Where will you live? How will you live?"

"I'll get a job."

"That's all well and good, but what kind of job can you do and are you really seventeen?"

"Yes," lied Harry. "I know I look young but I'm strong and can do all sorts of things. I can ride a horse. I know how to mend fences and how to help with mustering. I can even drive a tractor. I've lived on a farm and I'm not scared of hard work."

Alf laughed and declared, "Well, I'll hand it to you, young Harry, you've got guts, I'll give you that."

The next few hours, both Alf and Harry sat silently thinking about how things might pan out for them. Alf was grateful for the company and was glad that he would have someone with him to maybe help if he got into difficulties. He realised he would have to feed the boy but that was no problem, likewise he would have to make a bed for the boy.

Just behind the driver's seat was a space which Alf had made into a bed for himself but he realised there was not enough room there for Harry as well. He looked at the two seats in the cabin front and thought that if he could buy a blanket and a pillow, it might serve as a bed for the boy.

As they pulled into a small town for their evening meal, Alf put his proposition to Harry. "Look, young Harry, I've been thinking. Maybe you could come with me but it won't be a bed of roses. We can buy you a blanket here in town and a pillow and I guess a clean shirt wouldn't hurt. You would need to doss down here on the two front seats. It wouldn't be a first-class hotel but if you're up for it, I think we could do it. I'll feed you and see you right. As for the work, once we hit Sydney we'll see what happens. You'll be on your own after that."

Alf bought supplies for the long trip ahead in Coolgardie, one of the last towns before heading across the Nullabor. He bought petrol cans, water containers and plenty of food. He filled his cans with fuel and his containers with water. He bought Harry a shirt and a sweater as the boy had no luggage and wore only shorts and a grubby shirt. The pair had dinner at a roadside café and fell into conversation with the waitress who had no other customers to serve.

Throughout the meal, the waitress kept them entertained with stories of the gold being found in the area. She told them that for years people had been finding gold nuggets just on the ground around the town.

Both Alf and Harry thought the woman was exaggerating and dismissed her as a bit of a weirdo, however they both found that once outside they couldn't help scouring the ground around them and kicking their feet into the soft dirt at the side of the road hoping that someone might just have missed a bit. That was a forlorn hope. They spent that first night on the outskirts of Coolgardie and Harry was so tired that he fell asleep as soon as his head hit his new pillow.

After Coolgardie they drove through to Kalgoorlie where Alf had a parcel to drop off and which again, according to the Coolgardie waitress, was supposed to have gold just on the ground waiting to be picked up and again they kicked at the dirt on the side of the road, but they didn't find any. Harry was surprised to see the roads through both Kalgoorlie and Coolgardie were incredibly wide and when they stopped for lunch, Harry asked a storekeeper why the roads were so wide.

The storekeeper was only too happy to explain to the boy that years ago, the farmers would bring their stock through the towns as well as all the logs that had been felled and these would be loaded on a bullock train. The bullock trains had to have wide roads in order to have a turning circle and as a bullock train might contain ten bullocks or more, it had to be very wide. Harry found it difficult to imagine such a thing but had to accept the explanation.

The next day, the two intrepid travellers started on the Eyre Highway to cross the Nullabor Plain. They had plenty of water with them and passed many catchment tanks on the waterless plain. The wind started to blow and kicked up so much dust that at times it was difficult to see the track ahead. It could barely be called a road and in many places, was only wide enough for one vehicle. The Nullabor Plain lived up to its name and Harry noticed that there were very few proper trees: some low bushes and some stunted knarred old shrubs but hardly anything that could be classed as a proper tree.

Alf was curious about the boy and as they had hours and hours, days and days to talk about things, he quizzed Harry, first of all about life in England and then later about the long trip on the boat coming over. Harry found he could talk freely to Alf and related as much as he could remember about his young life so far.

Alf was fascinated. He had been born in Perth, Western Australia and his childhood had been pretty mundane. He had never had a girlfriend until he met Mavis, a glamorous waitress who tricked him into marrying her when she thought she was pregnant. Once she realised it was a false alarm, she started carrying on with other men.

Eventually, she left Alf for a used car salesman. Alf didn't sound particularly sad by this experience but he did warn Harry. "Be careful, young Harry, with women. You can't trust them, they'll get you if they can, twist you round their little fingers and then discard you like an old pair of shoes when it suits them."

Harry took note and agreed to be careful where women were concerned. For a boy who'd had absolutely no experience with girls, this was not a problem. He couldn't even remember ever talking much with a girl, except those at school, never mind actually dating one. Alf's parents, he explained, had both passed away and he was now, like Harry, alone in the world.

He had never travelled outside Australia and wanted to know all about England. Harry couldn't tell him much as he had been quite young when they left England. Alf then started to get quite philosophical and told Harry about his own life, growing up in the city. How he hoped to meet the woman of his dreams, not someone like Mavis, but a woman he could trust, someone he could rely on and love, but as yet hadn't met her.

He confessed he was hoping that the girls in Sydney would be more honest and decent than the girls in Perth. He thought a little about this statement and then corrected himself, saying, "Well, I guess that's not really fair, girls are girls no matter where they are, Perth girls are alright I guess, I mean I only really ever knew Mavis. I just haven't met one since that I could really fancy, you know, learn to love and all that. Maybe Sydney will be different. How about you, young Harry, have you ever had a girlfriend?"

Harry laughed at the mere thought. "Heck no, Alf. I don't even know any girls. I've hardly ever talked to a girl, never mind having a girlfriend."

Alf let the subject go and the two passed for a while in silence before Alf asked more questions and tried to get Harry to talk to him some more. "So, young Harry, tell me how come you're an orphan. What happened to your folks?"

Harry turned his head and feigned looking out of the window at his side before his tear-filled eyes betrayed him. After a moment, he collected himself and answered Alf's question. "Well, I never knew my mother; she was an American and died giving birth to me. My grandmother brought me up and told me she had never even seen my mother."

Alf nodded his head like an old sage. "OK, so what happened to your father? Where's he now?"

"Well, when the war in Europe broke out, he joined up and became a flier in the Royal Air Force. Grandma told me that he was a hero and shot down lots of German planes. Eventually, though, like a lot of pilots, he himself was shot down. All we got was a telegram. He was shot down and was missing in action. What they really meant was that he was dead."

Alf pursed his lips and phrased his next question carefully. "So all you know is that he was shot down. I mean, you don't know for sure that he's dead, do you? I mean, he could still be alive in the jungle somewhere or on a desert island."

"No Alf, he was shot down over Germany. I don't think there are any jungles or desert islands in Germany."

"Well, he could have been hit in the head and suffering from amnesia, you know, lost his memory. These things do happen sometimes."

Harry shook his head. "No, Alf, all the soldiers who were taken prisoner were released at the end of the war and they all had to wear identity discs which showed the authorities who they were. If my father had survived, they would have told us. If he had survived, he would have come to look for us. Even though our house was bombed out, he could still have found us. Everyone in England had to be registered so that the authorities could keep a track of where people were living, even after their houses had been bombed.

"No, Alf, my father is dead. But it is something that haunts me. I know he must be dead, but half of me wants to think like you think, that maybe, just maybe, he might have survived. You know Alf, I'd give anything to know that my father was still alive, anything. I dream about him sometimes. I know it's silly, but I dream that one day he'll come and find me.

"Actually, I nearly had a new father, well grandfather, well step-grandfather, I suppose you might have called him. He was Sam, the farmer, my grandmother and I stayed with. They were going to get married but then there was a bushfire and they both got killed. I even lost my dog. Well, he wasn't strictly speaking mine, but he loved me and I loved him. He was Sam's dog."

With that, Harry turned his face to the window and hoped that Alf couldn't see the tears that were threatening to fall. After a while Harry started again on the subject, "You know, Alf, I often have the dream, the one about my father, I know it's stupid and I know he's dead, but I sort of dream that one day he'll come and get me. I know it's stupid, it's just a kid's type of dream."

"Well, young Harry, we all have to have dreams, something to look forward to, something to cling too, even if we know in our heart of hearts that it's stupid. If we can't dream, then we're dead and if you don't have a dream, then your dreams can't possibly come true."

The road on the Nullabor was rough, rougher than Alf had ever thought possible and certainly beyond anything that Harry had ever experienced. The large van bumped and jumped around on the uneven ground and at one point slipped into and then out of a large rutted hole, followed by a distinct leaning of the van to one side accompanied by a loud thump, thump, thump of the tyres.

"Oh, bloody hell!" Alf swore. He pulled the van to a halt and both got out to inspect the damage.

"What's wrong with it, Alf?"

Sarcastically Alf answered him with much shaking of his head, "Oh, just a minor detail, young Harry. Say how are you at changing a tyre?"

"Err, I've never even seen a flat tyre, never mind change one."

"Well, here's where your education begins young man. I'm glad you came along for the trip. I'll certainly need your help and you can learn what every boy should know, 'how to change a tyre'. It's not so difficult, just tedious and annoying, especially in this hot wind."

Alf directed operations and Harry was keen and eager to help. He did all the fetching and carrying and between the two the tyre was changed and after only thirty minutes or so the pair were back on the road.

Each night, Alf would stop and prepare the evening meal, which just meant opening a can of whatever was on top of the box, opening a bottle of beer for himself and a soft drink for Harry. Harry would collect kindling and large pieces of wood and the two would sit on the ground, around the nightly campfire. Alf set Harry a challenge, each night he would let Harry start the fire, but he had to start it with one match only.

After his first attempts, Harry learnt to make sure his kindling was small and very dry. After three nights is was easy and Alf would always praise Harry for a "job well done!" It was the best time of day of Harry and Alf regaled the boy with tales of life in Perth, fishing, making rafts for the river, catching crabs and prawns, making tree houses in the old eucalypts and running wild, barefoot as a child. It was all beyond anything Harry had ever known and in his heart he wished that he too had been born in Australia.

"Tell me, Alf, did you really go around barefoot? Couldn't you afford shoes?"

"Yes, kid, we could afford shoes but we just chose not to wear any. Our feet were tough and we didn't worry about things like that. We were free, free to run where we wanted, down by the river or across to the beach, over to the marketplace, wherever we wanted. If we caught any fish or crabs, we'd take them home to my mother, who would cook them for our tea. We had to go to school, of course, but between you and me and the lamppost, I often skipped school. When my dad found out, I got a clip across my ear, but it was worth it. I never did like school very much. Have you ever been fishing or crabbing?"

"No, not really, but Sam took me marroning once and I caught three marrons."

"Blimey, kid, that's more than I've ever done. You don't get marron in Perth, you must have done it down south."

"No, the farm was north of Perth and the river was a secret marroning spot that not many people know about. It was not too far from where you picked me up."

"So did you cook the marron and did you eat them?"

"Oh, yes, Sam and I caught the marron and grandma cooked them when we got back to the farm. The marron were black when we caught them and guess what, when we cooked them they turned bright red. They were fiddly to eat and you had to know how to get into them, but they were super, absolutely delicious."

Three days on the road and the drive was beginning to get boring and monotonous. Alf tried to think of games they could play to help pass the time.

He started the ball rolling with, “Tell you what, young Harry, start with ‘A’ and then I’ll go with ‘B’, etc., give me all the animals that you know.”

“What do you mean?”

“Well, you start with ‘A’ for errrrrrrrrr alligator. Then it’s my turn to give an animal starting with ‘B,’ you get the idea?”

“Yes, but I don’t think an alligator is an animal. It’s a reptile.”

“Oh, my word, don’t be so pedantic; reptile, animal, what’s the difference? It’s close enough.”

“OK, I’ll go with ‘B’ for a badger.”

“Never heard of it. What’s a badger?”

“Well, in England, we had them in the woods. They’re sort of black and white animals about the size of a dog.”

“I’ll believe you, but can we keep it to simple animals that we both would know?”

And so the journey progressed, changing the list of things to name from animals to birds, on to countries, towns, girl’s names and boy’s names. It was a game they could both play and it helped to pass the time.

Alf had taken a pack of cards with him on the journey. He had intended to only play “patience” but now he had a second person to play with he determined to teach Harry how to play cards.

Once the pair had eaten and were sitting round the campfire, Alf took out the cards and asked if Harry would play a game with him. Harry had never played cards and so was keen to learn. Alf showed Harry how to play Canasta and then Gin Rummy. He wanted to show the boy how to gamble and play poker but thought it might corrupt the young mind and so decided against that and anyway, he knew Harry had no money and so it was useless teaching the boy how to gamble.

After a full week of travelling, bouncing around on the rough track, Alf drove the two of them, dirty and weary, into Ceduna, the first township across the border between Western Australia and South Australia. He declared a “job well done” and told Harry that he was going to book them both into a motel so that they could clean up, have a good meal and prepare themselves for the rest of the journey. Harry was happy to have any food that wasn’t served cold straight from a can and the chance for a shower and a clean, comfortable bed. The trip across the Nullabor had been an experience but Harry was really glad that, according to Alf, the worst was now behind them.

The next morning, Alf excused himself and went into the local post office to make a phone call. He hadn't told Harry who he was going to call but when he came out and met Harry by the side of the van, he related how he had called his aunt and that things were agreed.

"What things?"

"Well, my aunt is a widow lady and that's where I'm going to stay in Sydney until I get a place of my own. She has a three-bedroom house close to the centre of town and I will have one of her spare rooms. She has agreed that if you are, as I said you were, a decent young man, you can stay with her. You will need to get a job and she will charge you rent, but at least you will have a roof over your head, until you can sort yourself out. What do you think?"

"But I haven't got a job."

"I know, but you'll need to get a job and then you can pay your rent. But what do you think?"

"Err, yes, of course. That would be just great. Are you sure?"

"Yes, I talked it over with aunt Poll and she agreed. I'll be away most of the time, hopefully doing removal work and you can look around for a job. You won't need to pay her your rent until you get a job, but once you do, you'll be fine."

Chapter 33
Jack and Madelaine

Max was a regular visitor to Jack and Madelaine. He had fallen into a kind of depression following the death of Gladys and his friends encouraged him to visit them as often as possible. They all grieved for Gladys but Max was taking it really hard and they were worried for his mental health. His work gave him some solace and as he had now gained his commercial pilot's licence, he had been taken on by Qantas.

Madelaine was the first to notice that, at last, Max was beginning to take a real interest in the world and what was happening. Based on his excellent record with the Royal Air Force and then with the Royal Australian Air Force he had been given first the co-piloting of the Tourist (economy) class on the newly established Kangaroo Route to the United Kingdom and then in 1954 was selected to co-pilot the flights carrying the young Queen Elizabeth and the Duke of Edinburgh on their Australian Tour.

This honour jolted him out of his depression and it was all he could talk about as the date for the arrival of Her Majesty approached. He was instructed how to address Her Majesty, if called upon to do so and he was informed this was highly likely as she usually thanked her flying staff personally.

The new Queen Elizabeth and her husband, The Duke of Edinburgh, sailed on the Royal Yacht Britannia from England, stopping briefly in Fremantle, just south of Perth in Western Australia. The royal entourage then sailed around the southern coast of Australia and through the famous Australian Bight. For the last part of the journey, the royal couple left the large and impressive Britannia and boarded the much smaller Royal Ship SS Gothic to land in Sydney on 3 February 1954.

Jack and Madelaine, along with just about everyone in Sydney, lined the streets of Sydney and the harbour to welcome the royal couple. Jack had seen various members of the Royal Family many times in London and so was not particularly moved by the fuss and bother that everyone was making, but Madelaine had never seen Her Majesty and was as enthusiastic as every other Sydneysider to see the new monarch.

During their 58 days in Australia, the queen and her husband visited 57 cities and towns across all states and territories, except for the Northern Territory. It was estimated that seventy-five per cent of the population turned out to see their beloved queen. In Sydney alone, more than a million people lined the streets. The local newspaper described the welcome that the couple were given as "tumultuous."

Max, as arranged, co-piloted the royal entourage around Australia and after the tour, Her Majesty did indeed ask to meet the pilot and co-pilot. Max excitedly related every detail back to his friends. What was said, what the young beautiful queen wore, what the Duke said, everything. He had been instructed not to talk to the queen unless she addressed him first, but if she did, he was to bow slightly and reply to any questions with the answer to be followed strictly with the words, "Your Majesty."

He was further instructed that if he was to reply to a second or subsequent question, then he would answer first and follow this up with a polite "Ma'am." It was just what Max needed, some diversion, some excitement in his life. Her Majesty, as expected, did indeed ask to meet the captain and co-pilot of the plane she had been travelling in. She thanked them both for their skill and smooth take-off and landings. She shook their hands, as did The Duke of Edinburgh.

That experience lifted Max out of his depression and seemed to give him a new lease on life. Jack and Madelaine couldn't have been happier; their closest friend was, as Madelaine put it, "back on solid ground."

Max started to take an interest in the world around him and although he had always enjoyed playing the odd game of football, that is soccer and cricket, in his youth back in England, he had never been one to actually go to professional matches.

However, he now felt himself too old to actually start playing but enjoyed going to professional matches, either as a supporter for Australian Rules Football in the winter or cricket in the summer months. In the summer if Australia was playing, he would go out of his way to attend the international matches, as and when his flying schedule permitted. If the Australian team wasn't playing, then he would go to watch "The Blues" the Victorian state team, which he thought were the best in Australia, especially when they were competing in the Sheffield Shield.

He enjoyed Australian Rules Football in the winter and counted himself a "Magpie," that is a Collingwood supporter, which was a Melbourne team, but definitely preferred the cricket and counted himself an Australian cricket supporter, never mind that he was born in England. Since living in Australia, he had changed his allegiance and felt no conscience about that.

In the Ashes Series against England, Max watched in agony, biting his nails as Australia lost three to one to the touring English team. He roared with the crowd when Australia managed to bowl out a player or a good catch was made. He cheered with each run that Australia made and groaned with sympathy and misery when an Australian was run out, bowled or caught out.

Neither Jack nor Madelaine were really interested in the cricket but listened to Max and his commentary on the games with great patience and humour. They were just really happy that Max had found an outlet for his normal enthusiasm and nervous energy. Madelaine teased him by calling him "traitor" and "turncoat" but he just laughed and told her that he was now an Australian and as such that's where his loyalty was now.

The only thing that had marred the happiness of Jack and Madelaine had been her constant worry about not getting pregnant. They had agreed many months ago that they wouldn't bother getting married. As Jack explained to Max, it's only a piece of paper, you know, we're still committed to each other.

Max was more of the old school though and told them, "Well, you two will do what you want I guess, but it's my opinion that, if you're really committed to each other then you should prove it by becoming a legal couple, i.e. getting married; then when you do have a child, then he or she wouldn't be born illegitimately, it wouldn't be, excuse my French, a 'bastard,' that's just my opinion, of course."

To marry or not to marry was discussed constantly. Eventually both Jack and Madelaine agreed that, just to keep Max happy, they'd do the deed, get married. Madelaine was adamant that she wasn't going to get all dressed up in, as she put it, "a puffy meringue dress". It's not about getting dressed up, it's more about the commitment.

Jack was satisfied with the Registry Office wedding that Madelaine wanted and agreed with her that it was more about a marriage, not a wedding; he was not particularly romantic or flamboyant and these simple arrangements suited him just fine. He agreed to wear his best suit, as did Max, who accompanied the pair to the Registry Office and was a witness for Jack. Madelaine bought a simple silk dress with a tight bodice and pleated skirt.

As she explained to Jack, it would be something she could wear to dinner or to any formal occasion. It was not too weddingy, it didn't scream of wedding bells and she was perfectly happy with it. She carried a small posy of white orchids and her only concession to flamboyancy was a silly little hat that sat sideways on her blonde curls.

A witness for Madelaine was called in from the office staff at the Registry Office. There really couldn't have been a smaller, less fussy wedding, but it was the way Jack and Madelaine wanted it and Max was happy that they were now legitimate and any future children born would be legitimate too. Jack took them all to the best restaurant in town for dinner that night but there was no honeymoon and life went on as normal.

The months dragged on and the only worry for Jack and Madelaine was the fact that there was still no pregnancy. Madelaine visited the doctor who referred her to a specialist but there was nothing to be done and she was told that the more she worried about it, the less chance there was of falling pregnant. Jack was frustrated with the thought that, although he too wanted a child with Madelaine, in actual fact he knew that he already had a child, a son, somewhere. He never stopped thinking about his son.

When it was Harry's birthday on 2 October each year, Jack usually took himself off somewhere private; the beach or the park and he just contemplated what might have been, he thought extensively about how life could have been so different. He was happy with Madelaine but there was a part of his life missing and it played heavily on his mind.

Chapter 34
Harry in Sydney

With the Nullabor Plain behind them, the journey across Australia became much easier for Alf and Harry. The roads were sealed and it was a pleasant change from the bumping up and down that had been a constant aggravation for both of them. As they motored on, Alf noticed a sign informing the traffic that the town of Gundagai was coming up. “Look young Harry, we’re coming up to Gundagai. You know Gundagai?”

Harry shook his head. “You’ve heard the song, surely?”

Alf started to sing and Harry asked what was so special about Gundagai. “I don’t know that it’s special I’ve just heard the song. I don’t know it all, only a bit here and there but it’s and he started to sing again; ‘On the road to Gundagai, where the something something trees blossom, something, something, something, beneath the southern sky. Where my mummy and daddy are waiting for me, where the friends of my childhood, once more I will see. Oh, the something, something track on the road leading back, on the road to Gundagai.’ That’s all I know. Anyway, the town of Gundagai is coming up, so we’ll see what it’s like.”

Gundagai turned out to be like every other small town they had passed through and Harry couldn’t see why anyone would write a song about it.

Some miles further along the road, one sign did catch Harry’s eye. It was an information sign to the town of Bowral. Harry recognised the name and jumped up and down at the knowledge. “Alf, we’re coming to Bowral, we’ve got to stop. We’ve got to look at Bowral.”

“Whatever’s in Bowral, what are you getting so excited about? It’s just another small town, isn’t it?”

“No, Bowral is where Don Bradman was brought up. Don’t tell me you haven’t heard of ‘The Don’, you know, Don Bradman, the famous cricketer?”

“Oh, yes, I’ve heard of him, of course, but he probably doesn’t still live there, he’s very famous now.”

“Oh, can we stop, we might just see him, you never know?”

“Well, we can stop there for lunch but don’t get your hopes of young fella. If you see him, you could always ask for his autograph though, I suppose.”

For the one hour that lunch took Harry never stopped looking out of the café window scouring the pavement and parks for any smallish, slim built man who might just be “the Don.” He questioned the waitress at the café and was told that his family still lived in the area but she didn’t think that Don Bradman himself still lived there, she really didn’t know. Harry was disappointed but still thrilled to know that he had walked the streets that Don Bradman had probably walked. That he’d had lunch in a café that Don Bradman had probably eaten in. Just being there was a thrill for Harry.

Alf’s aunt Poll turned out to be Mrs Polly Pearson, a grossly overweight middle-aged jolly lady who greeted Alf with much kissing and hugging and welcomed Harry with a hearty handshake. She showed Harry the spare bedroom that she had allocated to him and instructed both Alf and Harry to get cleaned up and then come to sit down for dinner. She had prepared a meal, as Alf said, “With enough food for a small army.”

Harry settled in with Mrs P as he called her and Alf was off most days chasing work and his deliveries. Harry had no idea how to go about getting a job and knew that his only competency was with horses, old tractors and farming, but he was living almost in the centre of a busy city now and his small amount of knowledge of farming was not going to do him any good at all.

Mrs Pearson tried to help Harry but as he had no qualifications and no skills at all, it was proving to be quite difficult. He checked the newspapers every day but everyone seemed to want experienced workers. Harry was fifteen but looked seventeen and eventually just walked the streets of central Sydney, hoping something would turn up.

One day he passed a restaurant which had a handwritten sign in the window reading, “Kitchen Hand Wanted”. He had no idea what a kitchen hand would be required to do, but asked a waitress if the position was still open. The young girl took him into a back office where he met the owner of the restaurant. After a short interview Harry was informed of the simple duties that were expected of a kitchen hand, washing dishes, preparing vegetables and cleaning up generally. He readily agreed that he could do all that and was taken on immediately.

For Harry, it was like winning a gold medal at the Olympics. He ran home to tell Mrs P that he had a job. Granted, it wouldn't pay much, but it was a job. He felt he was a man now, not just a boy. He didn't care how difficult the work might be, he was now a "working man" and he felt on his way in the world.

Harry found the work tedious and boring but extremely easy. He got on well with the two chefs in the restaurant and tried to watch everything that they did. Although they didn't know it, between the two of them, they were teaching Harry how to cook. He watched carefully the making of each meal and the preparations that went into the production of the dishes.

As the months went by, Mrs Pearson allowed Harry to try his hand at cooking in her kitchen. She herself was a good cook and missed cooking for her four children, who were now grown up and living their own lives in other parts of Australia. She helped Harry master the craft of making bread and pastry and discussed her favourite topic, food, with Harry endlessly. She took him shopping at the local market and educated him in the finer points of choosing meat, fish and vegetables.

Christmas 1953 was different from anything Harry had ever known. He could remember being in England and how cold it always was at Christmas time. It never seemed to actually snow in London and if it ever did, it quickly turned to dirty slush, but in other parts of England it was usually snowing. Christmas cards and Christmas songs always portrayed the "festive season" as being cold and it usually was, just not snowing.

Mrs Pearson and Alf were determined to give young Harry a good introduction to an Australian Christmas. Alf shopped around for a Christmas tree and came home with something that looked like a fir tree, but Harry knew it wasn't really a proper Christmas tree, nevertheless the three of them enthusiastically decorated the tree with all manner of fancy things. Harry shared the chore of making paper chains with Alf and Mrs Pearson went overboard buying in, as Alf said, "Enough flamin' food for two armies."

There was no talk of Father Christmas but there were presents under the tree. Harry had bought a broach, a scarf and a new straw sunhat for Mrs P as he called her and he bought a pair of shorts and a carton of beer for Alf. It was agreed that after breakfast, they would all three go to the beach for a swim before heading back home to allow Mrs P to prepare the Christmas dinner.

Harry was terrified, he had never told Alf about the time he nearly drowned. The prospect of getting into the ocean was unthinkable. He made his first excuse, stating that he simply didn't have a pair of bathers. Alf immediately dismissed that excuse by offering Harry an old pair of his own.

"No, I can't go swimming," pleaded Harry. "I think I'm coming down with a cold."

"Rubbish."

"No, really, I don't want to go."

Mrs Pearson had a woman's intuition and looked sideways at Harry as she asked gently, "Can you swim, Harry? Do you actually know how to swim? Have you ever been swimming?"

Harry looked down at his feet, acutely embarrassed and mumbled, "Well not really."

Alf jumped in straight away with "Yea Gods Harry, everyone can swim. Why can't you swim?"

Mrs Pearson cuffed Alf across the back of head and admonished him for being so insensitive. "Alf, for goodness' sake, you were taught to swim when you were a kid, it doesn't come naturally. If no one's ever taught Harry to swim, well, maybe it's time someone did. How about we take him to the beach and show him slowly and gently how to swim. I used to be a good swimmer when I was a girl. I'll teach you Harry."

"No thank you, I really don't want to learn."

"Nonsense, I'll take care of you. You're missing out on a great pleasure. It's not difficult, really."

Reluctantly, Harry accompanied Alf and Mrs P to the beach. He wore the second hand bathers that Alf had given him and he was none too happy. The waves were not strong really but looked large and dangerous to the novice bather. Alf wanted to show off his prowess and dived under the breaking waves and struck out strongly. Mrs P as promised, gently coaxed Harry to the edge of the water and allowed him to get used to the breaking waves at the edge of the beach.

At that moment, a pod of dolphins started cavorting only about 50 yards from the edge of the water. Harry was thrilled to see the wild creatures; he'd seen pictures of dolphins and he'd seen some dolphins racing the ship when he emigrated to Australia, but he'd never seen them so close.

Alf hadn't seen them and as he came up for air, he was startled by a large black fin weaving towards him. His immediately thought was "shark" and he turned and swam back to the shore as quickly as any Olympic swimmer. He ran out of the water shouting "shark, shark!" Everyone else had seen the dolphins and Harry and Mrs P, along with others on the edge of the breakers, had a good laugh at Alf's expense.

Alf, when he realised his mistake and realised everyone was laughing at him, was cross and embarrassed. He dived back into the waves and wouldn't come out of the water for a long time.

Mrs P coaxed the very frightened Harry into the water, only to waist high. She gently cupped his chin and stretched him out on his stomach. The water was warm and slowly Harry relaxed. He allowed Mrs P to hold his head out of the water and following her instructions for moving his arms and legs. In no time at all, he was capable of doing a very rudimentary dog paddle. By the end of that visit, Harry realised that swimming wasn't so very bad at all. In fact, it was really quite enjoyable.

Alf soon got over his embarrassment and the three Christmas revellers returned home to enjoy the remainder of the Christmas day.

There were many presents for Harry. Mrs Pearson had made Harry a quilt cover for his bed and two new shirts. Alf bought Harry a football and a new shiny red cricket ball. There were so many boxes of chocolates that Harry thought he would be sick if he ate many more. Alf remember that Harry seemed to revere the famous cricketer Don Bradman and thought Harry might like to have a few goes at bowling in the back garden. After lunch, while Mrs Pearson was preparing the main Christmas dinner, Alf and Harry went out to the back garden to have a session playing football first and then cricket.

Alf tried to show Harry the finer points of Australian Rules Football: how to pass the ball by fisting it, how to catch or mark the ball. Harry didn't like the oval ball, which seemed to have a mind of its own. No matter which way he kicked or fisted it, he just couldn't control it. He was obviously not enjoying the exercise at all and so good naturedly Alf offered to change the game to cricket. With just the two of them, they couldn't have a game, of course, but Alf set up a makeshift wicket against a tree and the pair took it in turns to have a bowl and a bat.

At first it was just a gently affair as Alf bowled and Harry batted but after a while Harry asked if he could have a turn at bowling. He flailed his arms around in the air warming up a little and then took the ball and sent a slow, deliberate delivery to Alf. Alf laughed at him and jeered at him saying, "Come on young Harry, can't you do better than that, I could have hit a six off that delivery."

Harry smiled to himself, his muscle memory of bowling was coming back to him. He had been taught well when he was in school and now decided to give Alf a taste of what he could do. The next delivery was sent with a medium pace, but even so impressed Alf with its speed and accuracy. "Well done, young Harry, that's a good delivery. You obviously know how to bowl, I can see that."

Alf had hit the ball into a flower bed at the back of the garden. Harry retrieved the ball and then decided to show Alf how he could really bowl. The next delivery Alf hardly saw, it came at him so fast. "Blood hell, what was that?"

Harry laughed and retrieved the ball, ready for another delivery. "Hey, hang on a bit," spluttered Alf, "if you send me another delivery like that and it hits me, you'll knock my head off. Steady on young Harry."

The two played on for a further hour, taking it in turns to bat and bowl. Alf was terrified of being hit by Harry's fast delivery and was glad when his aunt Poll called them in to clean up and help her prepare some vegetables. Christmas night was spent playing cards with Alf drinking beer, aunt Poll eating two boxes of chocolates and Harry nibbling on various nuts, the names of which he had no idea. In England, he had only ever seen peanuts, but here in Australia there were many, many different kinds and they were all just delicious.

After Christmas, it was Alf who read out to Harry and aunt Poll from the newspaper that Queen Elizabeth and Prince Philip were coming to Australia. Harry had never seen any of the Royal Family, even though he had lived in London.

For Alf and Mrs Pearson, this was a real occasion. It was agreed that the three of them would go down to Circular Quay to watch the Royal Yacht Britannia sail in to Sydney Harbour. Mrs P bought a new dress for the occasion and wore the sunhat that Harry had bought her for Christmas. There were so many people there that it was difficult to find a good spot but Harry was quite tall and had no difficulty seeing over the heads of the crowd in front of him.

Apparently, the Queen and Prince Philip disembarked from The Britannia before entering Sydney Harbour and boarded the more manoeuvrable Royal Ship SS Gothic to make their first landing on Australian soil.

As the Royal Barge approached the harbour, the crowd started to cheer. The sound was loud at first and as the royal party approached Farm Cove, the cheering became almost deafening. There was a flotilla of small craft which had followed the royal party from the outer reaches of the main harbour and which were jostling each other for a closer position to the Royal Barge. As if the cheering crowds were not making enough sound, there was a very noisy "fly-over" from the Royal Australian Air Force and a round of cannon fire. It was all too much for aunt Poll, who declared that she was going to faint if she didn't sit down soon.

Alf was quick to ask a much younger woman who had found a park bench if she would mind giving up her seat for an old lady who was having difficulties. Both Alf and Harry fussed over aunt Poll, wafting her with some cool air with their hats and Alf sent Harry to find a cold drink for his aunt. Once the crowds had dispersed, aunt Poll declared herself fully recovered and the very happy threesome made their way home. The occasion of the queen's visit kept all three happy and excited for weeks as they followed the six-month tour in the newspapers and on the radio.

After two years with Mrs Pearson, Harry decided he knew enough to apply for a job as a cook, not a chef, but just a very plain cook. He knew the pay would be better and it would be a stepping stone for him.

Later, he could maybe attend a college or similar and learn how to be a real chef. A job was advertised in the local paper and Harry was taken on as a cook. The café only serviced an industrial area and there were no great expectations for "haute cuisine". His wages almost doubled and he was ecstatic. He was only required to cook simple things like bacon and eggs, sausages, chips, make sandwiches and such. The hours were easy although during the lunch hour rush, cooking was hectic, but he was young and fit and rose to the challenge. What the job meant though, was that Harry had time on his hands during the evening and also had his weekends free.

He passed a sign on the side of a park one day which read "Playing Members Wanted." It was signed by the Regency Cricket Club and a telephone number was given. Harry cast his mind fondly back to his school days with Mr Stone and decided to give the club a ring and see if he could join. Apparently, three members of the club had left at the end of the last season and the club was now recruiting new members.

Harry went along on the very next Saturday morning and met with the coach. He explained that he had played cricket at school but that was a long time ago and he was very rusty. The coach understood and took Harry to the practise nets to see what the boy was made of. Harry's first efforts at batting were a dismal failure and the coach shook his head in disappointment, however it was a different story when he asked Harry to show him how he could bowl.

It was obvious that Harry was out of condition and very rusty but the coach could see that Harry had been taught well and had the fundamentals of a good bowling style. He invited Harry to join the club and encouraged him to attend all the coaching sessions.

The coach questioned Harry about his age and playing background and it was at this stage that the now seventeen-year-old Harry decided to come clean and tell his real age. The coach was enthusiastic and optimistic about finding such a young player who had promise and he took Harry under his wing to start coaching him seriously. He could see there was real talent in the young man and was keen to bring him on and maybe join his team, which badly needed a good bowler.

That first season, Harry only sat on the sidelines watching his teammates but was itching to get on the field and show just what he could really do. The coach was sensible and held the boy back, not wanting to expose him to too much competition until his skills were up to standard.

During the football season, Harry practised on his own; bowling to a single stick in Mrs P's back garden, trying to hit it, first slowly and then fast and then stupidly fast. He pushed himself ever faster, always careful not to step over the line he had drawn on the pathway, after measuring out the length of the pitch. By the time the next summer season started, he felt he could give a good account of himself. The coach put him in the team, batting in the ninth position but halfway through the game, which was not going well, brought him out for bowling.

Harry had grown two inches in this, his eighteenth year and was now able to bowl as well as any adult. He was a fast bowler and took the opposition by surprise, taking two wickets in the first over. The coach was overjoyed and shook Harry's hand vigorously and patted him on his back as the boy came off the field. He knew he was onto a winner.

The Regency Cricket team did well that year and at the end of the season, the coach asked Harry to step into the office where there was someone who wanted to meet him. Harry was introduced to a Mr Joshua Jenkins, who was apparently a talent scout for the New South Wales cricket team. Mr Jenkins had been watching Harry for the last two matches and was seriously impressed with the young bowler.

He told Harry and the coach that it was highly probable that Harry would be invited to join "The Blues," that is the New South Wales team the following year, as a twelfth man. He wouldn't be expected to play any games for the first year but would be on standby in case he was needed as a substitute. Mr Jenkins said he couldn't make any promises, but he was going to recommend to his board that Harry be taken on, if that's what Harry and the coach wanted and would agree to. He emphasised that Harry would be expected to train alongside professional players and attend all the coaching sessions and the playing games too.

Mr Jenkins didn't pull any punches. "There's no room for slacking, young man," he said. "If you're invited to join it's either full involvement with absolute commitment or nothing at all, we've no room on our side for passengers."

Harry was ecstatic. He ran all the way home, back to Mrs P and Alf, who happened to be at home that weekend. They were all excited at Harry's news and Alf toasted his young friend with many a bottle of beer that night. Mrs Pearson didn't normally drink and neither did Harry, but this was a night of nights and quite an excuse for a big celebration.

As predicted, Harry was invited to join "The Blues" with the promise of an opportunity to play for New South Wales in the Sheffield Shield matches. He was over the moon with delirious happiness. He was not earning much money but life couldn't have been better. He now had a home and someone who cared about him and friends in the club who showered him with praises whenever he played well in the practise matches, which was most of the time or in coaching sessions.

The Sheffield Shield is a competition between the Australian states and eighteen-year-old Harry was now being considered for taking his place in the New South Wales professional side. He was still only acting as a stand in, the twelfth man, but his big chance came when one of his teammates was hit to the side of his head in practise. Simon, the batsman, had a suspected concussion and was kept in hospital for observation.

The big game was the very next day and so Harry was elevated to last man for batting but the coach assured him that he may very well be brought in for bowling.

The team was not doing too well and needed to take some wickets. Coach Martin decided that now would be a good time to bring in the novice bowler. The NSW team were playing the Western Warriors from Western Australia and no one had ever heard of Harry Singleton. The first batsman to face off against Harry had a sly smile on his face, he could see Harry was only a young man, a novice and he thought this would be his opportunity to knock out a few sixes. His confidence gave way to fear after only the first ball.

With frightening speed and deadly accuracy, the experienced batsman could only block and stop the ball. He had no time to swing his bat. The second delivery was made with the confidence born of youth and hit the bales with such ferocity that the batsman was glad to be called out and whispered to the incoming batsman that was replacing him, "Good Luck, Fred, you'll flamin' well need it! That kid's dynamite!"

Harry took four wickets in that game and suddenly everyone was talking about the incredible new talent called Harry Singleton, the brilliant young fast bowler. The reporters couldn't get enough of the young man. If Jack and Madelaine had been cricketing enthusiasts, they might have seen Harry's name and picture in the papers, but as they weren't, they never heard the name and never realised that this was whom Jack had been looking for.

His appearance at the Sydney Oval was normal in Harry's eighteenth year and he was being touted as the next big thing for the Australian team. Max had gone to watch the Sheffield Shield match and was interested in the young bowler, as most people were and wondered when the boy would be given his first opportunity to play for Australia and be given his blazer and "baggy green," the cap that all the Australian team wore. It was a badge of honour and Harry dreamt about getting one.

A few months after his debut playing for NSW, a letter was sent from the Australian Cricket Board. Harry was at work but Mrs Pearson emptied her mailbox and saw the letter for Harry and recognised the logo on the envelope as that of the ACB. She could barely contain herself all day; Harry was at work and when he arrived home she was hopping up and down, impatient for him to open the letter. Harry saw the logo too and realised this might be the most important letter he would ever receive. He sat at the kitchen table with the unopened letter in his hand, turning it over and over. "For goodness' sake Harry, open the letter."

"I can't, I'm too nervous."

"Do you want me to open it?"

"No, I can do it, just give me a minute." Harry's hands were shaking as he slowly opened the letter and even when he took it out of the envelope, he still couldn't read it. "I can't, please you read it for me, Mrs P."

"Oh, for goodness' sake, give it here." Mrs Pearson took the letter and started to read out loud. "Dear Harry, The Australian Cricket Board would like to invite you to join the Australian cricket team for the forthcoming summer season. If you could contact the CEO and manager of the team (see name and number listed below) arrangements can be made for you to sign an official contract and join the current touring team. We wish you well for your future career in international cricket and on behalf of the Australian Cricket Board, send you our heartiest congratulations.

Yours sincerely, etc. etc."

"Oh, Mrs P, I think I'm going to be sick."

"No, you're not. Well done, Harry, I'm proud of you. I know you did well playing for The Blues and I've seen you out in the back garden practising and practising day after day. You deserve this success. Well done. Wait til' Alf hears about this, he'll be tickled pink."

Chapter 35
Good News

At forty years of age, Jack was doing well in the bank and had been promoted to manager of the International Division covering the whole of Australia. Madelaine was proud of her husband and was beginning to think that she would be too old to be a mother, even if they did manage to conceive a child.

When her period stopped, she just assumed that at forty years of age she was going through a reasonably early stage of menopause. She started to feel quite nauseous in the mornings and started to feel listless and lacking in energy. She asked the chemist for a tonic or a pick-me-up and he recommended two different types of vitamin pills. They didn't seem to do much good and she was bemoaning the fact to Jack one evening as she was undressing.

Jack noted that Madelaine was putting on a little weight and was unthinking and none too careful in his asking, "Madelaine, are you putting on weight or am I imagining things?"

Pouting and slightly miffed, Madelaine went to the mirror and examined her reflection carefully, turning this way and that. "I am getting a little pot aren't I? I guess 'cos I've not been doing a lot these last few weeks, I haven't really felt up to doing much. Maybe that's what they call middle-aged spread. I guess I'm getting to be an old lady now, I'm forty."

"You're not old, forty's not old, my love." Jack kissed his wife and really didn't care if she was fat or thin, he still loved her, unconditionally. She didn't say anything more to Jack but decided that she should go to see her doctor the very next day.

"If this is menopause, I don't want it to make me get fat," she told herself. "I'll just have to get fit. Maybe I should join a keep fit class or go for a jog every day." She didn't feel like jogging though, she didn't seem to have much energy at all, for doing anything, never mind jogging.

The doctor asked Madelaine all sorts of questions and gave her a full examination. He asked her to give a sample of her urine and promised he would call her the very next day if there was any reason to see him again.

The phone call the next day left Madelaine shocked, excited, frightened, worried and elated, all at the same time. She went through a host of emotions and couldn't wait for Jack to come home from work. She prepared a special meal and had the table laid and looking beautiful. She brought in a bottle of really good wine and waited for Jack impatiently. She knew he would be thrilled with her news, that they were, at long last, going to have a baby.

When Jack came through the front door of their apartment, the delicious smell of roast lamb sent his taste buds reeling. "Oh, yummy yummy, do I smell roast lamb and roast potatoes?"

"Yes, my love, here have a glass of wine I have something to tell you."

"Wow, what's the occasion? You don't usually greet me with a glass of wine."

"Sit down, I have something to tell you."

"Well, I'm sitting down. What is it? Have you got a rise at work, have they made you matron?"

"No, it's better than that."

"Have you inherited a couple of million dollars from some long-lost uncle?"

"No, silly. I went to the doctor yesterday and he rang a while back to say, guess what?" she threw her arms up in the air as she shouted out to the world in general, "We're pregnant! We're going to have a baby."

"Oh, my god! Not really? Are you serious? Are we really going to have a baby? Oh, you clever, clever girl." She laughed as she sat on his knee and nuzzled his neck.

"I didn't do it all by myself, you know."

"Alright, maybe I had a hand in it slightly, but you are such a clever girl. Oh, my god! We're going to have a baby." Jack got up from the table and, taking Madelaine in his arms and kissed her over and over again. He danced her around the room, singing, "We're going to have a baby, we're going to have a baby. Oh, you'd better sit down, put your feet up. Can I get you anything? Oh, you darling, you clever, clever girl."

They were both laughing when Madelaine suggested they call Max and tell him the good news. "No," Jack put his fingers to her lips, "Not tonight. This is our night. Plenty of time to tell Max tomorrow or when he's next home on leave."

Chapter 36
Bundle of Joy

Madelaine had always loved working as a nurse but Jack was adamant and insisted she give up work immediately, as he explained, "Look Madelaine, I know you have always enjoyed your work and it's always been important to you but I am earning good money now and I want you to stay healthy. Once the baby is born, you won't be able to go out to work so we might as well start now as we mean to go on."

Madelaine agreed and was actually happy to give up work, it was becoming a problem as the last few weeks had been particularly busy at the hospital and she had not been feeling at all well.

Jack was old-fashioned and kept chastising his wife each time she did any housework or walked to the shops. He suggested one day that they get someone in to help with the housework and Madelaine readily agreed. Jack also wanted to discuss a new idea that he'd had in the night. "Listen, Madelaine, I know you like this apartment and it's close to town and everything but with the baby coming, how about we consider moving out to the suburbs and buying a house, you know a proper house with a garden and everything? A child needs a garden and room to run around."

"Oh, yes, Jack, I'd had the same thought but didn't want to bring it up as I thought you really loved this apartment."

"Well, I do, but it's just an apartment. We can do better. I think it's time we expanded, just like you're expanding." They laughed as Jack kissed her and gently patted her stomach.

When Max came around on his next leave, he was surprised to see flowers throughout the apartment. Jack had celebrated their news by buying lots of roses, Madelaine's favourite flower. "What's with all the flowers? Are we opening a florist shop?"

"No Max. Sit down, we have something to tell you. Jack, pour us all a glass of champagne." Madelaine waited until their glasses were filled and then with great deliberation, spoke softly and slowly, saying, "Guess what? We're going to have a baby."

"Oh, my god, really? That's wonderful. Oh, congratulations, you two. Well done. So when is it due? Can I be a godfather? What are you going to call it? Do you want a boy or a girl?" Jack and Madelaine laughed at Max's exuberance.

"Calm down, Max. Baby's not due for another seven months. Actually, Max, we haven't even had time to think about whether it's going to be a boy or a girl and we haven't any ideas yet for names." Madelaine, her face flushed with happiness, looked to Jack.

"So daddy, do you want a boy or a girl? Not that you get a choice really, we'll get what the good Lord gives us."

"Well, as you know, I've basically lost my son and I would really, truly, love our baby to be a boy. I would like to call him George, if that's alright with you Madelaine. George was my father's name and it would be nice to carry that name on and I would be honouring my father's memory."

"Well, what if it's a girl?"

"Well, we could call her Georgina and we could shorten it to Georgie. I'd sort of like that."

"OK, George or Georgina it is." Fill up our glasses and let's drink to that.

The following weekend, Jack and Madelaine drove out to the suburbs looking at various houses that were up for sale. They had no real idea of what they wanted, except that it had to have a garden and at least two bedrooms. They looked at large, two-storey modern houses and they looked at smaller older houses; some with red iron roofing and a bullnosed front veranda, some with coloured roof tiles and wooden picket fencing.

It was all so bewildering, however, there was one house which really took their fancy. It was a single storey three-bedroom house with a double garage at Chatswood, an outer suburb of Sydney. The road was on a bus route and there were shops within walking distance. It seemed ideal and the price was affordable. The garden sloped down to a pretty park which had a lake in the centre and black swans lazily paddling up and down.

The whole property faced west, which was ideal as Madelaine had always wanted a house and garden where she could sit of an evening and watch the sun go down. This property just seemed to be perfect.

Madelaine wanted to buy the house, sign the documents with the agent there and then but Jack advised that they wait a few days and maybe put in an offer slightly lower than the asking price.

After a week of negotiations, the agent advised Jack that his lower offer had been accepted. The happy mother and father-to-be were overjoyed and treated themselves to a night in the town to celebrate. Madelaine took along a pen and pad and during dinner they both made notes as to what needed doing to the house and what they needed to buy. There was so much to do, but both agreed it was an exciting time for them and they threw themselves into the exhausting task of moving house.

The new house needed repainting and the garden was in need of much loving care and attention. Jack was too busy with his work and wouldn't hear of Madelaine trying to do it all alone and so employed a team of workers to make the house presentable and to get the garden into shape. He fancied planting some fruit trees and maybe a grape vine or two. Madelaine found she had a flair for interior decorating and really enjoyed planning the colour scheme for each different room, ordering new curtains and generally getting the house into some sort of order.

The one room that Madelaine was really concerned about was the nursery. She wanted to paint it in muted colours, soothing and gentle for a baby. Jack, on the other hand, wanted it painted in bright, bold colours. He felt a child needed the stimulation of bright colours and wanted "his boy" to be bright and cheerful and felt the child's room needed to reflect that.

Eventually they compromised and had three walls painted in pale yellow, for Madelaine and the fourth wall was painted in bright green for Jack. Max found some pictures of farmyard animals and they cut these out and pasted them on the green wall, making a farmyard scene mural that Madelaine thought would be attractive as well as educational.

As the pregnancy developed, Madelaine became heavier and heavier and tried not to complain as her back and legs ached. She had an afternoon nap each day and Jack insisted on cooking dinner each evening to save Madelaine having to do too much work. Madelaine's doctor had given the couple an expected date of October for the arrival of the baby and had booked a bed in the hospital for that time, however the baby had other ideas and at the end of September decided it was time to come into the world.

Madelaine was out shopping when her waters broke unexpectedly. She cried out with the pain and the shopkeeper called for an ambulance first and then called Jack at the bank. Both the ambulance and Jack arrived at the hospital at more or less the same time and Madelaine was taken into the labour ward.

Her contractions came with annoying and extremely painful regularity and when they were close enough Madelaine was taken into the birthing room. Jack very much wanted to be there, in the room with his wife but according to the doctors, that was no place for a husband. He was directed to the waiting room and given a cup of coffee. The nurse in that department promised she would let Jack know if, as and when, there were any developments.

He sat for hours in that waiting room, frightened for his wife's safety, remembering all too well his past tragedy with Harriet. He was excited at the prospect of having a child, but worried that things were taking so long. He had taken to biting his nails and was drinking coffee, cup after cup, not really tasting the coffee. He chatted momentarily to another expectant father and together they paced the floor, worried, scared and frightened for their wives and jumped every time a nurse passed by.

The other father was eventually taken out of the waiting room by a serious-looking doctor and Jack got the feeling that all was not well with that poor man and his wife. The doctor hadn't told the man that his wife had delivered the baby. Jack was now terrified. What if he lost his wife again? He didn't think he could go through that agony a second time.

At long last a nurse came to tell him the good news, his wife had delivered a perfectly healthy baby boy. Mother and child were doing well. His legs went weak and he had to sit down before he could muster the strength to go and see Madelaine. When he did, Madelaine was asleep and by her side was a perfect pink little face with a whisper of red hair.

He desperately wanted to pick the baby up but a stern faced matron was standing by to stop any such nonsense. He tiptoed out of the room and walked out of the hospital, feeling ten feet high and with tears of joy streaming down his face, he shouted to the four winds, "My god, I'm a father, again. Thank you god, thank you god."

Chapter 37
George Singleton

Baby George was a gift from heaven. He was a good natured, placid baby who even smiled when the vicar poured the cold holy water over his head at the christening. Max was as proud to be the godfather as Jack was proud to be holding his son. There had been some heated discussion between Madelaine and Jack as to what George should wear for his christening.

Madelaine wanted him in a traditional long lace gown but Jack wouldn't hear of it, he didn't want his boy dressed in a gown, a frock as he called it; he wanted his boy in trousers. The child was only three months old and eventually Max was the one who came up with the answer. He brought to the little family his gift for the christening, a white satin romper suit which was neither dress nor trousers. Everyone was happy and the baby was thriving, even under the pressure of so much overpowering love.

There were so many toys in the nursery that there was hardly any room for the child and his cot. His bedroom drawers were full to overflowing with the most exquisite clothes, which unfortunately he grew out of so quickly that some of the suits he never even got to wear.

Every day, Jack would announce that George was doing something different. "Look Madelaine, he's laughing at me." or "Look Madelaine, he's trying to sit up." or "Look Madelaine, he's kicking my hands, he's going to be a footballer, I can tell."

Madelaine just took it all in her stride and answered the proud father with, "Yes dear, I know."

Max was worse than Jack and played constantly with the child. He would read him stories, taking on the voices of the various characters, especially any animals in the stories. His rendition of dogs barking and mice squeaking was funny but not half as funny as him imitating the voices of various ducks in one particular story. George was always quiet when Max was reading him a story and seemed to study Max's face intently, taking it all in.

Life for this little family (and Max was counted as family) was complete. There couldn't have been a happier set of parents. They had no financial worries. Jack was satisfied with his position at the bank and Madelaine had given up on any thoughts of returning to work. She was busy and contented with being a mother and wife.

George was nine months old and had started crawling first and after a few weeks, began pulling himself up into a standing position, using the furniture to lean on. He was into everything, his toys were scattered around the house and he was an active, noisy baby. He tried to grab the spoon when being fed and much of his dinner usually ended up on the kitchen floor. No one minded and Jack thought it might be a good idea to buy a dog, which would be a cheap sort of vacuum cleaner. Madelaine agreed, saying, "I'll think about that, at least with a dog it would save me keep having to pick up bits of food all the time."

Max was the one who eventually found a suitable little dog. It was in the window of a pet shop and as he explained to Madelaine and Jack later, "I couldn't help myself, he just sat in the window, all alone and his big brown eyes just melted me, he was whimpering, asking; begging actually to be rescued from the shop. Well, I couldn't leave him there, could I?"

Madelaine and Jack laughed at Max and immediately fell in love with the little dog. George didn't know quite what to make of the dog as it licked him and bounded around the house. He pulled at its fur and Madelaine was fearful that the dog would turn on George, but the little dog seemed to realise that this was a baby and he rolled around with George, accepting all the rough treatment. As predicted, the dog was a perfect vacuum cleaner and licked up all the messy food that kept coming his way during each meal. No one seemed to mind and it was a win/win situation for everyone.

Max was still following the football in the winter and cricket in the summer. He had bought George a miniature football and a red soft cricket ball. He was determined that he would teach George how to kick a football. George enjoyed playing with Max and gurgled happily whenever Max came to visit. Everything was wonderful until Max came to visit as usual on his first day off, following a long stint flying to Britain and back.

He sat reading to George when he noticed that George was not following the turning of the pages of the book he was reading and didn't seem to be paying attention to Max's usual silly antics, mimicking the animals and the various characters. He asked Jack, "Is George alright? He doesn't seem to be himself."

"Oh, I think he might be coming down with something, he threw up this morning, which is very unusual for him. After that, he wouldn't eat at all; normally he eats like the proverbial horse. Here, let me have a good look at him."

Jack picked the child up from Max's lap and kissed the child on both cheeks asking, "How are you my little man?"

George ignored his father and just looked blankly into space, unfocussed with his head a little stiff, sort of leaning to one side. "Madelaine, come and check out George. He doesn't seem to be right. What do you think?"

"Well, he did vomit this morning, maybe he's not feeling too well. I'll give him a bottle and see if he keeps that down. If he's no better tomorrow, I'll take him in to the doctor and get him to check George out."

Madelaine put the child to bed and the adults had dinner. After dinner, they played a game of cards and eventually, Max went off home, stating as he left, "I hope George is feeling better tomorrow. If there's anything I can do, just give me a ring."

"Sure, will do. Cheers, Bye."

Usually George woke up his parents at around 6 o'clock wanting his early morning bottle but this morning he just slept through until Jack had to go off to work. Madelaine wanted to wake the child but thought that if he still wasn't feeling too well, then maybe sleeping a little longer might be the best thing for him.

At eight-thirty, she started to get a little worried and decided to wake him. George didn't seem to mind being woken and just looked blankly at his mother. When she picked him up, she realised immediately that there was something wrong. George was normally quite a strong baby and held himself quite firmly against her, however now he was quite limp and wasn't holding his own body up. His head was at a strange angle and his eyes didn't seem to be focussing at all.

With all the sense of a good mother Madelaine realised something was definitely wrong with her usually bright and energetic child. She thought of taking him to the doctor but instinct told her to get him to the hospital. She rang Jack, who agreed to meet her at the children's hospital.

The nurse in triage was in no hurry; she asked if George was bleeding, "No," she asked if he was having trouble breathing, "No."

"Then could you fill out this form, both sides please and then take a seat, a doctor will be with you as soon as possible."

"Look, nurse, I think there's something really wrong with our baby. Could you have someone look at him in a hurry, it could be serious."

"I'm sorry but there's a lot of flu around and the doctors are very busy, you'll just have to take your turn."

Jack and Madelaine were frustrated and angry but there was nothing they could do, except do as the nurse directed, take a seat and wait. George was not crying, he didn't seem to be ill at all really, just listless and different to the child he had been two days ago.

Eventually, their turn came and they were called in to the attending doctor. After a short examination and some questioning, the obviously tired and weary doctor informed the anxious parents that he'd seen six infants that morning presenting with the same symptoms, George had obviously picked up the flu from somewhere or someone. Jack was relieved that it was no more than the flu and escorted Madelaine back home before he left for work once more. Madelaine was not so sure, she wasn't happy with the simple diagnosis and determined that she would take George to see their general practitioner.

She tried to give George a bottle and some soft baby food but he refused to eat anything. This was so unusual for a baby that normally enjoyed his food and had a huge appetite. She put him in his pram and walked him to the local doctor. After sitting in his waiting room for over half an hour, eventually Madelaine got in to see her usual doctor. He greeted her cheerily and had a good look at George.

At first he confirmed what the hospital had said, that it was highly likely that George had contracted the flu, however when he tried to get George's attention he realised that the baby's eyes were not focussing and seemed to be wandering, one eye going one way and the other staying still. Now he was worried; he realised he didn't have the expertise to handle this problem and so wrote out a referral to a paediatric specialist and picked up the phone on his desk to make an appointment for Madelaine.

The next day Madelaine presented at the same hospital for her appointment. Jack thought she was over-reacting and had left for work as usual. He was convinced that George was only suffering from the flu and would be better in a day or so.

Once with the paediatric specialist, it became obvious that there was really something seriously wrong with George. The paediatrician gave George a thorough examination and many tests. He looked at George's eyes with some gadget and into the child's ears with another. He tested the child's reflexes and tried to get George to sit up. The paediatrician told Madelaine that he would let her general practitioner know the results of his tests and she was to return to her doctor in four days' time.

Still, Jack was not convinced that there was anything seriously wrong with George but Madelaine was adamant, he was not the child he had been a week ago. George was hardly eating anything and when he did eat he generally threw it up shortly after. He would drink from his bottle but wouldn't take any solid food at all. Eventually Madelaine took George back to her own doctor and was met there by a very solemn faced doctor. "Sit down, Mrs Singleton, I have some things we need to discuss."

"Oh, just tell me, Dr Green, is it just the flu or is there really something seriously wrong with my baby?"

"Well, I'm really sorry to tell you but we think George has a parasagittal meningioma."

"My god, whatever is that? Is it serious?"

"Well, it's a type of tumour that develops within the membranes that cover the brain and spinal cord, which are called the meninges."

"So is it serious? Can you do something about it?"

"I'm sorry but, yes, it is serious, very serious and no, I'm sorry, we can't do anything about it."

"So what does that all mean? If you can't do anything about it, can anyone do anything about it? What will happen to George? Is it life-threatening?"

"I'm afraid so. It will almost certainly end his life prematurely."

"How prematurely?"

"Well, it's extremely rare that an infant of only nine months presents with this problem. I've never seen it and I've never heard of an infant having it either, but the paediatric specialist that you saw did quite a few tests and he assures me that your child has this kind of tumour. We wouldn't expect a child presenting with this tumour to survive more than say three or four months, six at the most." Tears welled up in Madelaine's eyes as she clapped her hand to her mouth in shock.

"So, is there anything, anywhere, anyone who can help me? Is there any treatment that can be given?"

“I’m really sorry. I think that at some point in the future there may be cures for tumours. They are always doing research into the various types of cancer, because that’s what it really is, but at the moment, there is nothing I can offer you.”

“So what am I supposed to do? Should I take George to the hospital or to some other hospital somewhere else?”

“There’s no point, Mrs Singleton. As far as we know, there is no cure or treatment for this kind of cancer. I suggest you take George home and make him as comfortable as possible and let him enjoy the time he has left within the loving confines of his family. I’m really sorry.”

Madelaine took George home and sat by his cot staring at her inert baby, wondering how such a thing could have happened and in such a short space of time.

Jack came home and was shocked to see Madelaine sitting by the baby’s cot with tears streaming down her face. He fell to his knees when she related what the doctor had told her. He couldn’t believe god could be so cruel. Here was the most beautiful baby, so good natured. Why? Why? It didn’t make sense to him. George had been so healthy only a few days back. How can this thing have happened and so suddenly?

George never cried, never whimpered, he just lay on his back with his eyes staring at the ceiling. His parents clung to each other for support, Madelaine’s tears flowed unrestrained, but Jack just couldn’t let the tears fall, he realised if he once started crying he would never stop.

Jack tried to ring Max to let him know what was happening but when Max came on the phone, Jack just couldn’t form the words. He stumbled through his distress and Max immediately realised something dreadful was happening. He put the phone down, saying, “I’m coming over.”

The three distraught adults sat around the baby’s cot keeping vigil that first night, each wondering when George might take his last breath. Madelaine had explained that it might be three, four or even six months, but the shock was so great that they all just sat around, sharing their mutual misery, watching their precious bundle struggle to keep a hold on life.

Both Max and Jack had to return to work and the nursing of George was left to Madelaine. After the first week, she realised the inevitable and started to accept what she couldn’t change. She looked after her boy, who was now reverting back to being a real baby again. He had lost the ability to sit up and no more gurgled, babbled or cried. He was as mute as a newborn. He couldn't or wouldn't take any solid food and would only take the bottle. It was a miserable time for everyone concerned and it seemed that they were just waiting for him to pass away, to leave them.

Emotionally, the parents felt that they had already lost their child, that first night, when they found out his life was limited. It seemed to them that they started to grieve for him, to grieve the loss of him from that time on.

Six weeks after that dreadful day, a storm was forecast for the afternoon. Max was on leave and visiting Madelaine and Jack. George was in his crib as usual, quiet and unmoving. There was no laughter these days in this house, no candlelight dinners, no celebratory wine, no games of cards, no joking, no silly voices from Max, no story telling. Max was listening to the football commentary on the radio and Jack was watching the storm clouds gathering in the west.

Eventually, the storm broke with violent ferocity. The little dog barked at first and then whimpered at each roll of thunder. He hid under George's cot and stayed there, terrified of the storm. They saw the lightening first following by frightening claps of thunder. When the torrential rain started, Max was the one who commented, "Hell's bells, the heavens have opened."

Madelaine picked up George, worried that the noisy storm would upset him and reverently declared, "Yes, you're right, the heavens have opened and they have taken our baby."

Chapter 38
The Meeting

Madelaine and Jack clung to each other physically and mentally through the next few months. Their love held them together and they relied on each other for emotional support during this terrible time. It would have been so easy to blame each other, to take out their frustrations and anger on each other but their love eased the burden and enabled them to carry on and to resume life without their little angel.

Madelaine was upset and sad, of course, at the loss of her baby, but her training as a nurse had given her an outlook on life and death that was prosaic, that was stoic. She had lost many patients as a nurse, especially during the war. She had seen wonderful young men taken in their prime and had often watched fascinated as the chaplain called upon god to save these young men, to help the soldiers, to ease their burden, to cleanse their souls.

It never seemed to do any good, so many of them died, anyway. She had been mostly religious but often had recourse to question god and his motivation for taking such young lives. It always seemed to her that the "good ones" were taken early and it all made no sense to her whatsoever. She now had lost her only son and most probably her only chance of ever becoming a mother. She couldn't pray to god, she felt that she'd lost any faith that she'd ever had.

Jack took his loss the hardest. His longing for a son and the loss of his sons, first Harry and now George, was almost too much for him to bear. He fell into a deep depression for a few weeks but Madelaine and Max between them coaxed him back into life and into the Jack that they both loved.

Madelaine tried to encourage Max to take Jack to a cricket game, even though she knew Jack was not the slightest bit interested in cricket, but she thought watching some sort of sport might just take his mind off his tragedy. Max was away so much it was difficult for him to time his leave with the important games that he loved attending.

However, Max was visiting Jack and Madelaine between his scheduled flights and one day started his ramblings on about the cricket. Jack was only half paying attention and let Max talk on, discussing this new kid on the block, a new fast bowler whom everyone had expected would be picked for the next Ashes Series and he was about to make his debut at the weekend. He asked Jack if he would like to accompany him to the game the very next day. It was touted as the most important game of the year. Jack was undecided. “Oh, I don’t know. I mean, it’s a bit like watching the grass grow, isn’t it?”

“No, it can be really exciting. We’re playing our old rivals England and it should be a great game.”

“Isn’t it over five days or so? I can’t just be gallivanting off for five days.”

“You don’t have to attend all five days. Just come along for one day and see how you like it.”

“I can’t really go. I mean Madelaine needs me here.”

“No, I don’t. You go, you need to get out now and then, all you do is go to work and back. No, you go and you never know you might really enjoy it.”

“Oh, I don’t know. I think watching cricket is probably like watching paint dry and I think you two are ganging up on me.”

“Yes, we are. Come with me, we’ll have a beer in the bar first and lunch in the marquee. You’ll see, it’s not as bad as you think.”

“Well, if you’re sure Madelaine, you don’t need me here for anything?”

“No, go, I want to get some gardening done. I’ve bought some seedlings and I want to get them in tomorrow before they die of neglect. Just go.”

“Crumbs, OK, I’ll go, if it’s only to keep the peace around here. What a pair of bullies you two are!”

The game was the first day of the match and Jack was surprised that it was actually quite an interesting game. Australia was batting and at the end of the day declared for 490 runs. Only seven players had batted and it was considered quite a good score. The young gun that apparently everyone was waiting to see was not a very good batter and so had not appeared on this the first day. He was expected to appear and do his share of bowling the following day.

Jack was not particularly interested and had never actually heard the name of this young player being mentioned, but he agreed it was a bit more interesting than he had expected it to be. He wanted to see if Australia could actually beat England and could this new kid really bowl well enough to get a few of his old countrymen out. Jack had been born in England and so of course still had British nationality but since living in Australia now absolutely counted himself as an Australian and barracked for Australia at every opportunity, watching soccer, rugby, swimming and any time the two countries met.

The next day was a Sunday and against his better judgement or so he said, Jack agreed to go to the second day of the match against England. It was a beautiful sunny day and the two friends had a beer before the game started. When they took their seats, Max turned to Jack and just conversationally started to talk about the new bowler that everyone seemed to be so excited about. "You know Jack, it's funny but this new kid is called Singleton, same as you. What did you say your boy was called, it was Harry, wasn't it?"

Jack stopped reading the local paper that he had picked up on his way to the ground, as his mouth went dry. "Yes, it's Harry. Why?"

"Oh, don't get your knickers in a twist, it's just a funny coincidence. I mean this boy, this new bowler, couldn't be your son, he's a negro or at least a half-caste."

Jack had never told Max or even Madelaine that Harriet had been a negress and that Harry was a half-caste. It wasn't important to him and he'd never felt the need to go into that kind of detail. Now his temples throbbed and his heart almost stopped. Max saw the colour drain out of Jack's face and put his hand on Jack's knee, concerned and worried. "Jack, what's wrong? That boy, he couldn't be your son, could he?"

"How old would he be?"

"Oh, I don't know for sure, eighteen or nineteen, I think."

Jack did some quick calculations in his head and broke out in a cold sweat. "Oh, my god, I think it could be him. Where is he? I've got to go to find out."

"But he's a half-caste!"

"Yes, so is my son."

"Are you kidding? You've got to be joking. You're not serious, are you? You had a half-caste son? Wow! You never told me. So Harriet must have been a negress. Wow! Well, he's about to play so you can't see him today, I shouldn't think. Maybe after the game, I don't know. They don't let players mix with the general public. I know some of the ground staff. I'll go and make some enquiries. You wait here, I have some friends in high places too, I might be able to get us in to the player's area after the game. Don't move, I'll be back soon."

Max was as good as his word and did his best to get the two of them an audience with the new young player, however nearly every reporter was scrambling to get an interview and the security staff were having a difficult time keeping them all at bay. Max did manage to talk to the junior coach who promised him that if he came by in the morning, before the warmup session, he might just be able to see the new player and maybe have a word or two with him.

The junior coach wanted to know what it was all about but Max couldn't tell him and just said it was a private matter. Max related all this to Jack, who could hardly contain himself. He wanted to rush home and tell Madelaine what he'd found out. However, at that moment, it was announced that Harry Singleton was about to come onto the ground for his debut game, playing for Australia.

Jack held his breath and watched emotionally as he saw an extremely tall young half-caste boy jog onto the field. Everyone applauded the new player as he took off his cap and acknowledged the crowd. Jack felt faint, he knew now this was his son, this boy had fiery red curls. Harry had a few warm up practise swings and then he started his international bowling career playing for Australia.

Jack didn't want to take his eyes off Harry but thought that as this was such an important day for Harry then, surely his grandmother might be in the crowd watching him. He scoured the crowd and those close to the change rooms looking for his mother but couldn't see anyone who might just look like Elizabeth. He tried to work out how many years had passed since he had seen her last and realised that, in all probability, she would look a lot older than she had when he last saw her. More than likely she would have grey hair, even if covered by a sun hat. Sadly, he couldn't see anyone who just might be his mother and so concentrated on his son starting his run up for his first international over.

Harry was shaking with nerves and his first delivery went wide, which made him even more nervous. The umpire stood by his side and whispered, "Settle down, son, you'll be just fine. Take a few deep breaths."

Harry took the umpire's advice and forced himself to take three deep breaths, rolled his shoulders to try and take out the tension and prepared for his run up. His second delivery was sent with a ferocity that surprised everyone, especially the batter on the receiving end. The batter managed to block the delivery but didn't make any runs. Now, Harry felt settled and ran down the grass for his third delivery and sent it whizzing through the air like a bullet fired from a gun.

The poor English batter had no chance, the hard ball came at him so fast he couldn't move out of the way in time and as the ball hit his pad, the umpire held up one finger and declared him "out". As this was Harry's first international scalp, the whole of the Australian team left their fielding positions and ran over to congratulate him, patting him on the back and ruffling his hair. The Australian crowd went wild, cheering and clapping. He was in seventh heaven and at the end of the day had taken three wickets, one to a LBW and two clean bowled to the stumps.

Jack was mesmerised and could hardly see through his tear-filled eyes. He was absolutely certain that this was his son and the pride that he felt was bursting within his breast. All this crowd was cheering his son. His son. He wanted to shout it out, to tell everyone, but he didn't. He just sat there, relishing the moment, relishing the anticipation of meeting his son tomorrow. Max, grinning from ear to ear, kept turning to watch Jack's face and judge his reaction. Jack asked Max, "How am I going to get through the night? Hell's bells, Max, why didn't you tell me before that my son was playing?"

"I told you, I didn't know he was your long-lost son. How was I to know? I mean, he doesn't exactly look like you, does he?"

"I guess not, but you might have told me that a boy, the new player, had the same name as my son."

"I just thought it was a coincidence. I never thought it could really be your son."

When they got back to the house, Jack ran inside and jumping up and down with excitement shouted into the back garden to Madelaine, "Guess what, guess what, you'll never guess what?"

Madelaine took off her gardening gloves and came into the house.

"For goodness' sake, Jack, let Max get through the door. Whatever is it?"

"Sit down, sit down. I have the best news ever. You'll never guess what's happened."

"Heavens above, Jack, calm down, whatever is it? I take it the team won?"

"Oh, I don't know, it's not over yet, but guess what? We've found Harry." Madelaine's jaw dropped as she looked first at Jack and then at Max. "You mean Harry, your son?"

"Yes, I mean Harry, my son. There's this young fellow making his debut in the Australian team called Harry Singleton. He's about the same age as my Harry would be; it must be him. And if he's been living in Australia, then that's obviously why I could never find him in England. What do you think?"

"Well, are you sure it's him? I mean, the name could just be a coincidence. You know Harry is not an uncommon name and neither is Singleton."

Max cut in then with, "Well, it appears that Jack didn't think to tell us that his first wife was a negress. This boy is a half-caste."

Madelaine's eyes opened wide with a questioning gesture of her hands and arms and looked at Jack for confirmation. "Is that right?"

"Yes, does it matter?"

"Err, I guess not, no, it doesn't matter, but what else haven't you told me?"

"Nothing, I never mentioned it before because I never considered it important. Harriet was an educated, good woman. The fact that she was coloured was absolutely immaterial to me. Is it a problem to you, in fact to either of you?" Max put up his hands in a defensive attitude and swore, "Absolutely no problem."

Madelaine shook her head as she answered more slowly, "No, Jack, I have no problem, but it makes me wonder what else haven't you told me, do you have any other secrets waiting to be brought out?"

"No, none that I can think of and it was never a secret, it was just something that never occurred to me to elaborate on, it's a bit like if I told you he was left-handed or had blue eyes, it's of absolutely no consequence."

Madelaine shrugged her shoulders and progressed to questioning Max about how he found the boy. "So Max, how do you know this is Jack's son? Have you spoken to the boy?"

"No and I don't really know that he is Jack's son. I just happened to mention to Jack that there's this boy playing cricket for Australia and he has the same name as Jack. I really didn't think it was Jack's son as this boy is sort of coffee coloured, but now I understand Harry is a half-caste and what's even more conclusive is this kid is a copperhead, he has flaming red hair, just the same as Jack. It all seems to fit in."

Jack looked at Madelaine with a worried look in his eyes. "Are you alright with this, Madelaine. I have to know that you're OK with this."

"Yes, of course, I'm alright with it. I'm thrilled for you, but it's all a bit of a shock. You have to give me time to absorb it all. It's not every day you find you might just have a stepson."

"I know, my darling, but if it is him, are you alright with that?"

"Yes, yes, truly yes, but before you get too excited, you have to find out if it really is him."

Jack sat Max down on the settee and started to quiz him about the cricket team. "So Max, where do they stay, the team? Where do they stay? I need to go and see him. I have to know if he is my son. Oh, my god, I can't believe it."

"They all stay in the same hotel. I don't know which one. You can't just rock up to his hotel and demand to see him. He's just made his first appearance for Australia, the media will be queuing up to talk to him. You'll never get anywhere near him. Wait until tomorrow and with a bit of luck, we'll catch him before the match."

"No, I want to go now. I can't wait until tomorrow."

"Look, Jack, be patient. You've waited a long time for this. A few more hours won't make any difference. Anyway, there's no way that security will let you get anywhere near him, he's a celebrity, everyone will be wanting a piece of him now."

Madelaine jumped into the argument next with the sensible realisation, "Look Jack, think about it, if this boy is such an overnight sensation then it's not really fair to him if he has to play an important match and you've upset him with an emotional reunion."

"Crumbs, I never thought of that. I suppose you're right. What do you think, Max?"

"I think Madelaine's right. In fact, I don't think you should approach him until this full match is over. That's another three days. It's not fair to the boy, he should be concentrating on his game, not getting upset meeting his father after all these years."

"Oh, you two, you're such bullies. How on earth am I supposed to contain myself, knowing that my son is within reach. It's inhuman, I tell you."

"So you agree, you'll wait until the full match is over?"

"Oh, I suppose so, but I'm not going in to work tomorrow, I have to go and watch the cricket and see how my boy does." They all laughed and Madelaine kissed Max and thanked him for taking Jack to the game.

The following day, Jack took Madelaine to watch the cricket, as Max had a flight to Indonesia booked. She was not the slightest interested in the game itself but was incredibly interested in looking at Harry and cheering on the Australian team. He batted in eighth place and made twenty runs, which was all that was expected of him. The following day Max was back and Harry was bowling again and took five wickets. He was an overnight sensation and Jack was bursting with pride.

Australia won the series and suddenly Jack and Madelaine became instant cricket fans. They needed Max to explain the finer points of the game and explain the rules and interpret the strange terms and language, but they were hooked and couldn't wait for the series to finish.

Max had friends who knew what the Australian team was doing after the series, where they were going and where they would be staying. He made arrangements for a private interview with Harry Singleton and when questioned, just told the security guard that it was a personal matter.

Apparently, Harry agreed to meet up with this Max Mulligan, whom he had never heard of. He wasn't told that a Jack Singleton would be part of the meeting. Harry had no idea what it was all about but agreed to meet with Max in a private room off the main reception area in the hotel. The meeting was scheduled for 10 o'clock in the morning before the Australian team was to fly out to South Africa that afternoon. Everyone was nervous. Jack had hardly slept for three days and couldn't wait to get to the hotel. He'd asked Madelaine and Max if they really wanted to be there. "Are you kidding? We wouldn't miss it for the world."

When the trio got to the hotel, they were told that Harry Singleton was not in the hotel he had sent his apologies but there was an airline strike and the South African flight had been delayed for at least six or seven hours. The team had all been taken to the Sydney Cricket Ground for a hastily convened coaching session. Disappointed, the trio drove out to the cricket ground and asked if they could watch the training session. They could see Harry in the nets and, of course, couldn't possibly interrupt him at this time. They sat and watched and Max offered to see if he could make arrangements for a meeting with Harry after the coaching session.

They all agreed that would be the best thing to do, if he could arrange it.

Again Max spoke to the security guard whom he knew quite well and who promised to do his best to organise a short meeting.

After the training session, the security guard sent a messenger into the changerooms to ask if Harry Singleton could meet a visitor at the main gate, the same person that he had missed that morning at the hotel. Harry was expecting it to be yet again another reporter but was surprised when the trio approached him. Jack asked him straight away, "I'm sorry for pulling you away from your session, but are you Harry Singleton?"

"It's OK, the session is finished now for the day. Yes, I am Harry Singleton. Who are you and what can I do for you? You don't look like a reporter."

"No, I'm not a reporter. This is personal. Can you tell me was your mother called Harriet Singleton, maiden name Watkins, an African American who died in London giving you birth? Were you brought up by your grandmother, who is called Elizabeth Singleton? And was your father reported killed in the war, that is, missing in action?"

"Oh, my god, yes. But who are you and how do you know all this?"

"I know because in 1937, I married Harriet Watkins; my name is Jack Singleton and I believe I'm your father. I was shot down in the war but kept against my will in Germany, even after the war. I looked everywhere for you and your grandmother. I never thought I'd find you in Australia."

There was stunned silence as Harry looked at this stranger in front of him. He felt a wave of emotion roll up from his stomach and through his lungs as he gasped for breath.

They say men don't cry, but no one ever said that to these two. They both just stood, immobile, mute, tears welling up in their eyes, not really knowing what to do, what to say, how to act. Madelaine had her hand over her mouth, watching the situation; holding her breath, waiting for someone to say something, to do something. Max held her other hand as they watched the drama unfold before them. Eventually, Jack raised his arms and Harry stepped forward into the embrace he had been dreaming about all his young life.

They clung to each other and sobbed, remembering their years of separation. They wept with unreserved passion and just cried. Yes, you could say, they cried.